THE PORTRAIT OF THE DEVIL OF ST. JAMES

A Historical Regency Romance

EMMI WEST

The Portrait of the Devil of St. James Copyright © 2024 Emmi West / Jenny Foster

This work is protected by copyright.

All rights reserved. No part of this book may be reproduced or transmitted in any form or by any means, electronic or mechanical, including photocopying, recording, or by any information storage and retrieval system, without permission in writing from the publisher, except in the case of brief quotation embodied in critical reviews and certain other noncommercial uses permitted by copyright law.

This is a work of fiction. Names, places, characters and incidents are either the product of the author's imagination or are used fictitiously, and any resemblance to any actual persons, living or dead, organisations, events or locales is entirely coincidental. The author acknowledges the trademarked status and trademark owners of various products referenced in this work of fiction. The publication/use of these trademarks is not authorised, associated with, or sponsored by the trademark owners.

ARP 5519, 1732 1st Ave #25519 New York, NY 10128

info@allromancepublishing.com

Cover Design: © ARP Cover Design

ISBN: 9798301271410

ABOUT THIS BOOK

Nash Burnwood, the Marquess of Arden, has returned from the war.

He brought with him a deep scar that – along with his near arrogant self-confidence and fiery temperament – has earned him the nickname "the Devil of St. James."

Now, at the request of the Prince Regent, he is to be compensated for his service in France with a beautiful young bride.

However, Nash has no intention of marrying and has devised a clever plan: he will send the unwanted bride a realistic portrait of himself to scare her away...

A Note to the Reader

This story is set in London, England, and follows British spelling conventions.

INTRODUCTION

On a summer's day, anyone strolling through St. James's Square will pass by Arden House. The handsome façade reflects the sunlight, and a gentle breeze cools the heated face. Peace and tranquillity reign here, in one of London's most prestigious squares.

However, appearances can be deceiving.

Behind the door of the mansion lives a man known as "the Devil of St. James" because of his disfigured face. And an encounter awaits him that will turn his life upside down...

I

NASH

It was the bead of sweat that pushed his patience to its limit. Of course, the bead itself was not something that usually robbed him of self-control. No, what infuriated Nash Burnwood, the Marquess of Arden – or, as the scandal sheets had dubbed him since his return from France, "the Devil of St. James" – beyond measure was the comprehensive failure of the man in front of him.

The signs were hard to miss: the trembling right hand that held the pen; the up-and-down motion of the left, which dabbed at the perspiring forehead with a lace-edged handkerchief; the glances the pale man cast everywhere except at the left half of Nash's face. Nash, who was familiar with his own reflection, had forgotten over the months how unsettling the sight of the red, inadequately healed scar must appear to the more sensitive souls of his time. But from one of the most famous painters of his era, Nash had expected more than this effeminate fuss. This dandyish man with the ridiculous little beard was now dabbing his sweaty forehead for the tenth time. Nash had been counting. What else was there for him to do to pass the time while he maintained the desired pose? His hand on his grandfather's ceremonial sabre – a wretched spendthrift, may he sweat in Hell – gripped the hilt tighter.

The painter's eyes bulged from their sockets as he followed the movement. Nash couldn't have imagined that an artist whose allegedly shockingly realistic style had caused a scandal in the ton would behave in such a manner. He almost pitied the man. If Nash hadn't needed this wretched portrait so urgently, he might have been more patient. But as he watched the tell-tale drop of sweat trickle down the pale forehead, he knew that even this artist wouldn't provide him with what he had commissioned.

Two seconds passed as Nash stared into the painter's wide, fearful eyes. The man abandoned all decorum, turned around, and made a run for it at the exact moment Nash leapt off the platform and closed in on the easel. While Nash ran, the sabre struck his thigh, but he ignored the ridiculous thing. He heard the painter stumbling down the stairs. Hopefully, the fool wouldn't break his neck in flight from the Devil of St. James. Nash had enough on his plate already; he didn't need a magistrate or – God forbid – a ponderous constable at Arden House.

A glance at the sketch confirmed his worst suspicions.

Like all the other painters before him, this idiot had tried to turn Nash into a damned pretty boy. He had to admit that the proportions were well done. His shoulders were broad, his waist narrow, and the legs, as far as visible, were strong and muscular. It was the face that drove Nash to despair.

It was an attractive face, there was no doubt about that. The chin was masculine and distinctive. The characteristic high cheekbones of the Ardens spoke of the justified arrogance that had been passed down from generation to generation, just like the blue eyes. Straight, dark brows and a nose, which Nash found to be proud, made this face one that would have suited a Caesar, a conqueror and subjugator, very well.

The only problem: it wasn't his face.

Not anymore.

His frustration erupted in a scream that caused passers-by on the street and even in the square across the way to pause before hurrying along at double speed. Ignoring the startled pedestrians, he sprinted after the incompetent painter, just catching sight of the pitiful creature leaving his property to fall into a woman's arms.

She wasn't very young, he could tell at first glance, even from the steps of his house, although her face was covered by a plain bonnet. It was her posture that revealed she was no longer a shy debutante – she stood upright and self-assured. Under her arm, she carried a rectangular package, which she had wrapped in a colourful cloth to protect it from the vagaries of the English spring weather, and clutched tightly to her chest as the bumbling man stumbled against her, almost causing her to fall. For a second, Nash was sure she would end up on the sidewalk with her rear end first, but at the last moment, she managed to maintain her balance. The preservation of her person, however, came at the expense of the package, which fell into the gutter simultaneously with the clumsy fugitive. Her precious cargo landed in the filth right next to the painter, who looked at the dirt on his breeches with a disgusted expression. The woman seemed frozen and unable to comprehend the misfortune that had befallen her.

With a sigh, Nash decided to come to her aid. The mishap wasn't his fault, but he wasn't entirely uninvolved in the chain of events either. He jumped lightly down the steps and heard the perpetrator of the mishap – the dilettante who called himself a painter, not Nash himself – showering the lady with a flood of accusations.

"...very well, madam. If your husband wishes to try his luck, by all means. I wish him and you good luck in taming this devil in human form."

Nash grinned. That was him they were talking about.

"I will send you the bill for cleaning my clothing. Are you still lodging in Lambeth—"

Whatever the painter had intended to say turned into a squeal as Nash grabbed him by the nape of his neck and gave him a shove. "Dare to blame the lady for your clumsiness, and I'll ensure you roast in Hell, you worm!" Worms didn't squeal, but comparing him to a barnyard animal in the presence of a lady was out of the question for Nash.

The failure staggered away. Nash watched him with satisfaction.

At the same moment, the frozen woman came to life and sank to her knees to retrieve her precious package from the gutter. "Allow me," Nash said, pulling the woman to her feet with one hand and reaching for the package with the other. The protective cloth had come undone and was soaked with liquid, so Nash left it and only grabbed the rectangular package. She raised her head, giving him the opportunity to see her face in its entirety.

Oho!

Not young anymore, he was correct in that regard. If he ignored the signs of exhaustion, such as the shadows under her eyes, she was in her mid- to late-twenties. Too old by conventional standards, but Nash had never been one to base his personal preferences on rapidly changing fashion. Honestly, who would want a shy, stammering virgin when one could enjoy the sight of a woman like her? She was a sight to behold, though not conventionally beautiful. Her mouth, unfortunately pressed into a disapproving line, was too large, and her nose was too straight. Her brows were dark arches, her eyes almond-shaped and of a bright brown that here and now reminded him of a hawk's piercing gaze. Her hair was concealed by the bonnet, but if Nash had to wager, he would bet it was red-blonde. She had the coolness of a fair English rose, but beneath that, he thought he could discern the passion of a redhead. How much charm would it take to dispel the severity from her striking face and replace it with passion?

"Thank you," the woman interrupted his thoughts, "for your... assistance."

Oh no, it wouldn't be much effort for Nash if she stumbled over her words in her first sentence to him. But his interest waned as suddenly as it had flared.

"If you would be so kind as to return my property now before it incurs further damage." Her words came from her mouth like alms, hard and cold; her tone suggested it was a command, not a question.

When was the last time a woman had left him speechless?

Perhaps it wouldn't be so easy to break her resistance after all. Nash looked down at his hands, still holding the rectangular package. The woman reached out with her gloved fingers. Instinctively, he handed her the package and watched as she closed her slender fingers around the now-soggy paper. "Once again, my thanks, sir." A cool nod, then she turned her back on him and surveyed the house he had just left. He observed her narrow shoulders straightening in the clean but long-out-of-fashion coat, as if she were summoning all her courage. In the next moment, she froze.

Nash understood.

The woman with the hawk-like eyes had realised he was the man to whom the house belonged. She was on her way to him.

Nash felt his lips curl into a broad smile. The movement of his facial muscles was uncomfortable; the stiff scar tissue refused to cooperate with his expression, but he couldn't stop. A nanny and her charge squeezed themselves between him and his prey. A furtive glance at his face was enough to make the governess turn pale. The boy's face twisted into a frightened grimace, and he began to cry as the governess dragged her charge across the street, clearing the view of the woman.

Her shoulders slumped forward, and she took an uncertain step toward the entrance of Arden House. Nash smoothly stepped beside her and offered his arm. "You're on your way to me, I assume." Although the wide-brimmed bonnet concealed most of her face, Nash thought he saw her grow a shade paler. A slight disappointment crept into his chest as he perceived her reaction to his disfigured face. *She's probably not a redhead after all. Too little fire and too easily startled.*

Yet in the next moment, he was proven wrong as she straightened her shoulders and lifted her chin. A promising spark flickered in her gaze as she looked at him for a deliciously fleeting moment.

How he would relish painting her cheeks with the fiery blush of passion! The brown eyes beneath the dark brows created a spicy contrast to her fair complexion, fuelling his imagination. "Allow me to introduce myself. I am Lord Burnwood." Some women were delighted when he offered them the more intimate "Arden" right away, but she seemed to be the type of woman who needed to be courted first. However, once she warmed up, there would be no stopping her...

She still refused to look at him. "My lord." She hesitated and clutched the precious package to her chest, which was more than hinted at beneath the grey coat and whose turmoil Nash didn't miss due to his towering height.

He bowed. Not so deeply that it would have seemed mocking given her low status, but deep enough to assure her of his appreciation. Finally, she accepted his polite offer and placed her arm on his. He allowed himself a tiny moment of anticipation as he felt her hand, light as a feather, on his arm, and led her into the house.

2

FREDERICA

She should have known that her streak of bad luck was far from over. Wasn't it enough that Frederica had run into the pompous fool Thomas Crawford of all people when she had undertaken the heavy task of going to Arden House? The last image she had left of Francis, so to speak, lay in the gutter, soiled and figuratively trampled on. Did it have to be Lord Burnwood himself, the highly esteemed Marquess of Arden, who rushed to her aid unasked, when she could have handled Crawford perfectly well on her own, thank you very much?

It took her strength she no longer possessed to accept his arm and follow him into his house. Now she had to try to make the best of the situation. Perhaps she should start by apologising for her rude behaviour. She needed his favour if she didn't want to find herself back on the street shortly. Or worse, in Sussex, in her father's house, buried alive under embroidered, framed Bible verses and sermons about a woman's duties.

His Lordship remained silent as the butler took her coat. When the grey-haired servant attempted to relieve her of her package, Frederica shook her head and said she wanted to keep it with her. A little too late, she realised that the man couldn't possibly know how precious it was and what it meant to her. Before Frederica could make a complete fool of herself and apologise to the butler, Lord Burnwood spoke up and ordered tea and pastries. In the salon. As if she were a proper guest!

As he attempted to take a seat, his sabre, which he wore on a belt around his hips, got in the way. With a sound of impatience, he jumped up and struggled in vain with the clasp of the lethal weapon. However, the butler was already on hand and effortlessly undid the hook with a practiced motion. Measured steps and carrying the sabre as if it were the Holy Grail, the man left the salon. Frederica was alone with Lord Burnwood.

After she had taken a seat hesitantly, His Lordship chose the seat opposite her. He crossed his strong legs and leant back, seemingly relaxed and not in the least embarrassed by the little scene. The chair with the high back had cobalt blue upholstery that almost magically matched the colour of his eyes. Lord Burnwood couldn't have chosen a more effective setting to showcase his unusual eye colour. A portrait of him should incorporate the cobalt, perhaps as a reflection in water or in the sky? His face... Frederica tried to muster the courage to look at his face. The fleeting glance she had risked before the house had given her a mighty shock. Before she could think further about it, the door opened, and a neatly dressed maid appeared. The silence in the salon was punctuated by the soft clinking of porcelain and the delicious scent of hot tea as the young maid filled the delicate cup. The girl curtseyed politely, first to her and then to Lord Burnwood, and then disappeared silently.

"You still haven't told me your name and the purpose of your visit." His deep voice made her jump.

"Forgive me," Frederica said, forcing herself to smile, a smile that matched her words – humble but not submissive. It felt fake. She looked at the cup in front of her without touching it, searching her heart for the courage she would need to look at the disfigurement. "I am the wife of Mr. Francis Fitzroy. My husband," she took a deep breath, "was awarded by the Royal Academy as one of the most outstanding portrait artists of his time, and I have come to request your commission." Internally, she cringed at the unabashed bragging, but humility would not get her closer to her goal. "If he is still available," she added because although she had witnessed

Crawford's expulsion, she could not know if Lord Burnwood had already chosen another artist.

It wouldn't get easier if she delayed the moment any longer. With all the courage she could muster, she looked into his face.

Frederica's intention was to glance at the scar with her eyes rather than rudely staring at it, but her intention collapsed like a house of cards. The malicious and poorly healed wound extended across his entire left cheek. It dominated his face, which was all the more regrettable because the rest of his features were quite attractive. Even she, who was not easily shaken, had to swallow. The streets of London were teeming with maimed war veterans who could no longer work and earnt their meagre food by begging, but Lord Burnwood was more severely marked than she had thought. Her stomach clenched.

A scar was so much more than skin that had grown over an old wound. A scar was a lasting memory, it told a story. What was the story behind his scar?

Frederica speculated it might have been the result of a lost duel. Was it about his honour or a woman?

Stop! She was speculating about things that were none of her business. All Frederica wanted was a chance to get the commission, despite her gender.

"Why doesn't your husband come himself, Mrs. Fitzroy?" The brows, a shade lighter than his black hair, lifted for a few seconds before furrowing slightly. Distance settled over Lord Burnwood's features like a thin cloth, turning a living face into a mask. Even his voice had lost some of its expressiveness. Was it due to the mention of her husband, the fact that she was another man's wife?

"He is not well," Frederica said, avoiding looking at the package that lay at her feet. When she had planned this conversation, the sentence hadn't sounded as flimsy as it did now, nor had clarification been necessary. "But there is nothing preventing him from completing your portrait," she added hastily. She silently prayed that His Lordship wouldn't notice how evasive her answer was.

"Where did you learn about my search for a painter?" He didn't respond to her mention of Francis.

"I read about it in the newspaper."

His dark brows rose even higher. "Which paper reported this?"

Technically, it hadn't been a report but a caricature that had caught Frederica's attention. Crawford was not the first artist of some renown to leave Arden House under the owner's vehement insults. She had immediately recognised the famous painter Archibald Leech in the image. The artist had captured Leech's bloated face quite well, as well as the horrified expression as he tumbled down the steps of Arden House, with the ominous Marquess towering above him. The caricaturist had likened him to Zeus and had him hurling a lightning bolt at Leech's rear end. She had encountered Leech a few times when accompanying Francis to receptions and dinner invitations and remembered the pompous little man well. The public display of his expulsion from Arden House had surely hit him harder than not getting His Lordship's commission. "It was the *Morning Star*." His Lordship hadn't been captured nearly as well as Leech by the caricaturist. He had nothing in common with the grey-bearded godfather. Rather, he looked like Ares, the God of War, always seeking the next challenge.

His Lordship snorted, a sound Frederica would never have expected from a nobleman. "Who would have thought that this paper would someday tell the truth," he remarked. Frederica breathed a sigh of relief. All was not lost yet!

"You have surely heard of my husband and seen some of his works," she resumed the conversation. "Mr. Fitzroy had the honour of portraying His Royal Highness the Prince Regent and his consort." Normally, this revelation would elicit awe, but with Lord Burnwood, it only produced the already familiar raising of his brows. "The painting earnt him a knighthood."

A steep crease appeared between his perfect black arches. Of course! For a Marquess whose lineage could be traced back to William the

Conqueror and who was remotely related to the royal family, a knighthood was nothing.

As if his thoughts had been occupied with something edible, he gestured with his long fingers to the selection of thinly sliced sandwiches and pastries that had come with the tea. Frederica straightened her back and thanked him. There was a good reason she had tasted neither the exquisitely fragrant tea nor the delectable treats that had been served with it, for once she started eating, she wouldn't stop until every crumb was consumed. Hesitantly, she reached for the sugar tongs and placed a moderately sized lump of sugar into the delicate porcelain cup.

The tea was delicious. Its dark yet floral aroma caressed her nose and restored some of the confidence she had lost piece by piece over the past weeks and months.

"Tell me more about your husband," Lord Burnwood urged. "I am not up to date when it comes to the fine arts." A cloud passed over his face, and he raised his hand to his scarred half, only to let it sink back immediately. His cobalt blue eyes darkened until they took on a cooler slate hue, which would be difficult to capture on a canvas. Frederica quickly averted her gaze. Staring into his eyes and considering what artistic techniques were needed to portray him would be like selling the bread before the flour was in the house.

"Mr. Fitzroy is primarily known for the expressiveness of his paintings," she continued and reached for her precious package. She placed it on her lap and untied the cord that held the damp paper together. "As one of the most outstanding artists of his generation, he managed to capture the essence of the subject and..." She looked up and fell silent when she saw the expression that divided his face into two halves. The unscarred half expressed mockery, while the wounded half twisted his features into an expression of hellish rage.

Fear gripped Frederica. It felt as if she were sitting opposite two men inhabiting the same body and vying for dominance. She felt her blood drain from her face and gathered all her remaining strength. There was no reason for Lord

Burnwood to be angry with her. She was probably misinterpreting his expression, and his smile, thanks to the scar, looked mocking, even if it wasn't. In her agitated state, she misread everything that came before her as rejection. "...to capture it on canvas," she finished the interrupted sentence and simultaneously removed the wrapping. For an embarrassing moment, she didn't know where to put the packaging, then she placed the soaked paper beside her on the sofa. Her mouth was dry, and her tongue felt as if it wanted to refuse its duty. With trembling hands, she lifted the painting with its humble frame from her lap and handed it to His Lordship. If he didn't like it, if she failed to get the commission, she might as well throw herself into the Thames.

NASH

The small woman had indeed brought him a work by her husband. She handed him the painting with the raw side facing him and seemed as though she might faint at any moment. Her cheeks were flushed, and her hands trembled. He accepted the painting, and for the briefest of moments, their fingers touched. The colour on her cheeks deepened in the same measure as his reservations. Mr. Fitzroy was either seriously ill, or he didn't care much about getting the commission for Nash's portrait, because why else would he have sent this delicate flower as a messenger instead of coming to him in person? The woman couldn't even look at him! She had sipped the tea but hadn't tasted the pastries, as if his presence had taken away her appetite. A little more flesh on her bones wouldn't have hurt. On the contrary, she was far from stately. Why didn't he put an end to the game and send her back into her husband's care?

Because you're the Devil of St. James, whispered the voice inside him that delighted in this diabolical game.

Nash turned the frame and examined it.

He had misjudged her. She was neither a delicate flower nor too thin. Her husband had portrayed her, not in her natural state, but in a way that showcased her figure extraordinarily well. More than that, Nash thought. He felt as though he could reach out and grasp a corner of the delicate fabric to see her in all her feminine beauty, even caress her creamy white skin. His gaze moved to the ornate signature. "FF" was boldly displayed there – Francis Fitzroy. Nash's eyes travelled further down to the bare feet, turned to flee, and back up to her thighs, waist, and breasts, covered by the colourful cloth. Only hesitantly did he tear his eyes away from the seductive curves and look into the face of the woman in the painting.

No. No shy flower looked at the viewer like that. The woman depicted there was an Amazon, a fighter, a Christian in the lion's den, ready to defend her life to the last drop of blood. Her brown eyes glowed and seemed to burn deep into his soul. The reddish-blonde hair curled in an almost palpable hot wind and concealed the curves that had escaped the covering cloth due to her movement.

Nash cleared his throat and tore his gaze away from the painting. He didn't know how much time had passed since he had taken it from her hands, but one thing he was aware of: she hadn't exaggerated when she spoke of her husband as one of the most outstanding artists of his era. Perhaps he really was capable of creating the portrait Nash so urgently needed. "Tell your husband that I would like to see him as soon as possible to settle the formalities," he said, realising that he still held her painting in his hands and handing it back to her with an abrupt motion.

Her shoulders slumped imperceptibly, causing her plain pale blue dress to wrinkle unflatteringly.

Nash closed his eyes to dispel the image that overlaid reality, in which no tightly laced gown restricted the freedom of her feminine form. He pressed his lips tightly together. He would never forget himself to corrupt a woman who belonged to another, no matter how much his fingers twitched and yearned to caress her soft skin and make her blush by bringing her to life.

Finally, she took the painting from his hands. This time, she took great care to ensure their fingers didn't touch. Her gaze remained lowered. Nash briefly wondered if Francis had sent his wife with this portrait to emphasize his application. That was not unlikely. The woman in front of him was clearly being used as bait – the question was just how far Mr. Fitzroy was willing to go.

"My lord, as I told you, that is not possible today. I am his representative in all matters, and am authorised to negotiate the price with you." The trembling of her hands had transferred to her voice.

"I understand," he said slowly, infusing his words with the arrogance and coldness that had grown in the Burnwoods over generations. "I insist, nonetheless." Were those tears shimmering in her eyes? "I assure you, my... husband will create the best portrait for you that you can imagine. Every detail will be executed according to your wishes. But," she took a deep breath, and this time Nash didn't succumb to the temptation to avert his gaze from her face, "it is you who would have to come to our studio."

"What changes for your husband if I accede to his request? You must forgive me, but your suggestions, tempting as they may be, do not pique my curiosity." *Liar*, the voice chimed in before Nash silenced it. Mrs. Fitzroy did not respond. "Surely you understand that your approach seems a bit... suspicious to me." There was something she was not telling him, Nash was sure of that. But what? There were as many possibilities as he had fingers on one hand. "Why don't you tell me the truth, Mrs. Fitzroy?"

4

FREDERICA

Was her desperation as clear as the fact that she was keeping the most important thing from Lord Burnwood? She had bared herself in vain, and not just in the figurative sense. She had failed. Frederica rose to her trembling feet. The truth? He wanted the truth? Of all people, this man who had stripped her with his eyes, compared the image in his mind to reality, and in the next moment forgotten that she existed? No, she could and would certainly not reveal the true intentions behind her appearance as a petitioner.

Through the veil of tears, she saw that he also stood up. Even now, in this moment of defeat, Frederica couldn't help but consider how to capture the athletic elegance of his movements on canvas. A dynamic portrait was hardly an option, not for a nobleman like him, but it should be possible to convey his powerful grace to the viewer in another way.

"Your husband is free to change his mind and present himself." He had stepped beside her and stared down at her from his imposing height. From this perspective, the disfigurement should have looked even more significant, but the opposite was true. Lord Burnwood's face was still frightening, but at the same time, Frederica felt a strange fascination taking hold of her. Someone had managed to hurt him and leave a lasting reminder of his defeat. Lord Burnwood was a human like any other. She noticed that she had raised her hand, as if to touch the scar, and hastily took a step out of his reach. What had come over her? Her head was spinning. Nevertheless, Frederica managed to gather her last bit of reason and reply to Lord Burnwood.

"Thank you," she said, and realised that the two words sounded anything but grateful. She reached for the painting and retreated further. Human or not, he was not someone she would willingly turn her back on. "I will convey it to my husband. Goodbye, my lord."

With that, Frederica fled from Arden House. She was no better than Crawford. At least she was spared the humiliation of being chased out of the house with profanities by His Lordship. She was already on the footpath when the sound of the slamming front door made her realise she had missed her very last chance. In the gutter lay the cloth in which she had wrapped the portrait before setting out. Francis had given it to her when he had returned from the palace, his wallet bulging, and with the joyful news that His Highness had promised him a knighthood for his services.

"Without your support, I would never have come this far," he had said and handed her the cloth made of exotic silk with its delicate pattern of blue flowers. At first, the remark had tasted bitter to her. *Without me, you would never have completed the painting*, she wanted to say, but after a look at Francis's radiant face, she laid her head against his narrow chest and muttered some non-committal words into his waistcoat. She should be happy that she was allowed anywhere near colours and canvas, rather than pitying herself.

Frederica reached for the cloth in the gutter and wrung out the dirty water. She would wash it at home and hope it hadn't suffered any permanent damage. Home. The word left a bitter taste. Without giving Arden House and its owner so much as a glance, she began her return journey. It was essential to look forward.

Only, in this case, "looking forward" meant taking a step backward. Frederica could no longer afford to keep the house in Lambeth that her husband had partially paid for with half of the Regent's payment – which truly deserved the title "royal" in terms of amount. She thought as she marched along George Street towards Westminster Bridge that she could have lived with that. She didn't need luxury to be content, even though the thought of never again stepping into the garden behind the house tore at her heart. Unfortunately, in his flight of fancy, Francis had spent the money faster than it had come in, accumulating debts under his "good name." The sale of the house would fetch a high enough price to clear the debt, but her future was uncertain. What would she live on? No one suspected that it was she who had painted Francis's most famous pieces. He had been an excellent artist, there was no doubt about that, but she was better. More inspired. More disciplined. Francis had been more talented than her, but he had never worked on his skills, so he had always painted the same pictures, usually landscapes. And stagnation, Frederica sighed, was equivalent to professional death in an artist's life. The audience wanted to discover something new in the familiar, to be surprised, perhaps even shocked. Francis's career had only taken a second wind when she had secretly started completing his works. The expressiveness of *his* portraits had been praised to the heavens by connoisseurs and patrons. Some critics had noticed the change in brushwork and had put her and Francis in some awkward moments. But then Francis had the brilliant idea of attributing the innovations in his portraits to a feverish frenzy in which the muse had kissed him. In fact, one of the most influential patrons had called the portraits "feverish in their intensity of emotional expression, almost indecently passionate," which, of course, suited them both.

Muse's kiss, my foot! Frederica snorted, earning her a disapproving look from a gentleman who passed her briskly. She ignored the wordless reprimand. To excel in an artistic discipline, it wasn't enough to wait for the muse's kiss. One had to drive themselves day by day, as Frederica had done. That was how you grew beyond yourself.

And what had it brought her in the end?

Nothing. Francis had received the knighthood, the money, and the fame that should have been hers. And then he had died. It had been a foolish, unnecessary death, and it had deprived Frederica of her husband in one stroke, as well as the one thing in her life that she was passionate about: painting. In the early days after Francis's death, she hadn't picked up the brush because it wasn't proper. As a newly minted widow, she wasn't supposed to think about anything other than her husband's death, let alone find joy in something during the mourning period. While hardly anyone knew that her husband was no longer alive, Frederica would have been ashamed of herself if she had been happy so soon after Francis's passing. But following convention had turned into truth because every brushstroke reminded her of Francis. The happiness she felt when she started a new painting had never returned.

In a way, it was a relief that Lord Burnwood had not agreed to her terms. Perhaps she was no longer capable of painting.

She wrinkled her nose as she stepped onto Westminster Bridge. With the tide, the Thames had swelled into a stinking brown stream that bore no resemblance to the lifeblood it was commonly praised as. Those like Lord Burnwood, who lived in St. James, benefited from the goods from the colonies that reached London by ship without confronting the city's filth. But those like Frederica, who lodged in Lambeth, not far from the river, lived with the dirt, soot, and stench. Someone had lit a fire on the left bank, and the wind carried the acrid smoke in her direction.

At the highest point of Westminster Bridge, Frederica stopped for a moment and looked down at the grey-brown water. It wouldn't take more than a bold leap to solve her problems in one fell swoop. Let others worry about what would become of the house. Whirlpools appeared in the water; with a bit of luck, the undertow would pull her beneath the surface quickly. Drowning would not be not a pleasant death, but it would still be better than dying a little bit every day, as she was doing now.

The eddies grew in size. Frederica stood on her tiptoes and leant over the railing. She closed her eyes and felt a trembling in her core that spread with every breath. The noise of carriages behind her and the shouting of the boatmen below merged in her head. It reminded her of the buzzing of the bees her father raised in the Sussex Downs. It swelled the same way, as if her father was approaching the hives with the smoking tool, growing louder and more aggressive until it suddenly fell silent. For a terrible moment, it seemed that the agitated surface of the Thames was reaching out for her. Frederica's legs gave way. Without thinking, she grabbed the railing with both hands. The painting and cloth slipped from her fingers and tumbled into the water.

NASH

"Have you once again forgotten your good manners?" Aunt Matilda's voice had, as of late, carried a disapproving tone. "I do not know what has gotten into you, my dear boy, but your behaviour leaves much to be desired lately."

Despite the admonishing words, Nash suppressed a smile as the grey-haired Lady Hastings tracked him down in the library and pulled the curtains aside uninvited. Dramatically, he shielded his eyes from the pale sun with his hand. Aunt Matilda was his late father's favourite sister and the only one for whom Nash, at over thirty years old, was still a boy. "That bungler wouldn't have been able to draw a straight line even if I had handed over half my fortune to him," he retorted and lowered his hand that had shielded his eyes. He pointed with his index finger to the disfigured half of his face. "I can understand that one needs time to get used to the sight," he continued, observing how Lady Hastings took her time sitting down opposite him. "But I managed it eventually, and this oaf doesn't have to live with this," he brushed his hand over the scar, "here."

"Stop with this nonsense!" Lady Hastings retorted. "You seem to take great pleasure in terrifying those around you. If you truly wanted the portrait so urgently, you would have already found a suitable painter."

Nash gave up trying to conceal his amusement. "You're not entirely wrong about the first point," he admitted and reached for the decanter of whisky his butler had brought before Lady Hastings' arrival. He poured himself a glass and raised it to his lips.

"Is it not a bit early for spirits?" Lady Hastings asked pointedly.

"On the contrary," Nash mumbled. "After this exhausting morning, I need something to lift my mood." Out of pure defiance, he emptied the glass in one gulp and poured another. He loved his aunt, but he was his own master and wouldn't let anyone dictate how he should live his life. In his opinion, Lady Hastings had no idea about the delightful sins that made life worth living, but Nash didn't want to discuss it now. He needed peace to think about his problem.

Lady Hastings sighed but refrained from offering further advice, for which Nash was extremely grateful. The encounter with little Mrs. Fitzroy was lingering in his mind more than he cared to admit. The tears in her eyes had been unmistakable and had left a strange feeling in his chest. It was as if he had missed something, without knowing what it was. He couldn't remember the last time he had felt so uncomfortable.

"Do not try to distract me," came from across the table. "I will refrain from making any more comments about your manners, at least for now."

Nash perked up. It was unusual for Lady Hastings to give up so quickly. Her rapid capitulation could only mean one thing: in reality, she had another topic on her mind, and Nash suspected what it was.

His aunt wanted to talk to him about marriage.

"Have you managed to arrange a meeting with Lord Stewart?" There it was, the question that had been giving him sleepless nights. His future father-in-law had suggested several dates and was growing impatient. Shortly after the last, more pressing letter, a portrait of Lady Annis Stewart had arrived, depicting Nash's intended in all her Scottish beauty. That had been the moment when the absurd plan had taken shape in Nash's mind: he would send his bride, who had never seen him in her life, a painting that would show her his monstrosity.

"No," Nash replied curtly and eyed the whisky decanter. It wasn't even afternoon yet, and whisky only offered a temporary solution. He wondered if a Scottish bride would supply him with the water of life, as the Scots called it.

"And when do you intend to fulfil your responsibility?" The questions didn't end. Nash could well imagine Lady Hastings in the service of the Inquisition. She pursued her goal relentlessly and wouldn't give up until she was satisfied, which could take a very long time, as he knew from painful experience.

"When I deem the time is right," Nash replied. "I don't like to be told how and with whom to lead my life."

"Prinny meant well," Lady Hastings said, wiping a non-existent speck of dust from the desk. Actually, the manoeuvre was meant to move the whisky out of his reach. Nash suppressed the impulse to gulp down the entire decanter in one long sip. That would be childish. Then again, what did she expect when she treated him like a boy?

"I know," Nash reluctantly agreed. He was related to the Prince Regent through a convoluted family tree, which had brought him little benefit but a lot of annoyance lately. Nash was fortunate, at least in his opinion, to be far down in the line of succession. He would only come within reach of the throne if the hundred people ahead of him all lost their lives simultaneously, which was highly unlikely. However, the royal family considered it their duty to provide for every distant relative, as long as they didn't make themselves utterly impossible. In Nash's case, disaster had struck when he had faced the Prince Regent for the first time after his return. George, who loved everything beautiful, had embarrassingly wept upon seeing Nash's once-handsome but now terribly scarred face. In vain, Nash had tried to explain that the scar annoyed him but didn't limit him in any way. George had set his mind on Nash being a war hero and deserving more than an award – a beautiful bride. Prinny – and here Nash deliberately thought of the ridiculous, brainless nickname for the Prince Regent – hadn't hesitated to babble about fairy-tale destiny, about Beauty and the Beast. Nash had barely suppressed the question of whether George fancied himself as a fairy godmother. Someday, his overflowing imagination would get him into serious trouble, but thank heaven it hadn't on that day. Nash had kept his mouth shut and told himself that he would manage to get out of this predicament.

Nash had been convinced that the idea of marrying him was just a whim of His Royal Highness and that he would soon forget it. George was fickle and often forgot his promises. However, in this case, Nash was mistaken. His Royal Highness the Prince Regent had already taken action, and it was too late for Nash to outright refuse. All his assurances that he was perfectly capable of finding a wife on his own had fallen on deaf ears. A week later, the letter from Lord Stewart had arrived, the father of the woman whom George had personally chosen for Nash. Lord Stewart held the title "Earl of Orkney" and was a true-blooded Scot and a Catholic to his core. As a direct descendant of the stubborn Scottish Queen who had ended up on the scaffold, he appeared surprisingly enthusiastic in his letters. He was so enthusiastic that Nash couldn't help but be suspicious and wonder why he was so eager to marry off Lady Annis Stewart to him. The girl was barely ten-and-seven years old and, if one could trust the portrait, breathtakingly beautiful. Surely there were plenty of suitors who would gladly take Nash's place. And Nash would just as gladly have thrown his status as a groom into the lap of the next best man.

Damn it, he didn't want to get married! Someday, but not now. But it was no longer just about offending the Prince Regent by flatly refusing to marry Lady Annis Stewart. Lady Annis's father had already announced the engagement and Nash's sense of honour prevented him from running away. He only had one option: Nash had to persuade his future bride to break up with him and continue her life without damaging her reputation. What better way to do that than to show the girl a portrait of a disfigured monster, giving her a clear picture of what to expect?

Nash didn't understand much about ten-and-seven-year-old girls because he preferred the woman in his bed to know what she was getting into. He left debutantes and virgins to other men. However, one thing Nash knew: no maiden, no matter how mature she pretended to be, dreamt of marrying a monster with a permanent reminder of war on his face.

"Nash? Nash!" Lady Hastings' voice reached him. "Heavens, I said it is too early for this devil's brew!" His aunt stood up and was about to ring for Ferguson.

"Forgive my inattention," he said quickly. "I was lost in thought about my wedding."

Lady Hastings took her seat again. She leant forward and patted his significantly larger hand. "My dear boy, please believe me, in the end, everything will be fine. I promise you. You are old enough to marry and sensible enough not to wait for the one who turns your head. In the beginning, your Uncle Hastings and I were also in an arranged marriage, and look how much I still miss him six-and-twenty years after his death." She pulled a lace-edged handkerchief from her neckline and dabbed her eyes.

His Uncle Hastings had been a damn rake and, if Nash believed his father's words, had died two years to the day after their wedding of the French disease.

Aunt Matilda would have made a great actress.

6

FREDERICA

"Watch out, lass!" A giant hand grabbed Frederica by the nape of her neck and pulled her away from the railing. "He ain't worth it."

Who was the man referring to? Francis or Lord Burnwood? Neither of them, Frederica realised as she looked into the flushed face of the beer cart driver who had stopped his vehicle in the middle of Westminster Bridge to save her from falling into the depths. He clearly believed she had been led to ruin by some man and wanted to throw herself into the river. The driver wasn't entirely wrong, but he wasn't entirely right either. If Francis had left her with a child, at least there would have been a reason for her to live. Frederica looked at him: the weathered face, the brown eyes surrounded by wrinkles, and the toothless but compassionate smile. Around her, the other drivers were shouting and cursing, unable to move forward, but this man stood calmly in front of her, meeting her gaze.

Frederica burst into tears. She had lost the first painting that Francis had started and she had finished; had sent it tumbling into the river! Countless memories were attached to that painting. Back when he had started to paint it, he had still loved her unconditionally. Money had been scarce, but they had been abundantly happy. Bread, wine, cheese, and a few loving kisses were all it took to make them content. But with the painting, much more than her memories of those good days had been lost. Now, she had nothing to present to a potential client.

"Now, now, lass, it ain't that bad," he grumbled and gestured with his hand towards his rickety vehicle. "Hop on. If you're headed to Lambeth, I'll take you part of the way. I'm headin' to the Red Hand Tavern at Halfpenny Hatch." He handed her a tattered but clean cloth to wipe away her tears.

"Thank you," said Frederica, unsure whether she should keep the handkerchief or offer to wash it for him, as wet as it was. "For everything. But I'll walk. I'm not far now." She leant forward, doing her best to ignore the growing commotion they were causing on the bridge. "What's your name?"

He gave a brief bow. "William Beresford, at your service, madam."

He was right. What had come over her to give up so easily? It was a good thing there were people like him to remind her that life was a gift. Frederica planted a kiss on his cheek. "Thank you, William. My name is Frederica Fitzroy, and if you ever want a portrait of yourself or your wife, please visit me. I live at 7 Charlotte Street, right by Nelson Square." She took a few uncertain steps, then turned back one more time. "Thank you, William Beresford." The man still stood calmly in the middle of the bridge, making no move to leave. Frederica returned his smile and raised her hand in farewell before finally leaving the bridge. From a distance, she could still hear him urging his horse on with a hearty "Giddy up!" and saw the wagon set into motion, then he was gone for good.

It was an encounter she wouldn't forget.

On her way home, she tried to look for beautiful things: the smile of a flower girl or the team of two bay horses, whose proud necks she should aspire to. She thought about the work that had kept her afloat since Francis's death, a job that brought her almost as much joy as painting. She had learnt to make soap, just as her mother had taught her, but it was her father who had shown her how to dip candles. For him, it had been a useful pastime stemming from his beekeeping activities, but for Frederica, every candle sold meant a few pennies earnt through her own labour.

She was grateful for that too.

Lord Burnwood's commission wasn't the first one she had lost, and it wouldn't be the last. Besides, she smiled faintly, she was in good company with her lack of success. The famous Leech and the no less renowned Crawford had also received rejection from His Lordship. So why should she be more disheartened than the gentlemen? Women, Frederica realised suddenly, always took rejection much harder than men. Gentlemen shrugged off defeat like a dog shaking water droplets from its fur.

When Frederica opened the door to her modest house and crossed the threshold, her tears had finally dried, and she was dog-tired but no longer despondent. Tidbit, her red-striped tomcat, was nowhere to be seen. He was probably roaming the streets again, in search of a feline lady to add to his ever-growing list of conquests. Millicent had prepared a meal for her on the kitchen table, consisting of two slices of bread and cheese, and the sight brought tears to Frederica's eyes once again. Another reason to be thankful! Millicent was more than a remnant of the good old days when Francis was still alive, but now she only helped Frederica in the mornings and worked at a tailor's shop on Halfpenny Street in the afternoons.

As Frederica placed a log on the hearth to heat the kettle already filled with water by Millicent, she took a deep breath. What was left for her to do? What were her options?

She could ask her parents to take her back in.

She could find a new husband to provide for her. Provided she found a man who wanted her at her advanced age of eight-and-twenty. Moreover, she was a penniless widow who brought only herself and a few minor crafting skills to the marriage, in addition to the usual household duties, of course.

Steam rose from the spout of the kettle. Frederica carefully poured the boiling water into the teapot and sat back down at the table, waiting for the tea to steep. It tasted bitter. After tasting sugar at Lord Burnwood's, it was hard to go back to her usual, cheap beverage.

After Francis's death, she had been horrified to discover that he had left her with exactly three things: the jewellery he had given her after selling each painting, the house, and debt. She had parted with all movable possessions first: silverware she never used, clothes she would never have the occasion to wear again, and, of course, the modest pieces of jewellery. She had tried to paint, and she had managed to sell two or three paintings as posthumous works of her husband, but she had felt like a fraud. When she had finally mustered the courage to try under her own name, she had failed. For days, Frederica had stared at the canvas without a single preliminary sketch coming to her.

No matter how hard she tried, she couldn't paint anymore.

Francis's death had been so... unnecessary.

She had postponed selling the house for as long as possible. To make ends meet, she had made candles, boiled soap, and sold both at the market with Millie's help.

The visit to Lord Burnwood had made it more than clear to Frederica how glaring the gap was that now separated her from her old life. Not that she and Francis had ever lived in such luxury as His Lordship, not even close, but they had been better off and lived more carefreely than most other people.

Tired of the ups and downs of her emotions and exhausted from the walk to St. James and back, Frederica pushed the wooden plate with the half-eaten meal away and rested her head on her arms. Would she have thrown herself into the Thames if Mr. Beresford hadn't spoken to her? She closed her eyes. Frederica knew the answer to the question, and it filled her with a nameless fear of herself.

7

NASH

"The afternoon post, my lord." Ferguson placed the stack of letters on the edge of the desk and silently withdrew from the study. Nash nodded, checked the sum he had just entered in the ledger for the fifth time, and closed the thick notebook. Most noble landowners entrusted their affairs to family solicitors and the direct management of their estates to estate managers. However, Nash preferred to handle things himself. It had less to do with not trusting his managers than with offsetting the recklessness of his father and grandfather by increasing the family fortune. Where would he find time for a wife amidst all his duties? A wife demanded more attention than a mistress, especially when she was only seven-and-ten and would quickly become bored. Nash had neither the time nor the inclination to waste his thoughts on playing the fool for a wife who had barely outgrown the nursery.

As if in response to his thoughts, his gaze fell upon the Stewart seal. The Scottish lion and the typical sailboat of the Earls of Orkney were proudly displayed at the top of the stack of letters, which his butler had neatly placed on the designated corner of Nash's desk. The ship reminded him more of a galley than a warship ready to conquer enemy coasts.

Heavens and hells, was there nothing else to do up there in the most remote corner of the Scottish hinterlands than write letters? His prospective father-in-law was constantly bombarding him with mail. The weight and size of this letter suggested that Nash would have several pages to deal with today. He pursed his lips, sighed, and broke the seal.

As he had expected, the letter consisted of six closely written pages, of which only two came from Lord Stewart. Lady Annis Stewart had written four more double-sided sheets. Absentmindedly, he rubbed his scar. The tissue was tight, but it didn't get any better by constantly running his fingers over it. Perhaps he should attend to the other letters first... no, he should get it over with. If he set off on a ride to Hyde Park now, which he longed for more than anything else, the letters wouldn't disappear.

First, Nash read the lines dictated by Lord Stewart to his secretary. After some back and forth about the merits of Scotland in general and the Orkney Islands in particular, which Nash knew well enough from the other messages and which he couldn't care less about, the most important part of the message was hidden in the very last paragraph. At first, Nash thought he must have misread it. The writing was cramped, as if the secretary had tried to save paper, but there was no mistake:

"As soon as my affairs permit, I will travel south with my esteemed daughter. It is time for me to personally thank His Highness for an arrangement that must fill you with the greatest happiness." At this point, Nash didn't long for a glass, not a decanter, but a whole barrel of whisky. This arrogant, self-absorbed Scotsman truly believed that Nash was beside himself with joy at the prospect of marrying a Scottish bride! No wonder the Battle of... no, Nash wouldn't get lost in historical considerations that would lead to nothing now. He let the sheets drop. Was there a possibility of benefitting from the impending arrival of the Stewarts in London? He rubbed his forehead and thought feverishly. If he could be sure that his appearance would frighten the young lady even more than his portrait, he would look forward to a meeting with more confidence. However, Nash knew himself well enough to know that he would never bring himself to add rude behaviour to his

deformity to deter Lady Annis and her father from the wedding. Stupidity or obtuseness, as in the case of the damned painters, quickly enraged him, that was true, but intentionally insulting a person... no, that simply wasn't in his nature.

He reached for the next sheets and looked for the beginning of the letter written by Lady Annis Stewart. Unlike her father, she had put the lines on paper herself. Nash recognised it by the round letters that looked as if they were painted, occasionally interrupted by a poorly concealed ink blot. He could almost visualise the girl, compelled by her father to write a letter to her betrothed, licking her lips and composing word by word. As for the content... he furrowed his brow. Lady Annis wrote pages about her homeland, but at least she did it in a way that could be described as entertaining. She managed to capture with words a sense of the wild beauty she saw when she looked out of the window. Against his will, he felt sympathy for the young woman who, if he could trust her words, was looking forward to her upcoming trip to London.

"Soon" was a word Nash had never paid much attention to, but in the context of this girl and her mentioned journey, it filled his chest with sheer terror. Neither of the Stewarts indicated how many days this little word encompassed. Were they talking about weeks or months? Perhaps even half a year? Couldn't that cursed Lord Stewart have used a few of his rambling lines to specify his arrival time?

Oh, how he hated not being able to plainly tell the Prince Regent what he thought of this marriage! Instead, Nash was forced to take complicated detours. The manoeuvre with the portrait of horror was not only dubious in its chances of success, it was also on the brink of failure. It was maddening!

Questions upon questions, and Nash couldn't answer any of them. His plan for the lifelike portrait had been repeatedly thwarted by the overly flattering portraits of the so-called artists, and he was no closer to his goal than on the day of his first attempt. At the beginning of his odyssey, he had been a model of patience. Time and time again, he had explained to the painters how important it was for the scar to be realistically represented in the portrait. Even when he pointed out explicitly, upon seeing their hesitant sketches, that he absolutely wanted the disfigurement to be visible in the painting, they all softened the scar instead of emphasising it. Eventually, he lost patience, partly because he didn't understand why they feared him so much. Now, the only artists of acceptable reputation he hadn't summoned were Marcus Fletcher and Francis Fitzroy, whose wife had visited him earlier this morning. Fletcher was out of his reach, painting damned animals and plants somewhere in the colonies. So, if Nash didn't want to settle for an incompetent nobody, Fitzroy was his last and only chance to frighten the Scottish bride convincingly.

He didn't like having to approach Fitzroy as a supplicant now, after harshly rejecting the painter's peculiar conditions just a few hours ago. It felt like crawling to him. On the other hand, it would cost him no more than admitting he had acted hastily. What was a little feigned remorse if, in return, he escaped the impending prison called marriage? Also, the prospect of seeing the painter's little wife again was rather a pleasant one. He wouldn't go too far with her, of course, just a little flirting, just enough to keep himself entertained and pass the time. Nash had to admit he was impressed by how quickly she had overcome the shock of his disfigurement. Moreover, he had found no trace of the disgust that gripped most people when they looked at him. Fright, yes, no doubt – heaven, he sometimes scared himself when he saw his reflection in a window – but not repulsion.

He imagined her joyful surprise when he knocked on the Fitzroys' door later today and informed her husband that he was giving him a chance. He was curious about this Mr. Fitzroy. Was he really as good as his wife claimed? If he was, Nash might be generous enough to buy the portrait of his wife that she had brought this morning. The more he thought about it, the more he liked the idea. Of course, presenting the portrait in public was out of the question, but perhaps Nash would hang it in the library, in a place Aunt Matilda wouldn't immediately notice during one of her occasional visits to Nash's realm. He imagined himself sitting in his favourite armchair, legs stretched out, a glass of whisky in hand, enjoying the sight of Mrs. Fitzroy's seductive curves. Was she really as flexible as the portrait suggested?

The idea of having an image of her that belonged to him and him alone was exceedingly tempting. It was a pity he couldn't lure her into his bed as a married woman, but it had its advantages. At least – Nash chuckled self-deprecatingly – Mrs. Fitzroy posed no threat to his bachelorhood. It would be too comical if he escaped one marriage only to end up at the altar with another. But more than harmless flirting with a married woman was out of the question anyway. His ideas of what was right and wrong were firmly rooted in his nature. Owning her image, occasionally looking at it and indulging in fantasies was not reprehensible. Nash's fantasies harmed no one, and what the owner ultimately did with it was no longer the concern of the artist.

When he glanced at the two letters, he felt some of the burden on his shoulders dissipate. Nash decided to have the horses harnessed immediately to visit Fitzroy and the charming woman. He could write the letters to Lord Stewart and the Scottish bride later when the solution to his marriage problem was in sight. He rang for Ferguson and instructed him to prepare the cabriolet. For the hopefully short ride within the city, this vehicle was more suitable than the more comfortable but less agile four-in-hand carriage...

Wait a moment!

Nash stopped in his tracks. Mrs. Fitzroy hadn't given him her address, and because of the – admittedly – unconventional way he had invited her into the house, she hadn't been able to leave her card. How would he find her? Certainly, he could set out and visit some of his acquaintances who had contacts in artistic circles, but that might take time he didn't have. Damn it! Fate seemed to throw obstacles in his path, one after another. When he had thrown that wretched Crawford out of the house this morning, Nash had considered his situation serious but not hopeless. However, it now felt as if the whole world had conspired to get him married. He resumed his way to the front door, where Ferguson was waiting for him, holding his Spencer so that Nash only had to slip into it.

"Thank you," he grumbled, taking gloves, hat, and cane, and considering which of his acquaintances would be familiar enough with Francis Fitzroy to know his address.

8

FREDERICA

When Frederica awoke, it was almost dark. Her neck ached due to the unfortunate position in which she had fallen asleep, but all in all, she felt better than expected.

There was a silver lining in having nothing left to lose. Now, she was entirely on her own. The soap-making and candle-making, which had kept her and Millie afloat until now, were yielding diminishing returns. Procuring the necessary ingredients was becoming more expensive, and one of her suppliers had presented Frederica with a fait accompli last week: she wasn't buying enough from him to make the effort of delivering worthwhile. He had given her an ultimatum: either pay double for the tallow in the future or find someone else to supply her with the relatively small quantity she needed. One of her beekeepers, from whom she obtained beeswax for the candles, had moved to Wales along with the beehives, and the few other beekeepers in the vicinity sold their wax to professional candlemakers. The exorbitant fee she had paid two years ago for the permission to make and sell beeswax candles was far from being recovered. Taxes and the high overhead costs added to the burden.

It was inevitable that she would return to brushes and paint. Painting was the only thing that would bring in enough money for her to survive. But before that, she had to muster not only the courage to do so, but also find a patron. Why hadn't she sold herself better to Lord Burnwood this morning? Her pride had prevented her from begging, but pride was not only a cold bedfellow but also a poor currency.

Everything the future brought would be a result of her own decisions. It was solely in her hands to change her seemingly hopeless situation.

Frederica got up, stretched, and lit a lamp as the familiar meowing of Tidbit made her turn around. "Well, in which dark alleys have you been roaming?" she asked and knelt down to pet him between his red-and-white ears. Tidbit didn't react but withdrew from her and strolled in a manner that could only be described as regal to his empty bowl, mewing. "One moment, Your Highness. Let me check the pantry to see if I can find something to your liking." She got up and took the milk jug from the shelf. Together with what she hadn't finished, it should keep the cat content for now. Frederica watched as he dug into the mixture of milk, bread, and cheese, then she took a deep breath and retrieved the key to the studio from the pot where she used to store sugar.

Her hand was wet, and her heart pounded against her ribs as she left the kitchen and tiptoed through the corridor. She stopped in front of the door, which she hadn't opened in two years. Although the studio was the most spacious and bright room in the house, she hadn't been able to bring herself to make soap and candles in there. In summer, she worked in the garden, and in winter, she used an unused adjacent room. But she couldn't ignore the memories that awaited her in the locked room any longer.

Francis was dead. He no longer minded if she painted on his canvases, wasted his sketch paper, and wore down his precious drawing pencils. He would never scold her again for offering unsolicited suggestions, which he would accept with a smile and a thank you but never put into practice.

Before she could change her mind, Frederica inserted the key into the lock, turned it, and pushed the door open. The foul smell that met her took her breath away. With one hand over her nose and mouth, and without looking, she hurried to the table, randomly grabbed a few sheets of paper and a single pencil, and rushed back out. Outside, she leant against the wall with trembling knees and looked back at the studio door, behind which an unfathomable darkness lurked. Even now, two years after burying Francis, she wasn't sure if her hand could actually wield the brush.

Once her fluttering heartbeat had calmed down, she straightened up and went into the modest sitting room. The room had earnt the honorary title of her favourite room thanks to the high window overlooking the garden. The sun would set in the next few minutes, which meant she would have to draw by the light of candles and the oil lamp, but she didn't mind. Of all the rooms in the house, Francis had been the least present here. He had never appreciated the garden, and the salon had been too small and, as he occasionally emphasised, too feminine in its decor. Not occasionally, but often.

She pushed the memories of Francis as far away as she could and smoothed the paper on the table in front of her. She loved the smell of wood and glue that emanated from it, but she loved the promise that emanated from the unspoilt sheet even more. Frederica picked up the pencil with her trembling hand. For a brief moment, she closed her eyes, then she opened them and smoothed a sheet of old sketch paper. On it she saw the hastily sketched outline of a heathland, which made her smile because it reminded her of her husband. Details like the crooked chimney, a cottage in the distance, and a few sheep guarded by a dog were typical of his paintings. Francis had always had a good eye for details.

Determined, she turned the sheet over to its blank side. She would never forget Francis, but it was time to make peace with the past. Painting the back of a drawing by her deceased husband seemed like a reconciliatory omen to Frederica.

Her right hand holding the pencil hovered indecisively – and trembling, if she were honest – over the paper. What should she draw? Tidbit's triangular, obstinate face appeared in her mind, but she dismissed the thought. The Tiger of Lambeth, as she secretly called him, she would draw another time. No cute animals, no tame scene of domestic harmony, but a true sign of a fresh start. Something wild, untamed, not easily captured on paper.

Something like Lord Burnwood's face.

Now or never!

9

NASH

In Nash's mind, finding the Fitzroys' address had been straightforward: he would simply ask his butler. There was nothing Ferguson didn't know, or so Nash had assumed. When it turned out that the butler couldn't help in this case, Nash was momentarily speechless, a rare occurrence for him. He weighed his options. Aunt Matilda had acted as a patron of the arts before her husband's death and was likely familiar with Fitzroy, but explicitly asking about the painter would arouse her curiosity – something he couldn't afford given his risky plan. No, Nash needed another way to obtain Mr. Fitzroy's address, one that excluded Aunt Matilda.

Surely, there must be someone who... Of course! Nash almost slapped his forehead.

What had the painter said to Mrs. Fitzroy when they had collided on the street just before Nash grabbed him by the collar? *I will send you the bill for cleaning my clothing. Are you still lodging in Lambeth?* All he needed was Crawford's card and a quick visit to the painter he had thrown out of the house earlier this morning.

Perhaps luck hadn't deserted him after all.

The journey to Bloomsbury Square, where Crawford lived, went smoothly at first. However, as soon as the carriage stopped at the given address, the difficulties began to unfold. His servant, whom Nash had sent to the door, informed him that Crawford wasn't home. Nash was sure this was the truth and not just a polite way of saying the painter was pretending to be out. After the spectacular eviction earlier, the man wouldn't dare. The painter's studio was – for some inexplicable reason known only to the Almighty – in Rotherhithe. Normally, Nash would have enjoyed the ride, but today, his attempt to be entertained by the bustling activity around him failed. He wondered if he had acted too hastily when he had thrown Crawford out. The man was obviously wealthy enough to afford a house in Bloomsbury Square and a studio. Artists didn't make money if they produced rubbish. Success required a certain tenacity and more than just basic painting skills – and with success came a steady stream of income. Charlatans, he knew from Aunt Matilda, could trigger hysteria, a short-lived fashion, but to survive the tough competition among artists, more was required – namely substance.

When he arrived on Jamaica Street, it was already late afternoon, and it seemed that Crawford had slipped through his fingers again. Nash was so impatient that this time he didn't even send the servant but knocked on the door of Crawford's studio himself and, when that didn't work, took a peek through the small windowpanes at the front. All Nash saw was an unusually tidy room and part of a painting that was not covered by a cloth, revealing a promising smooth ankle. *Damn*, he thought when he finally tore himself away from the exposed body part. All he longed for was to get his hands on Crawford to obtain the urgently needed information. He was about to admit temporary defeat and return to Arden House when a plump woman emerged from the door of the neighbouring house.

"You can knock as long as you want, the gentleman artist isn't here." She spoke loudly and clearly, as if addressing someone hard of hearing. Unlike most of his acquaintances, she didn't seem to be frightened by his scar; she neither turned pale nor avoided his gaze.

Nash's mood improved. "You don't happen to know where I can find Mr. Crawford, Mrs...?"

She tilted her head. "Dalford is my name, Daisy Dalford. And as for where you can find him..." She paused briefly before continuing, "Have you tried one of the five thousand taverns in town?"

"It's a pleasure to meet you, Mrs. Dalford." Nash tipped his hat. A broad smile appeared on her face. "Would it be possible for you to tell me the names of his preferred taverns?"

The smile widened. Her eyes wandered from his hand-sewn shoes up his breeches, lingered on his chest for what he thought was a second too long, before finally settling on his face. He understood. Winking, Nash took a coin from his purse and handed it to her with a bow. The coin disappeared at a speed worthy of an illusionist, and a minute later, Nash possessed the names of five taverns where Crawford might be found. Mrs. Dalford offered to accompany him, so that he, the noble gentleman, wouldn't get lost in the streets of Rotherhithe, but Nash politely declined and set off for the first tavern, which was just around the corner.

The sun had disappeared below the horizon when Nash finally located Crawford. Of course, it was the last of the five inns where he found him. After spending most of his afternoon and evening trying to locate Crawford, the apprehension was disappointing, even downright anticlimactic. While Crawford did try to flee through the back door at the sight of Nash, he was far from steady on his feet. Within five seconds, Nash reached him, posed the pressing question, and received an immediate response: 7 Charlotte Street. Since it was too late to pay a visit to the Fitzroys today, he had an ale poured for himself and Crawford. The beleaguered painter drank his beer cautiously as if concerned Nash had laced it with belladonna. Nash asked him a few questions about Francis Fitzroy, but Crawford didn't give any sensible answers. Either fear of Nash had rendered him speechless or he envied his colleague the commission but didn't dare to openly speak ill of Fitzroy. Nash watched the painter with a half-smile as he left the tavern unsteadily. For a man who had been ejected from the house in such a manner, Crawford was remarkably forgiving.

Nash hoped he wasn't chasing a mirage. If Mr. Fitzroy, like all the other painters, turned out to be unwilling to prominently feature the scar, Nash wouldn't have many options left. What was it about his straightforward words that seemed to go unheard? Could they not or did they not want to follow his precise instructions? Nash had almost asked Crawford out of beer-infused curiosity if his suspicion was correct, that the painters were afraid of hurting him, Lord Burnwood. As if he didn't know what he looked like! But then Nash thought better of it and decided not to ask the question. Only if Fitzroy turned out to be a more accommodating man and Nash gave him the commission would he inquire.

If Mrs. Fitzroy's husband wasn't the right one either... well, then Nash wouldn't have many options left. The last option was to outright refuse to marry Lady Annis. Nash would lose the favour of the man who would soon be on the throne, but he could live with that. George wouldn't throw him in the Tower just because he declined the Scottish bride. For Aunt Matilda's sake, he would regret it, as her star at court would undoubtedly sink alongside his. Aunt Matilda wasn't a sycophant, but she was a woman whose circle of acquaintances would shrink drastically if she lost the favour of the Prince Regent. It wouldn't be a matter of months, but rather years, before society forgot – if ever. Nash had once seen what happened when a formerly respected person lost the favour of His Royal Highness. It was not something he wanted to subject his aunt to. If it were only about him, the situation would be different, but it wasn't.

The girl, Lady Annis, was in a much more delicate position than he was. Not only because she was Scottish and the relationship between England and her homeland was extremely tense. Surely, Lord Stewart, given the generous dowry he provided, could easily find another suitor for his daughter. However, her reputation would be damaged. Not irreparably, but people would gossip about her and wonder what flaw had prompted Nash to reject her. He couldn't do that to the girl. She hadn't asked for this union any more than he had, and she had done nothing wrong to him. Even though he didn't know her, he couldn't bring himself to turn her innocent life for the worse. Especially now she had written him a letter, and he had a faint sense of her character. Lady Annis Stewart was too young for his liking, but she wasn't foolish and knew how to choose her words. It would be better for her to initiate the separation and dissolve the engagement.

Speaking of letters. He finished his ale, placed a coin on the counter, and left the tavern. It was time to deal with his correspondence with the Scottish bride's father. The task wouldn't become any more pleasant if he procrastinated. He would support the deterrent effect of the painting by showing himself in a less favourable light. Perhaps – he grinned wolfishly – it wouldn't hurt to mention his whisky consumption. What could sufficiently deter a girl of her tender age and make her move heaven and earth to avoid walking down the aisle with Nash?

10

FREDERICA

Frederica awoke with a sore neck and eyelids that refused to lift. Rubbing the sleep from her eyes, she sat up. The sofa she had curled up on was comfortable, but the goose feathers in the sofa cushion were clumped together and not soft enough to support her head for an entire night. Her tongue felt thick, and her head ached as if she had indulged excessively in wine the previous evening.

She had drawn late into the night, almost obsessively, her hand guided by the pencil as she created sketch after sketch of His Lordship. To be precise, of his face. She hadn't even come close to capturing the particular allure that radiated from him. Frederica found the profile view the most successful, capturing the curve of his nose and the strong chin quite well. Just a suggestion of the scar was enough to give his face an entirely different expression. Strangely, the scar enhanced his expressiveness, even though Frederica couldn't pinpoint the exact source of his almost irresistible charm.

She tore her gaze away from the scattered sheets on the table. During the night, it had seemed like a promising plan: she would draw Lord Burnwood, take the sketches to him, and tell him the truth. Frederica would confess that she, not Francis, was the one in desperate need of the commission. What did she have to lose? He had already rejected a male artist. If the sketches didn't convince him, he would reject her as well, and it wouldn't matter whether it was because of her gender – as it always was – or because he didn't like her style. But the promising plan to secure the commission was now disintegrating in the harsh morning light. She was not an artist, period. Francis had been right when he had praised her talent but pointed out that she lacked the mental strength and discipline to succeed in a field dominated by men. In moments like these, she wondered how her life would have turned out if her mother hadn't insisted on her taking drawing lessons. Would she be content, even happy, if this all-consuming passion had never struck her?

Frederica approached the table, gathered the sheets, and blindly piled them together. She regretted using the back of Francis's sketches, but she wouldn't forget Francis just because she burnt his hastily drawn drafts. Her pictures were only fit for kindling the fire. Later, she would ask Millicent to roll up the papers so she would never have to look at Lord Burnwood's face again, or ask herself "What if…?"

Frederica washed up and slipped into her favourite dress before heading to the kitchen. Like all her other garments, it was out of fashion and had become a bit too loose over time, but it could be cinched under the bosom to hide the excess fabric. The once-bright ultramarine blue had faded, but that didn't bother the dress or Frederica. She loved every shade of blue, whether vibrant or subtle.

"Good morning, madam," Millicent said, setting aside the cloth she had been using to scrub the floor in front of the hearth and rising from her kneeling position.

Frederica returned the greeting and invited the girl to sit with her at the kitchen table. Where should she begin? What were the right words to dismiss someone who had been coming to her for more than ten years, someone Frederica knew inside out, both at her best and worst? "Millie," she said, swallowing hard. "We need to talk." Frederica took a deep breath. "I'm sorry, but I can no longer afford to employ you. This week will be your last with me."

The young woman with the cherubic face nodded. "I understand, madam," she replied, doing something she had never dared to do in all her years in Frederica's service. She reached across the table and took her employer's hand. "Don't cry," Millicent said, tears streaming down her own cheeks. "I'll manage somehow. And you..." It was half a question and half an offered comfort. "I've already asked Mr. Solomon if I can work more than just half a day with him, and he said yes."

"That's wonderful!" Mr. Solomon was the tailor Millicent assisted. Frederica felt a weight lift off her chest. She didn't want to talk about herself in this situation but focused on Millicent's future instead. "I'm so glad, even though I'll be terribly sorry to lose you." Frederica would manage on her own. A smaller place to live, a room to rent somewhere – something like that would save her a lot of money. She could sell the candles she hadn't been able to sell so far. The same went for the soap. Both would keep her afloat for a while.

Millicent pushed a strand of her ash-blonde hair from her forehead, leaving a streak of dirt on her freckled skin. Frederica felt the urge to sketch the girl here and now, so full of life and optimism that never seemed to fade.

"Mr. Solomon has been asking for a year if I want to work more hours. So, you don't need to worry about me." She squeezed Frederica's hand again and then let go. "Mr. Solomon also said he wouldn't mind if I... if he and I... well, he wants to marry me!" she blurted, looking immensely surprised.

"Oh, Millie," Frederica whispered when she found her voice again. "You didn't hesitate and decline his proposal because of me, did you?" It would be typical of the girl to feel obliged by her kindness not to leave Frederica alone. A look at the girl's face confirmed Frederica's suspicion. "Mr. Solomon will be lucky to have you as his wife. He will be the happiest man in the world." And she wouldn't even have enough money for a wedding gift, even after selling the house! "I'm very happy for you," she said softly. She stood up, circled the table, and pulled Millicent to her feet. Then she hugged the young woman. When she noticed that the closeness was becoming uncomfortable for the girl, she released her and stepped back.

"I'm going out, and I don't know when I'll be back," Frederica announced. It was time to part with the very last thing that reminded her of her old life. "When you're finished, close the door as usual. If Tidbit shows up, give him the rest of the cheese." The Lambeth Tiger was a notorious late riser and probably wouldn't appear before early afternoon, but you never knew.

"What will you do now, madam?" Millicent followed her into the narrow hallway and handed Frederica her coat and bonnet. She folded back the brim a bit, examined Frederica, and nodded approvingly, like a mother hen sending her chick out into the world.

"I'll do what I should have done a long time ago," Frederica said determinedly. "I'll ask Mr. Kingston if his offer for my house still stands and, if he wants it, I will sell it to him." The sum would be enough to settle the rest of Francis's debts. That was all that mattered.

"And then?" Millicent knew the sum would not be enough to give Frederica a secure retirement.

"And then..." The image of beehives came to her, only to be replaced by the brown waters of the Thames. "Then we'll see."

She opened the door and walked out onto Charlotte Street, head held high.

II

NASH

The following morning, Nash could barely contain his impatience. He was eager to bring the vexed issue of marriage to a conclusion, and for that, he needed Mr. Fitzroy. If the painter could deliver the desired result to Nash, and if Lady Annis Stewart chose not to marry a monster, he would be free. If not... well, then he would at least enter the chains of marriage knowing that he had made a few people happy.

Of course, that was nonsense. While Aunt Matilda and his prospective father-in-law would be relieved, there was little chance for Nash himself or Lady Annis to find happiness together. Content, perhaps, after many gloomy years of marriage, once they had grown accustomed to each other, but happy? Never! Nash had studied enough philosophical writings to know that everyone sought personal happiness, but for people like him, of high rank and all its associated duties, it was rarely granted. Or, more precisely, it was difficult to maintain. If this marriage were to happen, he would have to redefine his notion of happiness. Although it looked worse for him with each passing day, he refused to give up.

An impatient glance at the clock on the mantelpiece showed him that he could finally make his way to Lambeth without arriving too early.

Normally, he would have left long ago and even thrown the painter out of bed, but this time, Nash reluctantly found himself in the position of a petitioner, even if the eccentric Mr. Fitzroy didn't know it. The painter's wife, however, was a different matter. She would know he needed her husband's services as soon as she saw him.

Why did he even care about her opinion?

He leant back into the soft cushions of the carriage and allowed himself to be lulled by the muted heartbeat of the city. The clip-clop of hooves and the calls of the coachmen warning or urging on pedestrians usually calmed him, but not today. The hooves on the road sounded like shots on the front lines, and the coachmen's cries like the screams of the wounded. Even though no one could see him, Nash discreetly wiped the sweat from his brow and didn't breathe freely again until he had slid the narrow window in the carriage door to the side. Light and air, even if the latter carried the musty scent of the Thames, were preferable to the stench of his own anxiety.

To make matters worse, they had now reached Westminster Bridge. The chronic congestion, caused by the carts of traders and numerous pedestrians, forced his coachman to a snail's pace. Nash wished he hadn't given in to his urge to impress and ordered the cabriolet instead of the closed carriage.

What was wrong with him? Since he had met Mrs. Fitzroy yesterday, he had been increasingly losing control of his emotions. She was just a woman, a wife, and not particularly pretty, according to the prevailing fashion. Or was he telling himself that to drive away thoughts of her? Mrs. Fitzroy had left a deeper impression on him than he cared to admit, and not just because of the seductive curves in the painting. He leant to the left to look out the window, but the much-too-narrow frame allowed him only a limited field of view. He was about to jump out of the carriage and cross the bridge on foot when it finally started moving again. Just a few more minutes, and he could get out of this damn cramped carriage.

It took much too long to reach his destination. The carriage had barely come to a stop when Nash jumped out, without waiting for the servant's help or sending the man ahead. Giving his surroundings hardly more than a fleeting glance, he headed for the door, and at the last moment remembered to change his demeanour from hasty to dignified and arrange his features so they reflected nothing but neutral arrogance – if such a thing existed.

He let the door knocker fall onto the metal sign, stepped back a pace, and waited. The little painter's wife would be surprised to see him. Perhaps... Much faster than expected, the door was opened from the inside, and a stout woman stepped toward him. Her eyes widened in shock, as if she had looked the devil in the face, and she jumped back. At first, Nash believed she would slam the door in his face upon seeing his scar, but with great effort, as reflected in her expression, she regained her composure. She held a broom in her chubby, reddened hands and seemed capable of doing more with it than just sweeping dirt from one corner to another.

"Good day," Nash began, trying to ignore the unexpected disappointment that had come over him when he saw the woman. Hardly had he spoken his greeting when a red-striped beast shot out from behind the wide-eyed maid and stood before him. What the hell was that? Perhaps the Creator had intended to confine the beast in a cat's form, but his adversary had clearly played a hand and turned it from a cute, cuddly housemate into a mixture of guard dog and ferocious tiger. Its sulphur-yellow eyes pierced Nash's blue ones. The oversized creature hissed and bared fangs worthy of its striped relative.

"Back off, Tidbit!" the woman said unceremoniously, and with the bristles of the broom, she half-heartedly slapped the cat on its furry behind. To Nash's surprise, the cat obeyed after giving the woman an offended look – and him an exceedingly revengeful one – before disappearing inside the house.

"Good day," Nash began again from the beginning. "Please inform Mr. Fitzroy that Lord Burnwood wishes to speak with him." He handed her his card, which she took hesitantly and examined, as if she were reading. Which, apparently, she could do, albeit slowly and with her lips forming the syllables silently. It took an unduly long time before she stepped aside and granted him entry. The aggressive cat was nowhere to be seen.

"My lord, my mistress has gone out, but I expect her back any moment," she said, curtsied, and closed the door behind him. The hallway was narrow and cramped, but the maid managed to pass him with her broom without him having to press against the wall to make way. "Please follow me to the drawing room, my lord. You can wait there. Would you like... tea?"

The hesitation before the last word caught his attention. There was no expression on the young woman's face, but she chewed on her lower lip. At the same time, he noticed the sparse furnishings and the stained walls. In the drawing room, there was only a sofa, a chair, and a table – just the essentials. There was exactly one piece of wood in the basket next to the fireplace. Mr. Fitzroy was clearly not doing well. Was he in such a bad state that he didn't even have tea in the house? Perhaps, perhaps not, but that would explain why the man had sent him this expressive painting of his wife. So Nash politely declined and explained that he would wait until Mr. Fitzroy returned from his business.

"If you require anything, my lord, there's the bell," the maid said, pointing to the cord hanging from the ceiling with the broom in her hand. Nash nodded and settled reluctantly into the chair, which seemed better suited to his tall frame than the dainty-looking sofa. As soon as he was alone, he leant back and stretched his legs out. Everything in this room had a feminine touch, from the faded rose-patterned wallpaper to the furniture. The meticulous cleanliness stood out to him, as did the sparseness of the furnishings. Clearly, the Fitzroy household had seen better days. As Nash sifted through his memory, searching for a scandal or offence that could explain Mr. Fitzroy's decline in his career, his gaze fell on a few crumpled sheets of paper. They were the only detail that stood out from the rest. Should he...? Why not?

Because one did not do such things. One did not snoop into other people's... sketches. Unless one had an urgent commission with princely payment to offer to a man one had not yet met and who exhibited rather suspicious behaviour.

Nash leant forward and picked up the first of the crumpled sheets. Carefully, he unfolded it and smoothed it out. He was about to set aside the drawing with the boring sketch of a dull landscape when he noticed the dark, translucent lines of another drawing on the back of the sheet. At first, all he saw was a tangle of dark grey lines, but after blinking several times, the lines formed into a face. *His* face, to be precise. Did he really look so stern? The brows of his likeness met above the bridge of the nose, forming a steep V. His mouth was nothing more than a line beneath a nose that, at least, looked just as noble as he remembered. Even the scar was there! Not just hinted at like in the paintings by other artists, but exactly as he wished it to be, namely, lifelike. Ha! No wonder the poor maid had recoiled from him. In the drawing, he looked positively intimidating!

He hastily set the sheet aside and examined the next pages. Some showed more than just a human figure, while others included details like an eye or a cheekbone, a strong neck, or a pair of hands, but they all belonged to him. In the hastily drawn sketches, the artist's passion for creating a detailed image was evident, but even an artistic novice like Nash could sense the frustration that had fuelled the artist in creating his work. Some areas of the paper were torn or had holes in them.

He paused and spread the sheets out in front of him. What had he done to incur the artist's wrath? As far as he knew, he had never met Francis Fitzroy and had done nothing to personally anger the artist. And, more importantly, how on earth had Fitzroy managed to draw him so accurately when they had never stood face to face?

He stared at the drawings. Bold curves alternated with sharp lines. There was a delicacy in the line work that was undeniably feminine.

How could he have been so blind? It wasn't Mr. Fitzroy who had created these sketches, but someone who had already sat face to face with Nash. Nash was so surprised by his realisation that he only noticed someone entering the drawing room when it was too late.

12

FREDERICA

Of course, Mr. Kingston had sensed Frederica's desperation and negotiated down the price of her house. Exhausted as she was, Frederica had had nothing to counter him with. On her way to Mr. Kingston, one of Lambeth's wealthiest men, she had felt the urgent desire to finally bring everything to a close. It hadn't been as bad as yesterday after her visit to Lord Burnwood when she had stared into the Thames and wondered what it would be like to put an end to it all, but she was still miles away from a feeling of a fresh start.

But she and Kingston had made a good deal. She was free of Francis's debts, and everything else would have to fall into place. One step at a time, Frederica told herself as she entered her house. *The* house, she corrected herself mentally. She had signed the purchase contract and received a down payment. Perhaps the sum would be enough for a high-quality wedding gift for Millicent and her suitor after all. Her maid was already trotting towards her, as if summoned by Frederica's thoughts. She was still here? Frederica had told her that she couldn't employ Millie anymore! But she didn't get a chance to express her joyful surprise because she immediately noticed that something had happened. Millicent promptly pulled her from the hallway into the kitchen, without taking off her coat and hat as she usually did.

"A lord is here!" Millicent's dramatic whisper was accompanied by her hands pressed to her bosom. Her cheeks were flushed. "It's him. The Devil of St. James!" Hasty breaths punctuated the pauses between her words.

"Who?"

"Lord Burnwood!"

Fine. Slow down. Lord Burnwood was called "the Devil of St. James," and he was here, in her house? Frederica pressed a hand to her mouth to contain the mad laughter tickling her chest. She would ask Millie where she had got this absurd nickname from in due course. She could imagine roughly how His Lordship had earnt that name. "Where is he? Did he say what he wants?" Millie's short, choppy speech seemed contagious.

"He's waiting in the drawing room. For *Mr.* Fitzroy!" The look Millie gave her was filled with panic.

"Good," Frederica said, lowering the hand she still held protectively over her mouth. Then she repeated, "Good. That means he wants something from us." She quickly removed her bonnet and coat and handed them to Millie. "How do I look?" She regretted asking even as the words escaped her.

Millicent grinned. "Like a woman ready to face the devil."

Good. At least she only thought this meaningless phrase instead of saying it out loud for the third time. Nothing was good, not even remotely. Even if His Lordship had changed his mind, it would be difficult to persuade him to give the commission without insisting on seeing Francis at some point during their negotiations. Frederica dismissed the macabre idea of leading Lord Burnwood to Francis's grave and introducing her husband to him. Did His Lordship fall for this new trend of summoning spirits? If so, she could pretend Francis was guiding her hand while she put the strokes on the canvas.

Enough now! After taking a deep, dizzying breath, she reached into her reticule and handed Millie a coin. "We need tea and biscuits, and we need them quickly! Better go to Mrs. Wheedon's and buy some from her. The bakery is too far."

Millie looked down at the coin in her hand and pursed her lips. "This is too much," she said. With a sigh, she turned and left Frederica to herself.

A deep breath. She was about to knock when she remembered that this was still her house, at least in name. With a jerk, she pushed down the latch and entered – and almost stumbled backward.

Lord Burnwood stood there, his dark head bent forward between his shoulders, studying his own face staring back at him from the paper, multiple times. He had smoothed out all the sheets and placed them on the table, one next to the other!

For a second, they both were frozen. The lord caught in the act, and Frederica equally caught, her chest exploding with a whirlwind of various emotions, were like captives in a sketch titled *The Unrepentant Sinner*. Then Frederica ran, stumbled briefly as she caught the hem of her dress, and tore the paper from his hands. Finally, she clenched her fingers around the sheets and crumpled them. Her breath was too fast, and her heartbeat throbbed in her ears as she staggered to the cold fireplace and threw the shreds into it, out of the reach of curious eyes. She wished for a dramatic burst of flames, so Lord Burnwood could watch his likeness consumed by fire, but of course, nothing of the sort happened. The paper balls lay untouched in the ashes where Frederica had thrown them. The impact of her gesture fizzled out. In a swirl of fluttering fabric, she turned around and crossed her arms over her chest. "What gives you the right to snoop through my private belongings?"

Lord Burnwood looked at her. "Good day, Mrs. Fitzroy. I apologise. My curiosity led me to violate your privacy. I'm sorry."

Frederica was by no means appeased, even though he had expressed his regret twice, but for the sake of fairness, she had to admit that part of the blame was on her. She should have put the drawings away or burnt them immediately. That was why she nodded stiffly like a marionette forced by an awkward puppeteer. Lord Burnwood approached her and extended his hand. It must have been her good upbringing that compelled Frederica to release her arms and allow him to lean over her hand. His fingers closed around hers, but he contented himself with a hint of a hand kiss.

As Lord Burnwood straightened up again, the distance between them had melted to half an arm's length. Tall and broad-shouldered, he loomed over Frederica before seeming to notice her discomfort. The mischievous delight in his eyes contrasted strangely with his empathy as he gestured towards the chair. "May I?"

Frederica nodded, still at a loss for words. Only the sound of the opening and closing front door snapped her out of her paralysis. Millie was back. "Of course. Please forgive my rudeness." The ironic undertone was so subdued that she prayed it would escape Lord Burnwood's notice. Frederica's hope was in vain. His lips curled into a mocking smile, causing her knees to weaken. She sank onto the sofa.

"I've reconsidered your offer from yesterday," he said so softly that she had to lean in to hear him. The blue of his eyes was stormy like the sea on a winter day. "I accept your offer." He placed a well-filled purse on the table in front of him. In Frederica's mind, the clinking of the coins was louder than the bells of St. Mary le Bow. Lord Burnwood didn't wait for her agreement but continued speaking. "I wish for a portrait by the artist who created these drawings." A single drop of sweat ran down her spine. "My only condition: it must be finished within two weeks." Finally, he leant back. Frederica could breathe, think, and speak again.

"That's impossible!" she croaked. To emphasise her voice, she cleared her throat. Then she began to explain, "Even if the artist managed to capture your unforgettable features on canvas in the shortest time, there's still the time required for the oil paints to dry. Depending on the thickness of the individual layers, it can take months before varnish can be applied." The jab regarding his appearance had come out of her mouth without her intending it. She continued when he frowned, "Varnish is the final layer that protects the painting and—"

"I know what varnish is," he interrupted. The sparkle in his eyes intensified. "Your husband, you said, will paint the portrait?"

Frederica felt the colour draining from her face. His Lordship's eyes darkened. The storm became a hurricane. "He's unwell at the moment." That was one way to put it.

"It's imperative that the picture is completed as soon as possible," he insisted. "Perhaps I could send my physician to your husband. He is a very capable man."

Frederica narrowed her eyes. Was this a trap? Lord Burnwood appeared as though he hadn't been sick a single day in his life. Her search for an answer had already taken too long, so she said, "Thank you very much, my lord." *Think, Frederica*, she reminded herself. "Rest is all my husband needs." She felt her cheeks flush. Francis certainly had rest. "In the meantime, I will begin the preliminary work. I am familiar with his working method, my lord. You need not worry that your portrait will suffer from my..." She hesitated before finishing the sentence. "From my involvement."

"I believe you," she thought she heard him murmur. Her heart skipped a beat. What did he mean by that? Had Lord Burnwood seen through her and was now playing a game with her?

"I am not one of those men who inherently consider a woman's work inferior, Mrs. Fitzroy. If your husband values your abilities highly enough to make you his assistant, it is not for me to doubt."

Could it be that she had lucked out again?

"Consider it a trade that will benefit both parties. You, Mrs. Fitzroy, will create my portrait and will be generously compensated in return."

Thoughts raced through Frederica's mind. He hadn't mentioned Francis but had referred to her specifically.

"From that perspective, you are right, my lord. I just wonder..." She paused and looked at him with narrowed eyes, as if she could see through his broad, smooth forehead. "What's in it for you, my lord?" Despite his words about his lack of bias, a lingering doubt remained in her heart.

"You needn't concern yourself with that, Mrs. Fitzroy." He mirrored her expression, narrowing his eyes as well. "I can keep a secret if that's what worries you."

He knew!

Her heart skipped a beat and suddenly seemed to be in her throat. With tremendous effort, Frederica swallowed, as if she could force the rebellious organ back into its place. "I'm sorry, but I don't know what you're talking about." If she repeated it often and long enough, he might not believe it, but he might accept it. The important thing was that neither of them would openly acknowledge that she was the one who would paint him. She stood up and added with a determined voice, "It seems you'll have to find another painter. I can recommend a few colleagues of my husband's who..."

When Lord Burnwood unexpectedly stood up, she once again felt reminded of a sleek predator. Or perhaps a toy devil springing from its box. Except that this man was no toy, at least not in her hands. "Enough of the theatrics," he whispered. Goosebumps crawled up her forearms and spread across her entire body. "I don't know where your husband is, Mrs. Fitzroy, and I don't care. If you're the one who created these," he gestured with a fluid motion toward the crumpled papers in the cold fireplace, "you're my first choice."

Hot pride brought tears to her eyes. He wanted her! And that, even though she wasn't a man, had no accreditation, and had no merits as an artist! He had said enough that she almost relented. As if sensing her hesitation, Lord Burnwood continued softly, "Come. I can tell you want it as much as I do. Follow your heart!" The shadowy blue around his black irises grew darker with each word.

"How did you find out?" Her voice was barely more than a whisper.

"The drawings gave you away," he said, stepping to the fireplace to retrieve one of the sheets. He smoothed the crumpled paper for the second time and held it out to her. "Firstly, your husband has had no opportunity to see me. The drawing with the scar can only be from someone who has stood directly in front of me, which means it's yours." With his free hand, he pointed to the disfigurement without any hesitation and smiled, strangely satisfied. It was as if he not only didn't mind that Frederica had portrayed him in such a lifelike manner, but that she had somehow expressed exactly what he desired. But Lord Burnwood wasn't finished. "Secondly," he began, flipping the sheet over, "this sketch here was made by a different artist." He turned the paper over so that her incriminating image was visible again. "The strokes here are bolder, but also more precise, and there are fewer of them."

"That cannot have given me away," she interjected, bolder now than just a few seconds ago. "The landscape, too, could have been drawn by me, perhaps years ago. My style might have changed."

"Oh no!" He shook his head. "This – my portrait – was clearly drawn by a woman. Women," he grinned devilishly, "may be considered the chatty sex, but that's not true in my experience. When a woman speaks, she can achieve a devastating effect with few well-chosen words. It's similar with a portrait: a few strokes can make an extraordinary impact. You can't deny your authorship, Mrs. Fitzroy." As if it had served its purpose as evidence, he casually placed the sheet on the table and stepped so close to her that she had to tilt her head back to look into his eyes. "Say yes! Paint me, Mrs. Fitzroy! I promise, I will not spill your secret."

Her exhaustion vanished in an instant, and heat surged through Frederica. This was her chance to step out of the shadows. This was the fresh start she had yearned for over the past two years! More than that, perhaps she could even earn a living with her own hands' work. She could do what she loved more than anything else in the world.

Now she understood why they called Lord Burnwood the Devil of St. James. Not because of the disfigurement on his face, but because he proposed a truly diabolical deal: his silence in exchange for the painting he apparently urgently needed.

13

NASH

Seeing her expressive face was like riding an untamed horse. Hope, distrust, a shadow of happiness and sorrow alternated rapidly, making it difficult for Nash to label her emotions. In these brief moments, Mrs. Fitzroy revealed her vulnerability, and Nash felt as if he were watching a beautiful woman sleep and dream. It gave him very little satisfaction to know that it was his words that had awakened these intense feelings in her – and that he had been spot-on in recognising her as the artist.

"There are three conditions," she said after an eternity. He met her open gaze. "First: my signature is on the painting, clearly visible, and you double the amount you brought with you today." Nash nodded. Without hesitation, he would pay ten times the usual fee if the painting was completed quickly and had a sufficiently intimidating effect. But how did Mrs. Fitzroy know what amount he considered appropriate payment? Probably, he thought with a healthy dose of admiration for her courage, she was going all-in. If he had brought fifty guineas, she would have agreed to double that amount. As for the first part of her condition, he had no objections. Of course, she could claim the fame for painting him.

"Before you agree and we come to terms," she admonished him with a hint of mockery in her voice, "let me explain the other conditions I am imposing, my lord."

"That sounds like we're sealing a legal agreement rather than the artistic act I want to commission you for."

Rose petals paled next to the colour of her cheeks, which his words brought forth. Without addressing Nash's comment, she continued. "Second: you must come to me for each session. There will be no substitution by one of your servants of similar stature, as is customary when portraying a nobleman." Her full lips curled mockingly. "I'm aware that this inconveniences you because it means neglecting your usual pursuits." The mockery in her expression intensified and conveyed to him without words what she understood by "usual pursuits" – namely gambling, drinking, and seduction. How he wished he could remove the taunting from her mouth and replace it with something more pleasant, but that would only provide her with evidence of her suspicions. "I will work as quickly as possible," she added, the black lashes around her brown irises deepening the intensity of her gaze.

"What is the final condition?" Nash leant back and steepled his fingertips together. He had borrowed this gesture from the Archbishop of Canterbury and used it whenever he wanted to express expectant confidence – or confident expectation, depending on the situation. Today, all his efforts were in vain because Mrs. Fitzroy, the beautiful impostor, was only paying attention to his face. "Please, I'm waiting!" He reminded himself that composure was the key to success here.

"Third: everything that happens within these four walls stays within these four walls." She extended her right hand with more than a spark of challenge in her gaze.

Nash allowed himself an ironic raise of the eyebrows, even though he spoke in a matter-of-fact tone. "I'm not a gossipmonger, Mrs. Fitzroy." That didn't mean he didn't want to unravel the mystery of the woman, which her every word was fuelling his curiosity of. What had happened to her husband?

Nash barely managed to stop himself from leaning forward in anticipation.

He took her hand and wondered if he had gone mad by forming an alliance with a woman in which they were almost equals. He would agree to her terms and pay her for a service as he normally would with a man. Could she deliver what her sketches promised? Why was she making such a mystery about her husband's fate? After all, she had insisted that her name be clearly visible on the portrait. Was the man ill, perhaps on the brink of death, and she wanted to secure her future by creating her own career as a painter? Every possible explanation led to another puzzle. It would give him great pleasure to solve them.

"We have an agreement." He picked up her phrasing and shook her hand – gently. After all, he wanted to see how her delicate fingers, which felt so fragile, wielded pen and brush. "As for the time... we start immediately. As I said, I need the painting as soon as possible." Beneath her index and middle finger, he felt calluses, the kind that someone who performed physical labour would have. "You've received the initial payment of two hundred guineas today, and the rest will be given to you upon completion. Agreed?"

Before she could respond, the maid entered, carrying a tray. Mrs. Fitzroy waited until the woman had set down her burden and signalled her that she would pour the tea herself. After an awkward curtsy, the girl left without even looking at Nash.

Mrs. Fitzroy's unconventional behaviour allowed him a glimpse of her ample bosom, which was concealed by her modest dress as she bent to fill the cups. Nash noticed that no sugar was served with the tea, which didn't bother him, as he preferred the taste of the brew pure. Other signs of meagre wealth were apparent, not only by his own luxurious standards. There was not much left that could be pawned, he suspected, given the Spartan furnishings. She hadn't sold the painting she had shown him yesterday, had she?

"I already mentioned that oil paints have a long drying time," she repeated in response to his comment, which he had almost forgotten. "An alternative would be watercolours."

He shook his head in horror. "Absolutely not! I don't want a tame, diluted version of myself but a vivid likeness that virtually leaps out at the viewer." A softened version of himself wouldn't serve the desired purpose of frightening Lady Annis Stewart. She might end up falling in love with him!

"My lord, using watercolours doesn't mean I will work with delicate pastel tones. These colours are just as vibrant as oil paints but less durable and lightfast. An oil painting can last centuries in the right place, while a watercolour loses its brightness over the years." Mrs. Fitzroy spoke with growing confidence. Painting seemed to be a subject she discussed with self-assurance and competence. "It would be highly unconventional, though, if you were to hang a watercolour portrait in a prominent place in your home." She furrowed her brow. "May I ask why you need the painting within this tight timeframe? Perhaps I can find a solution you haven't considered."

Nash choked on his tea and quickly held the thin napkin in front of his mouth, which the maid had brought in along with the tea and a bowl of pastries. "I will not inquire about your husband, Mrs. Fitzroy, and you will avoid questions about my motives in our conversations." That was an unmistakable command. He would rather model for her in the nude than entrust her with his desperate plan.

"You're making it unnecessarily difficult for me," she countered, not ready to give in yet. He tried to give her an intimidating look. She sighed. Sighed? Nothing more? Had his being in her house deprived him of his usual frightening effect? "But all right," she conceded. "You're paying, so you also get to determine what you receive. However, I warn you: if the layers of paint on the oil painting aren't fully dry, it can easily get damaged. A clumsy touch, and your face will be unrecognisable." She gasped and froze for a moment, then closed her eyes. It seemed she had become aware of what she had just said.

Nash smiled, doing nothing to hide his amusement. In some elusive way, it gave him fiery pleasure to have embarrassed her, even though strictly speaking, he had done nothing but sit there and let her talk.

"I-I apologise," she stammered, trying to regain her composure. "That was unspeakably rude of me." Somehow, she found the courage to look at him again. Whatever she saw, Nash didn't know, but it made the colour in her cheeks shift from a delicate pink to deep red. Unlike most women, she looked more attractive the more flushed she became.

"You will create the portrait in oil paints and hand it over to me. I will ensure that it doesn't get damaged."

"I could apply the paint in several thin layers," Mrs. Fitzroy said, stretching out her thoughts more to herself than to him. "That would simplify the drying process. Another option would be to use a thicker frame than usual to ensure that the packing paper doesn't come into contact with the paint."

"However you choose to proceed," Nash waved it off, "my proposal stands. You take care of the details of the painting process." For a moment, he thought his persistent urging might reveal how urgently he needed the painting, but Mrs. Fitzroy's next sentence told him that she was still thinking about the choice of colours. Did the woman have nothing else on her mind but these cursed paints?

"I could try Ackerman's Art Supplies," she contemplated aloud. "Their pre-made oil paints are said to dry incredibly fast."

"I will leave that to you," Nash replied, having received more information about the art of painting in one day than he had ever imagined. "So, when do we start?"

"Tomorrow," she informed him, indicating that she was giving in. Or that she agreed, depending on one's perspective. She had half-closed her eyelids. She was probably already painting him in her imagination. She had even forgotten to drink her tea. "Tomorrow morning at ten. That's when the light is good. If you want to be painted in special attire, dress accordingly. I assume your sword is to be included in the portrait?"

Ah, she was referring to his grandfather's ceremonial sword, with which he had driven her predecessor out of the house. "Yes, indeed, the sword must be in the portrait." He intended to convey a martial impression to Lady Annis, even though the scar would carry more weight on a pure bust. No, the combination of the sword and disfigurement was better suited for his purposes. If it weren't so difficult to obtain a human skull, he might even pretend to recite "Alas, poor Yorick! I knew him, Horatio…" and act as if he were speaking to the deceased. For a heartbeat, he imagined writing to his betrothed about generations of madness, but this story would be too easily debunked.

"Is everything all right, my lord?"

"Of course," Nash replied, tearing himself away from his dreams of insanity that would bring him freedom. "I'll be here on time. Until tomorrow, madam." He bowed and restrained his steps so his departure wouldn't appear as a hasty retreat. But then he remembered something he needed to address urgently: the painting she had shown him yesterday. "Mrs. Fitzroy, before I leave," he said, halting in the middle of his movement. "The painting you brought yesterday… is it for sale? I found it exceedingly appealing and would like to acquire it."

Her cheeks paled rapidly. "The painting has gone missing," she replied curtly.

He would have liked to inquire further, but her emotional turmoil was so apparent that he refrained. His sessions with the beautiful painter's wife – no, with the beautiful painter, he corrected himself mentally – would provide ample opportunity to demonstrate his persistence. She had no idea that her evasive answer only fuelled his determination to solve the many mysteries surrounding her. So he simply nodded and did what he had intended to do before the thought of the seductive portrait had occurred to him: he opened the door to the salon and stepped out into the hallway.

The maid must have been waiting nearby because she stumbled backward and cleverly reached for Nash's belongings. Hat, coat, cane. Had he forgotten something? No, the filled purse belonged to Mrs. Fitzroy. He was about to step out onto Charlotte Street when the striped cat shot out from hiding and blocked his way. Wonderful! First, he wasn't allowed in, and now the malicious creature wouldn't let him out. "Shoo!" He glared at the cat fiercely. A final hiss, which turned out to be an empty threat, and the path was clear for Nash.

14

FREDERICA

She had the commission! Frederica sat there holding her breath until she heard the front door close. Tears welled up in her eyes, and she couldn't be sure if they were tears of joy or sheer terror. What had she gotten herself into? She reached for the bag of coins on the table and withdrew her hand before her fingers touched the leather. She still had time to decline the commission and return the bag.

It was the bitterest irony. In one day, she had received more money than she had in the two years since Francis's death. If she accepted Lord Burnwood's offer, she might even be able to refund Mr. Kingston's down payment and undo the sale of the house. But did she want that? It had taken her an immense amount of strength to decide on a fresh start, and the idea of continuing to live with Francis's ghost would negate the feeling of a new beginning. If she sold the house and painted Lord Burnwood's portrait, she would have enough savings to take a breath for a while and plan her future. She could afford not to work day and night for a week or two, making candles and soap to earn her living. She wiped away her tears with her sleeve. No longer having to live from day to day, no longer having to worry if she would have a roof over her head the next week, and whether she and Tidbit would have enough to eat – that was heaven on earth.

Didn't they say the road to Paradise led through Hell?

Because there was no doubt about it: painting Lord Burnwood was already no pleasure, and she hadn't even started yet. It would be exhausting, not only because His Lordship would be difficult to capture on canvas, but also because his presence would be a constant challenge to her patience. He had – like any devil worthy of the name – something about him that drew her in and made her cross all sorts of inner boundaries, such as her comment about his disfigured face. Every second she spent in his presence, she had to be on guard.

Frederica stood up and went to the fireplace. She carefully picked up one of the sheets she had angrily crumpled up and thrown on the grate earlier, and unfolded it. For a few heartbeats, she looked at the face of the man who had offered her the opportunity to reshape her future. Could she sit across from him day after day?

The answer was: yes! She wanted to, and she could. Just a few challenging days, and then she would be free. Once she had captured his face and his pose, Lord Burnwood wouldn't need to come to her anymore. She took a deep breath, knelt in front of the fireplace, retrieved the remaining sheets from the ashes, and pressed them to her chest. Who knew if she might need her very first impressions again. On her way to the door, Frederica reached for Lord Burnwood's advance payment.

She had made her decision. But before she made the first brushstroke, she had some preparations to make. The first thing she wanted to do was share the good news with Millie. When she found the young woman in the kitchen, scrubbing the stove, the excess of emotion almost choked her. "Millie," Frederica said, hearing her own voice as if from a distance. "I... There is... If you want, you can stay. I can pay you! I have a commission!"

"That's wonderful!" Millie threw both hands in the air as if she wanted to hug Frederica but let them drop again, apparently embarrassed by her own overflow of emotion. However, this time Frederica overcame the distance between them with a determined movement and hugged her girl in return.

"Thank you, Millie! I couldn't have done it without you." She leant her forehead against Millie's and felt the young woman reciprocating the embrace. "Thank you." Frederica felt like she couldn't say it enough.

"Oh, nonsense," Millie grumbled. She began to fidget in embarrassment. Frederica smiled inwardly and let go of her. She would come up with something very special to express her gratitude. Not just a wedding gift for Millie and Mr. Solomon, but also something that conveyed Frederica's gratitude and that only she could give to the newlyweds. With this feeling of finally being able to give back some of the support that Millie had given her, Frederica felt strong enough to enter the studio for the second time. Last night, she had only darted in briefly and had quickly retreated because memories had threatened to overwhelm her. Now she had to face these thoughts of Francis, whether she wanted to or not.

Frederica had to do this on her own. If she failed now, she might as well admit that she was incapable of painting. She recalled Lord Burnwood's mocking smile and imagined telling him that she was declining the commission. He wouldn't be satisfied with merely accepting her withdrawal, but would dig until he had extracted the truth from her.

Frederica felt her heartbeat all the way to the small hollow between her collarbones. Her hands were sweaty, and her knees were trembling. Thinking of Lord Burnwood had done nothing to strengthen her resolve. *There are no ghosts,* she told herself, *only those that exist within me.* The door handle beneath her palm had become warm by now, and her whole body was trembling. What about the foul smell she had noticed in the studio yesterday? It had smelled sweetly rancid. Did her thoughts of ghosts stem from that? Francis had no reason to return as a bodiless spirit. Besides, how could he leave such a stench behind if he – as Frederica had just thought – no longer had a body?

Enough with these morbid thoughts! She was only scaring herself even more, and there was absolutely no reason for it. A thorough airing and dusting should drive away all ghosts, whether imagined or not.

The handle almost slipped from Frederica's fingers as she pushed it down and gave the door a determined shove. However, she managed to step over the threshold and not flee immediately. Heaven, the stench was almost unbearable! Just as blindly as she had walked to the table yesterday, she headed for the narrow sliver of light between the curtains today. Frederica coughed as she pulled the heavy fabric aside, and the stirred-up dust from the past two years tickled her nose. The lever to open the floor-to-ceiling windows seemed to be jammed. Frederica struggled in vain to breathe shallowly. Finally, the windows swung open, letting in light and air, dispelling the last bit of fear of Francis's ghost.

The view of the garden was soothing for her soul. Here, too, there were memories, but mostly good ones that warmed her heart. She turned around resolutely. The room had once been her favourite. When her gaze brushed over the vase of dried cornflowers that she had brought back from a countryside excursion, she couldn't help but smile. The blossoms had faded, the leaves and stems were more grey than green, and when she approached the dried bouquet and gently ran her hand over the flower heads, the delicate petals crumbled and fell to the ground. Francis had been a stickler for colours, and at that time, he had painted a portrait of her as the Queen of Summer, with a wreath of flowers in her hair, in front of a wheat field. When he had failed to achieve the blue of the cornflowers to his satisfaction, Frederica had brought him the bouquet. In return for the sale of the painting, he had thanked her with sapphire earrings, which she had sold last.

She turned to the empty easel, inspected the probably dried-up paints, and bent down to pick up a fallen cloth. The strong smell of turpentine had dissipated to a faint hint, but that was enough to transport Frederica back to the time when the scent of balsam resin, oil paints, and varnish surrounded her daily. She was about to straighten up when she again smelt something unpleasant – something spoilt – and with a stronger intensity than before. She searched for the source and found it within a few seconds: it was a dead mouse, barely recognisable as such by its naked tail and grey-brown fur. Tidbit, the cursed thief, must have somehow made his way into the studio and left his prey here for bad days. She couldn't even blame the cat, as hunting mice and rats was, after all, his job, even if he sometimes seemed to believe that his true duty was to defend Frederica – and Millie.

Before going to the kitchen to arm herself with a bucket, cleaning cloths, and a dustpan, Frederica checked the painting supplies. Except for the canvas and a few brushes, everything had become unusable in the two years of her absence. If she wanted to start painting Lord Burnwood tomorrow, she had a lot of work ahead of her. It was unthinkable to receive His Lordship in this dusty room, not to mention that she preferred to work in a tidy, clean environment. Frederica also needed fresh paints, brushes, and much more, which thanks to Lord Burnwood's generous payment of 200 guineas, was not a problem. The sum exceeded anything she would have dared to ask for herself. She promptly asked Millie to go to Ackerman's Art Supplies, where she would get everything she needed.

At least, she thought so. Millie came back in a carriage and immediately directed the heavily loaded driver to the studio, but she had not been able to buy everything Frederica needed. Apparently, a customer had been in the shop before her and had almost bought the entire stock of oil paints. Green and yellow had come along, which she couldn't do much with, and at least black and white. Well, Frederica thought as she unpacked the delivered materials, it would have to do for now. At least she had canvas and primer, so she could start preparing for the oil painting. If necessary, she would mix the colours herself, which took time but had an undeniable advantage. The ready-made oil paints wouldn't suffice to capture the blue of Lord Burnwood's eyes and the special blue-black tone of his hair. A palette and disgracefully clean cloths, which had once been a bedsheet in their former life, were ready, as were a range of brushes, pencils, and sketchbooks.

With a sudden realisation, she knew that this was truly a new beginning for her. For the first time in her life, she owned her own paints and paper. She no longer had to use the backs of discarded sketches from her mother, or later her husband, to scribble her pictures.

It was almost dark by the time Frederica had everything prepared to her satisfaction for the first session with Lord Burnwood. Part of her confidence had returned with the clean-up. Painting had been her everything for many years, and she might be a bit rusty, but she hadn't forgotten how to do it. What she needed was routine and the courage that would come with the familiar movements.

She pressed a hand to her heart to calm the turmoil inside her, but all she felt was the racing of her excited heart. Should she call it "happiness"? And why did it feel like betrayal to Francis? She opened her eyes and surveyed the studio. She and Millie had taken the last paintings of her husband to the attic, where the sun wouldn't harm the colours. The walls were bare. The table with the paint containers was meticulously arranged. There were two seats and an easel for later when she had completed the preliminary work and started on the oil painting. The windows and the glass terrace door were clean, so that tomorrow they could let in even the faintest rays of sun.

Frederica looked out into the garden that she had designed for Francis after his failing health had first become noticeable. How long ago had she planted the honeysuckle with its sweet-scented flowers, the lilies, and the moonflowers? How long had it been since she had sat out there in the evening hours, just to savour the scent of the flowers? She would also lose her garden once she had finally sold the house.

But at some point, the sadness had to end. Perhaps tomorrow, when her head and heart had grasped that she had landed her first independent commission.

15

NASH

After a detour through the town, Nash retired to his study to make time for his meeting with Mrs. Fitzroy tomorrow. He still had some bills to check and correspondence to catch up on, not least the cursed letter to Lady Annis. He hoped that writing would come easier to him now a solution was in sight. Nevertheless, he postponed composing the letter once again. His duties as a landowner took precedence. It was not only his own prosperity and indirectly that of his aunt that depended on his sense of duty; his numerous servants and the farmers on his estate also relied on him. He owed it to these people to take care of them. After a while, he had fulfilled his duties, and he could turn his attention to the letter to Lady Annis.

He had difficulty finding the right tone. Rudeness and impoliteness were out of the question; they contradicted his nature. It was not in him to hurt a lady, even if she was his unwanted wife-to-be and, moreover, a Scot, and thus, as Nash imagined, accustomed to the rough language of the male sex. In his experience, Scots were either taciturn or cursed without restraint.

An hour later, Nash was still struggling with the salutation and running his hands through his hair in frustration. *Dear Lady Annis* seemed too optimistic, even if it was polite and rather cold-sounding. *Lady Annis? Beloved Lady Annis Stewart?* No, no, and again no! With a sound of displeasure, he placed the quill back in its holder, where it could sit until doomsday. Moreover, Mrs. Fitzroy kept finding her way back into his thoughts. He wished he could see her face when she unwrapped his gift and discovered that she no longer needed to worry about the drying time of the paints.

He allowed himself a moment of reflection. What had happened to the beautiful painter's husband? Was he ill, perhaps due to his extravagant lifestyle? Had she left him? Nash knew that divorce was not impossible in his circles, but most couples preferred to simply go their separate ways and ignore each other. If one didn't care about the scandal that inevitably came with divorce, then one had to have a lot of money to separate from one's spouse. Only the truly wealthy could afford a divorce. In the lower classes, there was another, more practical method for husbands to part from their wives: the husband led his wife to the market by a halter and sold her. Nash knew the poor often had no other option than to resort to such a harsh method. What he couldn't understand, however, was the total, comprehensive indifference of the authorities to this barbaric humiliation of a woman. Heaven, if he imagined the beautiful painter with a leash around her neck from her husband... No, impossible! Surely there was enough fire in the copper-haired beauty to turn the tables.

With her dark eyes and the reddish shimmer in her blonde hair, she promised both English coolness and Southern fire, even though restraint took up more space when she was facing him. What colour were the tips of her breasts, he wondered – rosy like a blonde's or darker like a brunette's? He imagined closing his lips around the small buds and gently sucking on them until they were ready for further caresses. Only then would Nash let his hand roam over her skin, revelling in the softness of her, sliding further and further down until his finger touched her moist pearl, and... He moaned softly as he realised that his manhood was making its presence felt. *It's my own fault*, he thought. Why had he let his imagination run wild instead of tending to his duties?

For the first time in his life, he toyed with the idea of hiring a secretary to take some of his duties off his hands; someone who could compose a polite but nondescript letter to the Scottish bride, without stumbling over the salutation. How difficult it was to find a trustworthy and independently thinking man who wouldn't be put off by Nash's sometimes gruff manner! He shook his head. If he couldn't even convey his ideal portrait to a painter, it wouldn't be any easier with a letter.

At this point, a cacophony of unusual noises interrupted his thoughts, finally destroying his concentration. He jumped up, secretly grateful for the interruption of this drudgery, opened the door to his study, and sprinted out into the corridor. He really had to be careful not to make a habit of rushing through the corridors of Arden House like the runner of Marathon once had. That was undignified.

Nevertheless, curiosity won, and Nash leant over the balustrade to look down into the hall. The source of the noise was a delivery of crates that were not placed at the servant's entrance as usual, but rather at the front entrance. "Can't one write a letter in peace in this house for once – just once?" he thundered down. "And why doesn't the deliveryman use the back entrance?"

"I asked the gentlemen the same," Aunt Matilda called from below. She had appeared out of nowhere and tilted her head back to look at him. From up here, her face looked like a sun with grey-streaked rays. Without looking, she sidestepped a man in rough clothing who was carrying another crate inside and then looking around. "The answer was that the items were to be handed over to you personally." She paused briefly. "It would be nice if you came downstairs. Then I would not have to shout so much, and my neck would not be strained from looking up at you all the time." Nash hid his amused grin because, contrary to her words, Aunt Matilda was doing just fine.

He bounded down the steps and as he reached the halfway point of the landing, spotted the logo on the wooden crates: Ackerman's Art Supplies. At the same moment, Aunt Matilda also realised where the delivery had come from. "Have you become an artist, by any chance?" She regarded him with a sceptical look. "Painting, my dear, is not as easy as it may seem at first glance. The skills must be honed over the years, and no matter how barbaric these Scots may seem to you, they have produced some of the finest artists. You should consider abandoning the idea of a self-portrait." Nash had told Lady Hastings about the gift for Lady Annis, and, of course, she had noticed painters coming and going lately. However, he had kept the true purpose of the painting hidden from her.

Annoyed, he raised his hand. The gesture was directed at both Aunt Matilda and the men who appeared to be finished, as the stream of crates they were bringing in had come to a halt. "One at a time," Nash said without raising his voice. As if by magic, all heads turned towards him, including those of his servants. "This delivery has gone to the wrong address. My servants will help you load everything back onto the cart. After that, you will deliver the art supplies to the correct address. It is 7 Charlotte Street." One of the workers pulled out a rather crumpled note from his jacket pocket and studied it.

"Forgive me, my lord, but here it says the customer is Lord Burnwood, Arden House, St. James' Square, with the instruction to deliver everything into the house and hand it over personally."

Nash had told the seller where the paints, canvases, and most importantly, his most significant discovery, should be delivered, and since he didn't want to burden Mrs. Fitzroy and her maid with carrying the heavy crates into the studio, he had requested everything to be delivered into her house. Only the fools had mixed up the buyer's address with the recipient's address. As calmly as he could, he corrected the mistake, reiterated the correct delivery address, and supervised the return of the items outside, just to be sure. He waved to Lord Roxleigh and a pretty woman who were looking over from an open gig with wide eyes, and then turned to his aunt. Curiosity was her greatest weakness, and she was eager to cross-examine him.

"If this vast amount of art supplies is not for you, then who did you buy them for?"

"You know I was searching for the right artist for my gift to Lady Annis Stewart," he replied. "I've found an artist I like, and to start as soon as possible, I arranged for the painter to be provided with everything necessary."

Aunt Matilda narrowed her eyes. His evasive wording had clearly aroused her suspicion. Nash shrugged nonchalantly and offered a casual explanation. "The artist's circumstances are somewhat limited, and as I mentioned before, I didn't want to wait. I want to reciprocate Lady Annis's kindness as soon as possible."

Unfortunately, Aunt Matilda didn't take the bait he had subtly placed before her. Instead of focusing on Lady Annis, she remained on the original topic of conversation. "Who is this artist?" she asked. "Perhaps I can also do some good and help him."

Anything but that! His aunt had a soft heart, but chaos followed her good intentions like a faithful dog to its master. Imagine what would happen if she took Mrs. Fitzroy under her wing. He linked his arm with hers and steered her like a swaying ship towards the drawing room. "Peace and focus on art are the most important things," Nash deflected. "The creator of the painting is not yet ready to present themselves to a wide audience."

"Oh, so it is an unknown painter then?"

Blast it. She was more astute than was good for him. Nash had to be careful about what he said, or else his and Mrs. Fitzroy's secret would come to light. The delightful knowledge of their conspiracy belonged to him alone, and he intended to savour that state for as long as possible.

16

FREDERICA

Her intention to stretch the canvas onto the frame, prime it, have a meal, and then go to bed early was thwarted by loud and irritated banging on the front door. At least she had managed to prepare the canvas. Since Frederica had not inquired about the size of the painting Lord Burnwood wanted, she had chosen the standard format for a bust portrait, which would depict him slightly smaller than life-sized. The thought made her smile, for if she had asked him, he would surely have chosen an oversized portrait. If he insisted on having the sword in the painting, she would have to reconsider, but so far, they had only discussed a portrait.

The knocking intensified, so Frederica cast a longing glance at Millie's stew and the fresh bread before she hurried to the door. The last feeble rays of the sun still illuminated the city streets, so Frederica opened the front door cautiously but not fearfully.

"Am I at Fitzroy's residence?" The man standing before her was as massive as a bull and just as irritable. All that was missing was steam coming out of his nostrils.

"Yes," Frederica replied, peering past his broad figure. There was a wagon on the street, loaded with wooden crates, under the supervision of a thin man who leant boredly against the rear wheel.

"Where should all this go?"

"Just a moment, please. I didn't order anything." Frederica raised both hands defensively.

"Listen, Missy." The bull didn't roar, but he came close. Apparently, the burly man had reached the end of his patience. But Frederica had also had a nerve-wracking, exhausting, and tiring day, which was why she stood in a defensive posture before him. "I've already wasted enough time. Don't make a fuss, and tell me where all this should go."

"*Mrs. Fitzroy*," she clarified. "Until you tell me where *all this* came from and who sent it, don't set foot in my house."

The man raised his hand and pushed back his greasy hat. Respect did not glimmer beneath his bushy brows, as Frederica had hoped, only growing annoyance. "Ackerman's Art Supplies," the man grumbled and continued, "paid for and sent here by some fancy pin..." He cleared his throat before going on, "By Lord Wetwood. Burnwood, I mean. With a scar across his fine little face."

"Lord Burnwood?" Frederica echoed and took a step back.

"Well, there you go. Hey, Pete, come on, the way is clear!" The man ruthlessly took advantage of Frederica's moment of weakness and beckoned to the other, who immediately grabbed a crate and trotted away. So be it, Frederica thought. If she couldn't resist the flood, then she had no choice but to go with the flow. "This way," she said and led the two men into the studio. It felt strange to see other people in her sanctuary, but strangely in a good way, not a frightening one. Almost as if the studio were now truly her workspace and no longer that of her late husband. "Please stack the crates against the wall."

The invasion was over in a matter of minutes. Now she had to make sure that the incursion into her life did not become a hostile takeover.

"What on earth was that arrogant devil thinking?" Frederica muttered. Finally, there was silence again. After the men had bid her farewell with a nod, she returned to the studio. She looked thoughtfully at the crates of various sizes, each bearing the Ackerman's logo. From a safe distance – she absolutely didn't want to succumb to the temptation to inspect the delivery – she counted six wooden crates. Her heart raced madly as she imagined the treasures hidden inside the wooden boxes.

Brushes. Oil. Wooden frames. Canvas. Paints. Above all, paints. Was Lord Burnwood the one who had snatched the essential colours from her in the shop this afternoon? Once, Francis had come home from Ackerman's with six different shades of blue when he had attempted a seascape. She didn't want to know what colours His Lordship had bought for her.

Yet, deep down, she wanted nothing more than to open one crate after another. Perhaps just one? Just to see if Lord Burnwood had blindly bought everything he could get his hands on, or if he had acted with reason. How long did she intend to stand here and stare at the crates? Once she had opened one, it would be infinitely difficult to reject his gift. Did she feel obligated to Lord Burnwood? No, definitely not. On the other hand, behind the wooden slats surely lay much of what she had wanted to buy this afternoon. Only he had been faster and had snatched the items from under her nose. Theoretically, this was her purchase, which she would have liked to make, even if she would have significantly narrowed her selection. Would, could, should – this couldn't go on.

Before Frederica could change her mind, she went to her husband's worktable and picked up the rolled bundle of tools. The chisel fell into her hand as if of its own accord. Was this a sign? Perhaps. But first, she needed more light. She hadn't even noticed that night had fallen. There were, of course, more than enough candles, and she found the tinderbox right away.

Take one last breath. Hold the chisel. Insert it into the gap between the lid and the body. Move it downward. Don't cry.

But despite her best intentions, the tears came, as they often did lately, without Frederica being able to do anything about it. She placed the chisel on the worktable and pushed the wood shavings aside with trembling fingers, revealing the contents of the open crate. Her heart already knew what Lord Burnwood had chosen for her. It didn't need confirmation.

The painter's box was almost too heavy for her, especially in her shaky, distraught state. She lifted the precious mahogany box to her chest with both hands and almost let it fall to the floor. Then she knelt down and caressed the reddish-brown wood that glistened blackish in the candlelight – like spilled blood. Frederica couldn't suppress an exclamation of delight as she opened the expensive drawing box and reverently ran her fingers over the treasures hidden inside. Colour blocks that dissolved in water and could be diluted to the desired shade; a sketchbook that belonged to her and her alone; paper that was perfect for absorbing watercolours; a marble palette, pencils, small glass vials with vivid pigments... This time, they were definitely tears of joy that ran down Frederica's cheeks. She held the water glass in her hand and looked at the star that had been engraved on the underside.

Lord Burnwood had sent her a treasure. No, not just one, but several, if she imagined what was in the remaining crates. Surely he knew that she couldn't use the drawing box for his portrait because these were the materials for watercolour painting. So why had he given her this precious gift? It was almost enough material to paint for a lifetime.

Warmth spread in her chest and took possession of the rest of her body in stormy waves. Hot gratitude choked her throat. He may be an arrogant devil, but on this day, Lord Burnwood had made her very, very happy.

She pushed the mahogany box aside and opened the remaining crates one by one. Each revealed its valuable contents, including not six, but seven pre-mixed shades of blue. Ultramarine, the precious blue of the Virgin Mary. Cobalt blue? Did she hold one of the colours mixed from the new, artificially produced pigments in her hand? It was too much for Frederica. The leaden heaviness in her limbs, and especially in her head, made a closer inspection impossible.

That night, Frederica dreamt of the sea, the sky, and the blue depths in the eyes of the Devil of St. James.

17

NASH

Punctuality was the courtesy of kings. It was not beneath Nash's dignity to knock on the door of 7 Charlotte Street at precisely ten o'clock in the morning. She personally opened it and wore an expression he had last seen on the face of a lady who had unexpectedly found herself face to face with the ill-tempered tiger in Lady Castlereagh's private zoo. The Lady was a family friend, and Nash liked her, although – or perhaps precisely because – she was one of the most eccentric ladies in the entire Empire.

In any case, Mrs. Fitzroy looked at him as if she didn't know whether to run away or embrace him. At least she wasn't crying again. For heaven's sake, she lived with an aggressive tomcat, so she shouldn't be afraid of him, should she?

"Please come in, my lord," she said in a timid tone and stepped aside. The expected tears did not appear, although her brown eyes glistened suspiciously. The girl with the bad habit of appearing out of nowhere appeared and took his hat, coat, and cane. Mrs. Fitzroy walked ahead, giving him a chance to admire her straight back and the graceful curve of her delicate neck. A few reddish-blonde strands had escaped from her tightly bound hairstyle, curling against milky-white skin. The piquant contrast between skin, hair, and the pale blue of her dress was more than enticing. It made Nash want to step behind her, ruffle the fine curls at her nape with his warm breath, and then watch as the tell-tale vein below her earlobe started to pulse nervously. He would place the tip of his index finger on it and feel the excited flutter of her heart before bringing even more turmoil with a kiss. Before he could continue his dreams, the orange-and-white striped monster shot in front of his feet and almost knocked him over. A threatening hiss and a raised claw made it clear to Nash that this beast was not only the master of the house but could probably read minds. How else could the cat's aversion to him be explained?

"Tidbit, behave!" his owner scolded him sternly. Not stern enough for Nash's taste because instead of obeying, the cat threatened him again. She opened a door, and the smell of fresh bread wafted towards him. "Off to the kitchen with you!" Mrs. Fitzroy pointed in the appropriate direction with her index finger, and the delinquent reluctantly complied with her loving command. Someday, they – he and the cat – would settle this matter face to face, but not today.

"Forgive me, Tidbit is a bit suspicious of strangers," Mrs. Fitzroy explained. She led him into her studio and closed the door behind them. Blinded by the sunlight pouring into the room through the generously sized windows and the glass door, Nash shielded his eyes with his hand.

"I would say he suffers from pronounced territorial behaviour," he replied and lowered his hand when his eyes had adjusted to the brightness. "Are you sure he's a cat and not a dog?"

"As sure as I can be," Mrs. Fitzroy replied. The fear in her eyes had disappeared. For the first time since he had met her, her smile seemed genuine. "I call him the Tiger of Lambeth," she confessed. "He has the heart of a fighter."

Nash swallowed down the words that were on the tip of his tongue: *Why don't you accompany me to Loring Hall soon and together we'll face Lady Castlereagh's tiger?*

"There's something else we need to talk about, my lord, before I start the initial sketches." She sighed and gestured toward the Ackerman's crates. All of them had been opened, but as Nash approached, he saw that not a single sheet of paper or brush had been unpacked. "I cannot accept your generous gift."

He turned around. "Why not? Your false pride is misplaced, Mrs. Fitzroy. I see that your husband is not taking good care of you." He bit his lip. His temper had led him to say the wrong thing. "Forgive me. I didn't mean to imply that I wanted to take your husband's place. It was…" he hesitated for a moment, trying to find a way to convince her to accept his gift without hurting her pride, "nothing more than an investment. I just want to ensure that you have everything you need to complete my portrait in record time."

She stepped closer to him. Mrs. Fitzroy was so near that he could smell the scent of almond soap and rosewater emanating from her. She raised her hand. For a moment, it looked like she would touch him, but after a barely noticeable hesitation, she brushed a strand of hair away from her face. Mrs. Fitzroy tilted her head and looked him straight in the eyes. "It was more than what you claim, my lord," she corrected him gently. "After you vehemently rejected a watercolour painting out of fear of a diluted version of yourself, it was absolutely unnecessary to send me all the equipment for an enthusiastic watercolour painter." One corner of her mouth twitched. She bit her lip and, presumably realising that she was providing him with intimate knowledge of her feelings, her smile faded and was replaced by her usual expression. "Distant" and "on guard" were the words that came to mind. "Therefore, I cannot accept your gift. You are paying me generously for my work. That's where I would like to leave it." She took a deep breath and exhaled.

"As you wish," he replied smoothly. "I will have the box of watercolours picked up at your convenience and returned. However, I insist that you use everything you need for my oil portrait. Consider it a shrewd investment on my part, not a charitable gift." *And don't be so damn stubborn!*

She opened her mouth to say something, but Nash wasn't finished yet. He lowered his head. "Have you discovered the quick-dry substance?" he whispered.

She nodded, at a loss for words, and let her gaze drop from his eyes to his mouth. A longing expression appeared in her brown eyes. She blinked a few times but otherwise remained in position. "I've heard of it," she finally replied. "They say it dries the paint within days." Her mouth formed an astonished, worshipful O. Nash was overcome with the desire to be the one responsible for her breathlessness, not that damn substance.

"Mr. Ackerman said that if the mixture doesn't produce the desired result, he'll supply me with all the colours I need for a lifetime," Nash recounted. These were exactly Ackerman's words. The man was deeply convinced of his product. "It has something to do with the interaction of lead and paint or with the air, I believe. In any case, Mr. Ackerman also told me that when applied to the canvas, the substance allows you to apply additional layers of colour without mixing."

"I see," murmured Mrs. Fitzroy. Something seemed to be working feverishly behind her forehead. Instead of pushing her further to accept the miracle substance, Nash let his words have their effect. Some women became weak at the sight of jewels, while others were lured with honeyed words. She was the first person he had thought to seduce with colours and a tiger.

18

FREDERICA

It felt like a victory not to have accepted the box of watercolours. "I accept your proposal," she said. Would every day with him be a challenge? If so, she could only hope that the drying substance would do its job as Mr. Ackerman had promised, so she wouldn't have to spend a minute longer with Lord Burnwood than necessary. He confused her, and this was something Frederica couldn't afford. "I'll take what I need. You can return the rest."

Lord Burnwood did not look like a man who had just lost a skirmish, thought Frederica with a hint of suspicion. His crooked smile was unsettlingly confident, as if she had done exactly what he had expected. It was high time to switch roles.

"Let's do what you came here for," she said. "Have you ever sat for a portrait?"

"Only for a family portrait, and that was quite a while ago. My father commissioned it, with him, his favourite hunting dog, my mother, and me." He furrowed his brow. It was strange how the scar disappeared from Frederica's field of vision when he smiled, and how it came to the forefront when he looked grim, like he did now.

"And you hated it because you had to sit still the whole time," said

Frederica, directing him to the chair she had placed by the terrace door earlier. She reached for her sketchbook and tucked pencils of various thicknesses into the neckline of her dress. The artist's smock for women, with as many pockets as the one for male artists, was yet to be invented. "Today I'll make a few sketches of you so I can get a feel for you."

The hint of a smile flickered across his face.

"For your proportions and movements," Frederica quickly corrected herself. She managed not to blush. At least, she hoped so. She took a seat opposite him, opened the sketchbook, and grabbed a medium-strength pencil. "Tell me, how do you envision the painting?" she said, starting to put the first strokes on paper.

Lord Burnwood sat up straight. "I primarily want a lifelike representation of my face," he said. Frederica nodded and continued drawing. Out of the corner of her eye, she saw that barely a minute into their first session, he was already shifting in the chair.

"If it's more comfortable for you, you can stand," Frederica suggested, and he took the opportunity to rise.

His eyebrows were perfectly arched. They were dense, not so round as to appear feminine, and tapered evenly towards the ends. Not quite in the middle, but slightly closer to the bridge of his nose, they had a slight point, giving his face a fittingly devilish quality. Perhaps it wasn't just the scar – and his temperament – that had earnt him his nickname. Even without the wound on his face, Lord Burnwood would never have looked tame.

Frederica raised her head. "Why didn't you bring the sabre?"

He shrugged and immediately became stiff again. Without interrupting her drawing, she said, "You can move, my lord, and above all, don't forget to breathe."

"I remember posing differently as a child. I couldn't move for hours. As for the sabre... I changed my mind. I don't need it." He made a dismissive gesture with his hand, and Frederica didn't need to be a mind reader to know what was going through his head.

"Even without the blade, you present an imposing figure," she agreed and lowered her head for a few seconds to hide her smile.

His gaze turned piercing. "Imposing? That sounds like I'm an inflated rooster." He snorted, but it sounded more amused than angry. He puffed up his chest and challenged her with a defiant look. It was the twitch of his lips that revealed to Frederica that Lord Burnwood was joking about himself! A man who could laugh at himself was a rarity, and she loved that trait in the opposite sex. Who would have thought it would be His Roughness who would surprise her with this characteristic!

"I'm fine with that," Frederica replied, surprised. He was quite imposing with his broad shoulders and chest above his slender hips, and his face was extremely attractive. She almost regretted his decision to be portrayed without the murder weapon because there was something in Lord Burnwood's appearance that seemed to demand a sabre. She could easily picture him as a pirate, standing at the bow of a ship, leaning against the ample bust of the figurehead, gazing into the distance as the wind ruffled his black hair. His shirt collar would be open, revealing slightly tanned skin. Only the sky above him and the waves below would be his limits. She looked at the sheet in her hands and quickly turned it over so Lord Burnwood wouldn't see what she had drawn. "Where will the painting hang? In the entrance hall?" Frederica's attempts to get him to talk failed. He seemed fine with her looking at him, but as soon as she had brought up the purpose of the painting, he had become tight-lipped. He changed the subject.

"Isn't your approach a bit unusual? I thought the sitter had to remain as still as possible and hold the pose until the artist was satisfied."

"It's the way I work," Frederica replied, emphasising the "I." "Since you haven't told me how you want to be painted, I'm taking the liberty of immortalising you according to my taste." She shrugged, less elegantly than he did, but just as indifferently.

"I've told you what matters to me. I don't want embellishment, but a lifelike representation. And why do you need more sketches when you made enough of me yesterday?" Impatiently, he leant forward to take a look at her drawings. She pressed the sketchbook against her chest and tried to conceal as much of the mockery in her smile as possible. "When will you start with the actual painting?"

"As soon as I have enough material to capture you." This time, it was a slow lowering of her eyelids that hinted at the double meaning of her words. "Take a few steps back, towards the terrace door, please."

He did as she asked and didn't notice that his face was reflected in the glass. The light caught a glint in his hair, giving it a bluish hue. Frederica detached herself from his face and started drawing him from behind. The broad shoulders and straight back posed no challenge, but the back of his head did. How did he manage to look bold, even from this perspective? Lord Burnwood's eyes bore into hers. The fact that it was his reflection that Frederica was targeting did little to reassure her.

19

NASH

It turned out to be fortunate that he had forgotten the ceremonial sabre, Nash thought. In his self-assuredness, he had almost overlooked the essence of this painting. Why would he present himself proudly with all his physical advantages if he wanted to deter Lady Annis? No, that was not the purpose of this painting. Mrs. Fitzroy's comment about his imposing stature had made his mistake quite clear to him. If she painted him as a vain fop, he was fine with that. It didn't dent his self-confidence to be depicted in this unflattering way. He had chosen a talented painter precisely because she wouldn't spare his ego. The matter was progressing well, and even though it would take a little while to complete the painting, Nash was convinced he had made a lucky choice with Mrs. Fitzroy.

Nash didn't know how much time passed before she finally allowed him to inspect her initial sketches. As he walked over to the worktable where she had spread out selected sheets, he looked outside. The patch she called a "garden" was surrounded by high walls. The sun was high in the sky and easily overcame the man-high brick wall. It must be around noon.

He positioned himself slightly behind her. Mrs. Fitzroy was small enough that he could look over her shoulder, but she stepped aside. "Which pose do you like best?" she asked. Nash took his time examining them. Strangely, he found himself well represented, even though the sketches didn't go into detail, and she hadn't yet drawn his face.

"I like them all," he said, surprising himself. "But if I had to choose one, I would go with this one." He pointed to a drawing that showed him standing upright, facing the viewer with his hands on his hips.

"Fine," Mrs. Fitzroy agreed. She frowned. "If we limit ourselves to not depicting you from head to toe but only your upper body, the painting will be finished even faster. In that case, we need to think about the background and your arms." Unconsciously, Nash directed his gaze to the mentioned body parts.

"What's wrong with my arms?" He sounded too defensive even to his own ears.

"Nothing's wrong with them," Mrs. Fitzroy replied, turning her head away, but not quickly enough for him to miss her fleeting smile. "The pose is unconventional. Which isn't necessarily a bad thing, my lord. However, it's a posture that's a little..." she trailed off.

"Out with it!" Nash urged, sensing that she was censoring her words. "I can handle whatever you have to say."

Mrs. Fitzroy took a deep breath and stepped a pace away from him. "It's a defiant pose," she stated bluntly. "Look." She took another step back and mimicked the pose he presented in the sketch. She slightly widened her feet, raised her chin, and put her hands on her hips.

Damn. She was right! Did he really present himself this way to others? Nash stared at Mrs. Fitzroy. She met his gaze without blinking. "What do you suggest?"

She reached for her tools and turned to a fresh page in her sketchbook. "Stand up straight, Lord Burnwood. Arms relaxed at your sides." She tilted her head. Even before she continued speaking, Nash knew she wasn't satisfied yet. The charming crease between her brows gave it away. "My lord, turn your upper body slightly to the left. A little more... stop. A bit back. Stop. Good, and now cross your arms in front of your chest."

Nash felt silly. Not because he was following a woman's instructions, but because he had become overly aware of his body. A brief glance at Mrs. Fitzroy's drawings made him see himself through her eyes: his sheer size, the breadth of his shoulders, his arms that could easily envelop her, and finally, his hands that could delicately clasp her waist. Before the scar, he had never thought about how he appeared to other people, and after the scar, he had taken pleasure in playing with the discomfort most people felt at the sight of him. Frederica Fitzroy's gaze was neither that of an enchanted woman nor that of someone embarrassed by his physical injury. She looked at him, absorbed his appearance, and put her impressions on paper.

Nash turned his head in her direction. "Please don't move, my lord!" Groaning inwardly, he turned his head back just a tiny bit. Her sigh echoed his feelings, reflecting the same strained patience with her subject.

Stay resolute, Nash reminded himself. He needed this painting, and if he stopped now, he would have to start the search for a suitable painter all over again. So far, her drafts looked promising. Only the standing still was wearing on his nerves. If only he had something to distract him! He could start by unravelling one of her many secrets... Which one intrigued him the most? He didn't hesitate long. It was the mysterious Mr. Fitzroy, about whom she stubbornly remained silent. Nash glanced discreetly – or so he thought – in her direction. No, it was too early to inquire about her husband. He decided to wait a little longer until he got to know her better.

"Lord Burnwood, please!" Mrs. Fitzroy's resonant voice brought him out of his daydreams. She stood in front of him, holding the sheet up to his eyes. "Look. I have something like this in mind."

"All right. That looks good." His voice sounded hoarse. He made sure she hadn't downplayed the scar and only briefly glanced at the rest of the drawing in her hands. Nash cleared his throat. "You are the artist. See you tomorrow at the same time." He shrugged to loosen the stiff muscles in his neck. Finally, he bent over her hand and breathed in the scent of rosewater and almond soap. Nash found it difficult to resist the temptation that had just awakened in his mind.

AFTER A DETOUR TO HIS CLUB, Nash felt better. He had dined, drunk, and engaged in conversation where neither colours nor canvas, nor even quick-drying techniques played a role. Additionally, he had played a game of cards and taken a few sovereigns from Laffen Hetherington. When he entered Arden House, he felt much calmer and ready to face his usual routine. However, as soon as he sat down behind his desk with the firm intention of finally writing that cursed letter to Lady Annis, there was a knock at the door, and Lady Hastings entered. "Do you have a moment for me?" she asked.

"Of course," Nash replied, rising from his seat. "Shall we go to the drawing room? Or to the library? You could have tea brought in." The mention of the library reminded him that he hadn't asked Mrs. Fitzroy about the painting she had shown him yesterday. He mentally noted to bring up the topic again tomorrow. He already knew exactly where he would have the painting hung.

A smile deepened the many small wrinkles on Aunt Matilda's face. "It is so kind of you to take time for your old aunt, despite your many duties," she said. She took a seat opposite him in the visitor's chair. "Tea is not necessary, my dear." Nash perked up because her exceedingly friendly address aroused his suspicion. "I would like to host a small evening gathering again, if you do not mind."

"You know you don't need my permission for that," Nash replied. He leant forward and took his aunt's slender hand in his. Her rings were looser than usual, and if he looked closely, he could see age spots mixed with the freckles on the back of her hand. Aunt Matilda's eyes became moist. "I hope I never made you feel unwelcome, no matter how much you tyrannise your adult nephew," he said, attempting a lighter tone.

"Oh, my dear, dear boy, you never did." She visibly swallowed. "I just feel that my time in your house is coming to an end." The silvery gleam in her blue eyes intensified. "Once you are married, I will not have a place in Arden House anymore."

"But..." Nash bit his tongue. *I will not be bringing a bride home anytime soon to challenge your position,* was not a truth he wanted to reveal at this moment. Instead, he said, "Nothing will change as long as I am the master of Arden House."

Aunt Matilda gave him a look that said more clearly than a thousand words: *You might be mistaken there!* She reached into her bodice for a handkerchief and dabbed at the corners of her eyes. "I will get in your way once Lady Annis is your wife," she declared. "No matter how amiable she may be, no woman wants to be merely the lady of the house in name. But until then," she took a deep breath and put the handkerchief away, "I thank you from the bottom of my heart for your generosity. Not every grown man can bear to live under the same roof as his old aunt."

Nash racked his brain for another topic of conversation and was about to dismiss her excessive gratitude, but decided to keep his words to himself. It was obviously important to Aunt Matilda to be able to thank him, and downplaying what he did for her would also belittle her. For his aunt, living in Arden House and feeling at home here was no small matter. "I'm glad to have you with me," he said in a soft voice.

"You are such a good boy!" She reached across the table, took his hand, and squeezed it for a brief moment. "Lady Annis will be lucky to have you as her husband."

There it was, the change of subject Nash had been hoping for just a moment ago that now didn't sit well with him. What was so moving about a marriage that brought tears to her eyes, especially when it wasn't even her own? Nash grunted something unintelligible, but Aunt Matilda wasn't ready to drop the topic.

"I am sure she will be delighted with the portrait," his aunt continued. "I assume the artist you have chosen will start the portrait as soon as possible? Did he like your gift? And when will the first sitting take place?"

Nash chuckled at her attempt to extract the identity of the artist from him. To avoid revealing his emotions, he stroked his chin with his hand. "When the time comes, you will be the first to know the artist's name," he promised her, trying not to take her visible disappointment to heart too much. He had given his word to Mrs. Fitzroy not to talk about the sittings with anyone, and he intended to keep that promise.

"I have been thinking about reopening my salon," Aunt Matilda continued so casually that Nash perked up. "I still remember how fascinated you were with Lord Byron before he ignited all those scandals and became unbearable. He and Lady Caroline Lamb, and then the unfortunate affair with his sister... But let us not talk about that distasteful love triangle. What I wanted to say was something else. I can imagine it would be a pleasant change for you if Arden House became a meeting place for painters and poets."

A change from what? From managing his estates and the duties that came with his seat in the House of Lords? But she was right. Heated debates on artistic and philosophical matters had brought him great pleasure before the war. Nash enjoyed the intellectual challenge of engaging with others, and perhaps he had indeed lost some of his mental agility in recent years. Engaging in the same activities day in and day out did not exactly foster mental flexibility. A ride on Rotten Row was all well and good for physical exertion, but it was no substitute for a real challenge. "That's a wonderful idea!" he exclaimed, and was immediately rewarded with a radiant smile. Nash felt warmth in his heart, seeing how little it took to make his aunt happy.

"Excellent!" Aunt Matilda replied. She stood up and headed for the door. With her hand on the doorknob, she turned to him. "Perhaps it is too early for a salon, so close to your wedding," he heard her mutter. "I think I will postpone the revival of my regular salon and focus on a single soiree for now. You have made me very happy. Oh, by the way, if you do not mind, I would like to invite your artist." Before Nash could react, she stepped out and closed the door behind her.

Before the war with France, Aunt Matilda had been an enthusiastic patron of the arts, and Mrs. Fitzroy deserved artistic recognition. When the painting was finished, he could introduce the two of them to each other, assuming the beautiful painter gave her consent. Nevertheless, Nash couldn't shake the feeling that Aunt Matilda had skilfully outmanoeuvred him.

20

FREDERICA

Lord Burnwood's hasty departure left Frederica puzzled, but not for long. He had probably grown bored. Convincing him to hold a pose for longer than half a minute was difficult, and it wouldn't get any easier once she started painting with oils. Since they had agreed on a bust portrait, it wouldn't be necessary for him to remain in the same stiff pose, but at the very least, he would have to keep his head straight. Had she truly looked forward to the challenge? Frederica sipped her tea and looked at all the sketches she had drawn today, as well as the ones she had pulled from the fireplace. She liked the one where Lord Burnwood was looking at her with his legs slightly apart and chin held high – the image she had described as defiant. It wasn't entirely defiance, Frederica thought. It was more as if he was issuing a challenge. "Come if you dare," he seemed to be saying to the viewer. The pose was indeed unsuitable for an official portrait, but if she was honest with herself, Frederica was more afraid of being subjected to that silent challenge for hours, even days on end.

It wasn't Lord Burnwood who scared her, but herself and her unpredictable reaction to him. Frederica was no longer an inexperienced young girl and could give a name to what sent tingles through her body and put her in a state of perpetual restlessness: desire. It was the desire to feel a man's lips on her mouth, on her skin, to feel his rough fingertips becoming familiar with her body in a way only a husband was allowed.

To distract herself, she got up and took Mr. Ackerman's quick-dry substance from one of the crates. Lord Burnwood had bought five whole bottles of it. She held one of the transparent glass containers up to the light and shook it. The contents had a jelly-like consistency and a golden-yellow colour. Once she had recovered from the morning's session with the devilish Lord, Frederica intended to experiment with the magical substance's effects. Before leaving for Mr. Solomon's, Millie had, as usual, prepared bread and cheese for her. Frederica had little appetite, but she needed to eat something. It would be unthinkable if she were to faint during one of the strenuous sessions. She ate her meal hastily and thought all the while about the colours she would use for Lord Burnwood's portrait. The nervous tingling she felt when she looked at the blank canvas made it impossible for her to think of anything else.

THE NEXT MORNING, when she opened her eyes, her first thought was of the test painting she had created the previous evening. On a sample canvas, Frederica had applied oil paints in various thicknesses and coated them with Mr. Ackerman's drying substance. She grabbed her morning robe and hurried to the studio to inspect the results of her experiment. Tidbit followed, meowing, and nearly tripped her up as he veered into the kitchen, getting between her legs. "Soon, my tiger," she reassured him and approached the canvas with a pounding heart. Carefully, she extended her index finger and brushed it over the layers of paint she had applied yesterday. "Oooooh," Frederica sighed. "Tidbit, this is wonderful! Mr. Ackerman has worked a true miracle in his alchemist's kitchen." The oil paint in the lower corner was not dry yet, but the surface remained unaffected by the touch of her fingertip. That was truly remarkable! The portrait would dry much faster, which, in turn, meant that the Devil of St. James would disappear from her life more quickly. She picked up the pencil and closed her eyes for a moment. Her mother had done the same before making the first crucial strokes. Francis, on the other hand, had never pondered for long when he painted; he simply started. "Close your eyes and visualise exactly what you want to paint," she heard her mother's voice. "Engage all your senses, not just your eyes. You must know how the flower you want to put on paper feels. You know its scent, the delicacy of the petals, the roughness of the stem."

Frederica's heart raced. The first thing that came to her mind were his colours. Black hair, cobalt blue eyes, pale red lips. And then the scar, whose colour was as irregular as its structure. What would it feel like to touch his cheek with her fingertips?

Before she could change her mind and withdraw, Frederica opened her eyes and began sketching the initial contours in cautious, barely visible strokes.

Half an hour later, she danced into the kitchen. The scar, which had given her the most trouble because she was unsure whether and how clearly she should depict it, had only been hinted at lightly. Once she had figured out how Lord Burnwood saw himself, she could either portray the injury realistically or soften it to avoid offending his vanity. After all, he was the one paying a substantial sum for the painting. Despite all artistic freedom, she had to keep in mind that this was a commissioned work – with the emphasis on "work."

She fed Tidbit a mackerel that Millie had brought from the market yesterday and set the kettle for tea. She couldn't wait for His Impatience to arrive so she could begin the foundational structure on the canvas. The mackerel had started to smell a bit, but that didn't deter the Lambeth Tiger from playing with it for a while before devouring it in four big bites.

Millie came in, laden with groceries, including a new teapot. The old one was so thin at the bottom that you could almost see through it, she explained. Frederica put her arm around Millie's shoulders and reassured her that it was perfectly fine to spend money on a new teapot. "I just don't know who's going to eat all of this," she said, gesturing to the groceries piled on the kitchen table. She smiled so Millie wouldn't misunderstand her words as a reprimand. She had given the girl enough money the day before to buy half of Lambeth, with strict instructions not to hold back.

"I'll make a stew," Millie said, placing the vegetables on the right side of the table. "It'll last for a few days."

Frederica groped her way to the stove and rekindled the fire. Then she took a jug and fetched water from the cistern in the garden. The container wasn't large, but the rainwater tasted a hundred times better than the broth from the rivers. It was even more flavourful than the water from the public wells. "Nevertheless, this is all far too much for us," Frederica remarked when she returned. "If you don't want half of it to go to waste, you'll have to take some of it home with you." She put on an intentionally indifferent expression so Millie wouldn't get the idea that Frederica was doing her a favour. Millie was proud, despite – or perhaps because of – her poverty, and found it difficult to accept what she called "charity." Frederica believed that even marrying the wealthy tailor wouldn't change that. She bent down to pet Tidbit between the ears, but the Lambeth Tiger was more interested in the meat for the stew than in affection.

"Let's see," grumbled Millie, unexpectedly yielding to Frederica's offer. Before Frederica returned to an upright position, she allowed her smile to linger on her lips for a moment. It had been a long time since she had done more than just grimace when a smile was expected of her. When she straightened up again, Millie gave her a probing look but didn't protest. Not even when Frederica handed her a cup of tea, which she had lightened with milk. She was about to reach down and lift Tidbit onto her lap when the cat raised its head, pricked its ears, and emitted a hiss that even overshadowed the steam escaping from the kettle.

"If that isn't His Lordship," Millie remarked and wiped her hands on her dress before making her way to the front door.

"You do not care for Lord Burnwood?" Frederica asked the cat and also got up. "Well, then we're two of a kind." She knew that wasn't entirely true for her, but Tidbit wouldn't hold the small falsehood against her. "But don't forget, he's the one paying for your mackerels, so behave!" The cat tilted its head. Its tail twitched nervously back and forth, but after a moment of hesitation during which the gaze from its golden-yellow eyes bore into hers, it padded over to the stove and curled up in front of the hearth.

Just in time, because Lord Burnwood's loud footsteps were approaching. Frederica hastily drank the last sip of her tea and then hurried out of the kitchen. She locked the kitchen door to make sure Tidbit didn't launch a surprise attack, then hurried into her bedroom. With vigorous strokes, she brushed her thick hair and tied it into a knot at the back of her head. Her green dress gave way to the colourful attire from the day before. She took a deep breath again, ready for the encounter with Lord Burnwood.

In the hallway, Millie approached her. "Tea?" She stopped and wrinkled her freckled nose. "We also have some ale that I was planning to use for the stew."

"Then he'll have to make do with tea," Frederica said, considering the matter settled.

"I could send Georgie from next door to fetch a jug from the Merry Whistle."

"I don't believe Lord Burnwood will care whether it's ale or tea on the table," Frederica remarked. It was uncharacteristic for Millie to offer an alternative, especially if it involved additional trouble like sending the neighbouring boy on an errand. "He hardly touched his tea yesterday, and besides, he's here to model for me. This is not a social visit."

Millie chuckled. Not long and not loud, but hearing the young woman laugh was unusual enough that Frederica took notice. What was wrong with her? Normally, she was more than reserved. It had taken months for Frederica to coax more than an expressionless "Yes, madam" or "As madam wishes" out of her. Not that Millie had never smiled in the eleven years they had known each other, but today she seemed more approachable than in all those years combined.

The sound of footsteps came from the studio. Lord Burnwood was probably pacing impatiently back and forth. Frederica knew it was impolite to keep him waiting, but he had arrived earlier than agreed, and she needed to find out what was going on with Millie. "Is everything all right with you?" She put a hand on Millie's sturdy arm. "You're so different this morning. You're... happy?!" It came out half as a question, half as an observation. If an answer had been required, the radiant smile on Millie's face would have been answer enough.

"We've set a date for the wedding," Millie revealed. "In two months, we'll be man and wife."

"How wonderful!" Frederica shared in her happiness. She would miss Millie because once her housemaid became Mrs. Solomon, the young woman would no longer work for her. But if anyone deserved this happiness, it was Millie.

"I think His Lordship is waiting." Millie reverted to her usual reserved manner before Frederica could say anything else. Yielding to the impulse, Frederica kissed Millie on the cheek to express at least a small part of the joy in her heart. Then she took a deep breath and hurried into the studio. How strange it felt to enter the room she had avoided for so long!

Lord Burnwood had stopped pacing like a caged tiger. He stood by the terrace door, looking out at the small square she called her garden. Frederica was about to wish him a good morning when something about his posture made her pause. The pale sun hadn't yet risen above the walls, but it was bright enough that she had to blink for a moment to see more than his broad-shouldered silhouette. Above his black hair, a halo with a bluish shimmer flared up and dazzled her. A saint from behind, a devil from the front. Normally, it was the other way around: most people didn't hide their good side but showed it off and basked in the good opinion of their fellow human beings. Lord Burnwood, on the other hand... Frederica recoiled as he turned around and his deep voice sounded. "Good morning, Mrs. Fitzroy. I took the liberty of inspecting your work." His eyes sparkled. It seemed that her startled expression amused him. "I'm surprised you started without me," he continued. Was that praise? "I assume you'll add the details later." The gleam in his eyes intensified. "I don't want to go down in art history as the Marquess without a face."

Was that some kind of joke? "What you've seen is... how should I explain it... something like the concept of your portrait." She waved him over to her. "Come, I'll try to put it into words."

Within seconds, he stood beside her. The scent of soap and something earthy filled Frederica's nose. Combined with the warmth of his body, it created a disconcerting mixture that made thinking difficult. She discreetly took half a step to the side and gestured towards the canvas. "What you're seeing now is sort of my idea of your personality." She couldn't describe it any better, especially not when Lord Burnwood was standing right next to her, and she was the centre of his attention. "It's more of a feeling than reality. That's why you don't have a proper face on the painting yet. But don't worry," she added hurriedly, "it will, of course, unmistakably be your face."

"Are you saying you need to get to know me before you can paint me accurately? Or does it mean you don't stick to the facts but paint what you feel?" He sounded horrified. Frederica risked a furtive glance upward. Her head only reached his shoulders. "I did say it's not easy to explain," she defended herself. "Painting a portrait, even if it's a faithful reflection of the subject, never happens without emotion." She took another step away from him. He followed her, nullifying her attempt to escape his orbit. "If you were to commission one hundred artists to paint this painting, you'd get one hundred different images of yourself, as each painter would incorporate their own view of you, my lord, into the image. Regardless of their artistic abilities, you'd see one hundred versions of your personality." Frederica fell silent and bit her lip. Finally, she made another attempt. "Ask one hundred people to describe a sunset. The tavern keeper will use different words to your valet. They'll express themselves differently to my maid or me. I'm sorry; I cannot make it any clearer."

He stared at the faceless painting for a few more seconds, then shrugged. "As long as I get what I want in the end, I'm fine with it." After a short pause, he changed the subject. "Have you tried the drying substance?"

Frederica went to the table and took up her brushes and palette. "Yes, and it's excellent. Why don't you take the same position as yesterday?" she asked. The canvas was primed, the rough sketch completed. "I know you value a speedy completion. You can talk to me while I paint, but I may not always respond immediately." Perhaps he would stand still longer if he talked? It was worth a try.

Resignedly, he trudged – truly, his gait bore no resemblance to his usual brisk walk – to the centre of the room and assumed the exact position she had asked him to hold yesterday. The light fell on his face from the side, emphasising the distinctive features that made him so unmistakable. "Excellent!" she commented and returned her gaze to the lavish array of colours ready on the table. "I'll work from light to dark," she said in an attempt to involve Lord Burnwood in her work. "That means I'll start with your face. Specifically, your skin." She put red, yellow, two different shades of blue, sienna, and umber on the palette and began to mix.

"Blue for the skin?" Lord Burnwood, even from the distance between them, observed with his eagle eyes what she was doing.

"Every skin tone contains blue, even if only a tiny hint," Frederica replied. "I'd mix more blue into a fair, cool skin like mine than into yours. Your skin is warm and needs more yellow than blue and white, but in places where your facial skin is thin or where a shadow is visible, like under your cheekbones, I'll mix in a bit more blue." He lifted his hand from his hip as if he wanted to touch his face and feel where that thin skin was, but under Frederica's stern gaze, he let his hand drop again.

She didn't hesitate and made her first brushstroke. Too bright, and the colour wasn't rich enough. It needed more depth, more gold in the skin, but not so much that Lord Burnwood's skin tone clashed with the unusual shade of his hair. Yes, that was closer to the desired result.

For a while, she mixed colours and painted in silence, but the blissful state of forgetting, which had always been the most beautiful part of painting for her, wouldn't come. Even when she had portrayed a person before, after a certain time, she had forgotten who was sitting in front of her. Not today. Her fingers trembled, and her heart raced. Filling the canvas, along with the tentative contours, with life suddenly felt like a task she had overestimated. After two years without a single brushstroke, the beginning was much, much harder than she had expected. Although Lord Burnwood stood remarkably still for quite some time, each time Frederica looked at him, his personality intruded into her thoughts. His eyes seemed to miss none of her movements, and surely he wondered, given her obvious nervousness, if he had made a mistake in giving her the commission. Far too often, she pondered what was going on behind his furrowed forehead, why he knit his brows, or why his lips curled.

If his skin alone was causing such difficulties, how would it be when she captured his eyes on the canvas?

21

NASH

Surprisingly, Nash found it less difficult to stand still today. Mrs. Fitzroy had told him he was *allowed* to speak and sit down if he remained seated, so the lighting wouldn't change. Nash preferred to stand. This way, he could watch her better, which was enough to dispel his boredom today. In a way, he didn't even need to see what she was painting to follow the creation of the image. He only needed to look at her face to know how she was progressing.

At first, she encountered some difficulties. She raised her eyebrows, narrowed her eyes, dabbed a blob of paint on the canvas, stepped back, and then closer again. She even shook her head before turning to her palette to mix the colours again. But the longer he watched, the steadier her hand became. With each brushstroke, she seemed more confident. The crease between her brows didn't entirely disappear, but to Nash, it seemed like a promising sign. Mrs. Fitzroy wasn't easily satisfied; she continuously worked towards a better result. Her movements, which had been jerky at the beginning of the session, became smoother. Nash wondered what kind of lover she would be – the fiery one who pounced on a man like a predator, threatening to devour him completely, or the shy one who barely dared to breathe in a man's arms? Neither, he suspected. Frederica Fitzroy, with the reddish-blonde hair of an angel and the dark eyes of a passionate woman, was both. His imagination heated his blood, and Nash was grateful for his loose breeches, which concealed the all-too-visible evidence of his desire for this woman. He focused his gaze on her face again.

Occasionally, the reflection of a smile appeared on her features, something that would have escaped a less attentive observer. Not Nash. He felt like a predator on the prowl and enjoyed observing all the tell-tale details that revealed more about her character. Her pale skin took on a rosy hue. Her brown eyes repeatedly shifted between him and her work, but while an hour ago – at least, Nash believed an hour had passed – they had seemed rather nervous, they now held a more distant expression. It appeared as though she was taking in all the details of his appearance without truly seeing him, as if he were... an apple or a flower.

"You're frowning," Mrs. Fitzroy's voice sounded with more than a hint of sternness. Her admonishment only made him furrow his brows even more, so Nash made a deliberate effort to relax his facial muscles.

"I had no idea how exhausting it is to maintain the same expression for more than three minutes," he commented.

"I can imagine," she replied without looking at him. Something on the canvas, invisible to him, held her attention. "You're not a woman, after all." Barely had the words come out of her mouth when she closed her eyes, but not quickly enough. Nash recognised in them an expression of pure horror, and he saw her cheeks flush deep red. "I apologise, my lord."

Her embarrassment was highly appealing, and the sight of her was enough to stir his masculinity once again. He straightened his shoulders. Slowly, not only because of the effect it had but also because his muscles were a bit stiff from the prolonged immobility, he turned his upper body in her direction. She opened her eyes and, as her gaze met his, all colour drained from her face.

A strange feeling welled up in Nash's chest, sank down, and settled sharply and bitingly in his stomach. It took only a heartbeat for him to identify it: shame. What had he been thinking, scaring her like that? "You have nothing to apologise for, Mrs. Fitzroy," he said and approached her with measured steps. He reached out his hand – conciliatory or apologetic, he didn't know, and didn't want to know what exactly he intended to do. "But an explanation would be..." he swallowed the "appropriate" he had wanted to say and replaced it with a loudly spoken "welcome."

She lifted her chin. Then she sighed, set the palette and brush aside, and stepped towards him before he could get a look at the canvas. "You want an explanation, my lord?" She looked up at him with a sceptical expression. She was so small! He could probably span her waist with both hands if he wanted. "May I remind you that you wish to have the painting in your hands as soon as possible?"

"Yes, you may, Mrs. Fitzroy. And I'd like to remind you that anyone who works hard deserves a break."

The scepticism on her face deepened. "I'm not tired yet." She narrowed her eyes, as if she could read his thoughts this way. "If you'd like a short break, by all means! My maid has prepared tea." She was about to go to the table, perhaps to pour him a cup, but he stopped her.

"I'm neither hungry nor thirsty." At least, he wasn't hungry for something that could be satisfied with a meal or a sip of tea. He wanted to know what was going on behind that smooth, fair forehead. "I just get extremely bored very quickly." In a semicircle, he walked around the easel. Mrs. Fitzroy followed him with her eyes. "Why don't you allow me to see your work?"

Mrs. Fitzroy picked up the palette and dipped the brush into one of the colours. As she spoke, her features became expressionless, almost as rigid as those of a doll. "You can see it tomorrow, after our next session. Until then, I ask for your patience."

Getting her to speak was as challenging as extracting a pearl from an oyster. But Nash was persistent, and he was patient – if the prize was worth the effort. "Can you at least allow me some diversion? Didn't you tell me earlier that I was permitted to speak?"

She let the brush drop and looked at him. "I must have been out of my mind," she mumbled, but Nash heard every word. She raised the brush again and dabbed paint on the canvas. "How can I capture you if you constantly distract me with indiscreet questions?"

"Let's make a deal," Nash suggested. "For every question you answer, I'll stand and remain silent for five minutes heroically." Before she could reprimand him, he returned to his original position. She gave him a critical look, set aside her brush and palette, and approached him. As she touched his cheeks with her fingertips and gently turned his face to the left, desire surged through him once again. Involuntarily, he lowered his gaze and looked directly into her dark eyes. Her pupils were dilated, and her mouth was slightly ajar. The tips of her fingers still rested on his cheeks. Fuelled by her touch and the warmth of her body, his masculinity began to stir. He cleared his throat at the same moment she, with flushed cheeks, retreated to the easel. The rustling of her skirts and the gracefulness of her movements were enough to set his lower half on fire. Within seconds, he was painfully hard, and once again thanked his tailor for the comfortable, wide-cut trousers that concealed the visible evidence of his arousal.

"You are..." Her lips twitched, but her eyelids remained half-lowered, seemingly focused on the portrait.

"Impossible? Breathtakingly charming? Persistent? A true hero?" he suggested. "The first," came from her mouth. She blushed again, but this time only faintly. "Fine, ask away!"

"What do you prefer to paint?" Most women painted to pass the time and chose familiar subjects like flowers, children, or tame animals.

"Faces," she replied straightforwardly. Their gazes met. Nash raised an eyebrow. He would abide by the agreement and remain silent for the next five minutes, but nothing prevented him from expressing his opinion with his gaze.

Come on, he lured her in his thoughts, *tell me something about yourself, you enchanting, reserved lady*. Once or twice, the beautiful painter opened her mouth, and Nash thought she was softening, but he was mistaken. The only response he received was a downright challenging look.

Generous as he was, Nash waited a few more seconds beyond the agreed five minutes. He didn't have a timepiece, but he relied on his innate sense of time passing.

"Do you prefer to paint male or female faces?" was his next question.

"I don't have a preference," was the answer.

Time passed agonisingly slowly. Finally, Nash was allowed to speak again.

"Where did you learn to paint?"

Mrs. Fitzroy sighed inaudibly but didn't interrupt her work. "My mother was a talented painter." She briefly closed her eyes, and a wistful smile played on her lips. "One of my earliest memories is the smell of paint and the sight of my mother sitting at her easel, her hand hovering over the palette as she searched for the right colour."

"So, your mother was—"

She raised the hand in which she held the brush. "Five minutes!" she reminded him.

Nash smiled inwardly, only to keep his composure, even though he longed for another touch of her delicate hands. He silently counted the seconds until the next permissible question, which he had already formulated in his mind.

"What about your father? Is he an artist too?" After inquiring about her parents, Nash believed that the next question – about her husband – wouldn't sound unusually nosy, or so he thought. It was all a matter of the right tactic.

"No," Mrs. Fitzroy replied. A charming little crease appeared between her arched eyebrows. "My father is a clergyman. He oversees a small parish in Sussex and raises bees."

Nash refrained from even blinking, but he carefully stored away the precious information she had provided. The next few minutes flew by as he contemplated the perfect, unobtrusive phrasing.

"Why did you request my services in your husband's name?"

She ran her tongue over her lips. "I wasn't sure if you would hire a female artist," she confessed. "Most gentlemen don't believe a lady can deliver artistically demanding work."

Oh, how Nash wished to assure her that he wasn't like other men! But anything he said now would sound like foolish boasting, so he remained silent and juggled words in his head to formulate the next crucial question.

"Will your husband have any involvement in the painting?"

"No." The answer came without the slightest hesitation.

Nash knew he shouldn't change his facial expression, but he couldn't help raising his eyebrows.

Mrs. Fitzroy lowered the hand holding the brush and scrutinised him with an expression Nash couldn't decipher. "I am responsible for your painting. Francis... my husband... is not."

Did that mean she and her husband were living separately? In his mind, Nash reviewed his path through the house. Except for the darned cat, there was not the tiniest indication that a male being lived here. No coat on the rack, no scent of tobacco in the parlour, nothing! Every fibre of Nash's being urged him to delve deeper into the question of the absent husband, but he knew that if he applied too much pressure on the beautiful painter now, he would lose her. After five minutes, Nash asked the next consciously harmless question: "What does a face need to arouse the desire in you to paint it?"

She raised her head. "It must..." She lowered the brush. Now, not only her cheeks but also her décolleté turned pink. The swell of her bosom moved as her breaths became more frantic – and he was the cause of it. She quickly averted her gaze and hid behind the canvas.

Five minutes had never seemed so long and simultaneously so entertaining to him. Mrs. Fitzroy didn't spare him a single glance, so Nash passed the time by thinking of his next questions. Just like a trail of breadcrumbs lured the bird into the trap, he would lead the stern beauty into his ambush.

22

FREDERICA

Gradually, Frederica began to feel that she was paying a high price for Lord Burnwood's patient posing. Sure, he compensated her with gold, but for the cost, he wanted more of everything: more influence, which was perfectly normal for a noble patron. More information about her process, which was unusual but ultimately acceptable. What bothered her was... this insatiable curiosity that extended to her person. Half the time, she felt flattered; the other half, she was on guard, even though she didn't exactly know why. After the completion of the painting, they would never see each other again. They didn't move in the same circles. Even if Frederica rose overnight to become the most famous painter of her era, this would remain the case.

She had been able to answer his questions about her beginnings as a painter and her parents in relative peace. But then he had inquired about Francis, and she had been on the verge of confessing the truth to him. Didn't he have a right to know that the famous Francis Fitzroy wouldn't even look at the portrait? Frederica had obtained the commission under false pretences, she was aware of that, but Lord Burnwood didn't seem to care who did the painting, as long as it was done according to his terms. So she had hoped to sweep the topic of Francis under the rug.

It seemed such a thing would be impossible.

His next question caught her completely off guard. She had often wondered herself what it took for a face to capture her interest, and for a moment, it felt as if she and Lord Burnwood were more deeply connected than their brief acquaintance allowed. Immediately, she remembered the day she had come home and feverishly sketched his face. "It must..." *fascinate me. It must tell me stories without words. It must mirror its owner's life, their joy, and their personality*. But all of these were inappropriate answers. At the last moment, she managed to end the sentence innocuously: "... engage me," she concluded.

The time until the next question passed too quickly. With each answer, Frederica took longer to regain the necessary concentration. How would she ever finish if she was forced to ponder something that had once been as natural to her as breathing? And if that was the case, if painting was truly a part of her essence, why had she yielded to Francis's pleas and stopped?

"What appeals to you? Is it beauty that you want to capture?"

With conscious effort, Frederica dabbed her brush on the canvas where she wanted to work on the chin. The result was lacking: too round, too soft, too feminine, but she forced herself to make the strokes. "Beauty?" she repeated, to buy more time. She didn't want to know why she felt the urge to capture a particular expression on a face. Couldn't Lord Burnwood be content to let her paint? Why did he lead her deeper and deeper into the heart of darkness with his questions? "Beauty is relative," she said, not looking in his direction, but she could have sworn that a diabolical delight flickered in his eyes at her words. "It takes more than regular features or balanced proportions to engage me. Although," she continued, "in nature, the harmony of form prevails, and I believe that the perpetual presence of the ideal instils in us a certain longing for regularity." She set her tool aside and wiped her forehead with her hand.

Lord Burnwood seemed sceptical. Rightly so, because her words were only half the truth. "So, the pursuit of beauty is not innate in us, but out of habit, we long for symmetry?" He shook his head. "I understand that a rose is aesthetically pleasing, or a noble horse, even a dangerous predator in all its threatening splendour. But what about injured animals or those that have been hurt in battle?"

When Frederica left the protection of the easel, Lord Burnwood broke out of his rigid pose and rolled his shoulders. The dark blue fabric of his Spencer glimmered. His features showed no self-pity. Perhaps there was a touch of self-irony, but although he obviously alluded to his scar, there was no trace of self-indulgence in his cobalt blue eyes.

"Beauty is so much more than symmetry," she said, drawn out. "A disruption of harmony can be precisely what captivates our gaze. The wild, the extraordinary, rivets our attention and conveys to us the knowledge that we are alive. To live includes suffering as much as joy. It takes shadows to make the light shine. Beauty is the knowledge that the sun will rise tomorrow, regardless of how dark the night is." She went to him. Lord Burnwood's steps were as silent as a cat's as he followed her to the window, through which the garden could be seen. "Even in the darkness, there is beauty. Look at this plant." She pointed with her hand at the moonflower climbing up the wooden trellis. "During the day, it's the most inconspicuous of flowers. No one who enters my garden would give it a second glance." Frederica considered asking Lord Burnwood to leave, but decided against it. This was the garden she had designed for Francis, and every step in the square was filled with memories that were more carefree than those in the studio. Now was not the time to dwell in the past. "At night, however, the petal unfolds and emits a distinctive sweet scent. It also attracts insects. When the moonlight touches the leaves, they shimmer like opals. Over there is the honeysuckle, and behind it, you see the evening primrose. All these plants reveal their perfect beauty only in the darkness. They don't need the sunlight to come to life."

Behind her, she felt the warmth emanating from his body, but this time it didn't feel intimidating or threatening.

"There's a plant called the 'Queen of the Night', which blooms only on a single night. Its fragrance is said to be intoxicating, and the beauty of the spectacle when it opens is unforgettable." She sighed. "I've been waiting for years for it to bloom. Beauty," she said, smiling modestly, "is always in the eye of the beholder, my lord. The more rarely it reveals itself to others, the more precious it usually is."

"I understand," he said softly. Frederica closed her eyes and was relieved that he couldn't see her face at that moment. She no longer knew if she was only talking about the flowers or about herself. Like the night flowers, she remained hidden. No one saw her, no one recognised the fire that burnt within her, and she herself had been trying to extinguish it for years. The bitter realisation burned in her throat like poison. Breathing became difficult; it felt like she couldn't get enough air, no matter how hard she tried.

"Let's continue working tomorrow," Lord Burnwood suggested in a still-muted voice. The hairs on Frederica's neck stood on end. Escape or attack? It was too late for both, she realised. "You've answered every one of my questions," he continued. "Even the one I didn't ask."

23

NASH

As Nash stepped onto the street, he felt more invigorated than he had in half an eternity. He instructed the coachman to drive alongside him while he took a few steps on foot. There was an air of excitement in Lambeth that one would search for in vain in Mayfair. The air was mild, the sun only partially obscured by a few thin clouds, and Mrs. Fitzroy's infernal cat had granted him a free retreat.

Sometimes, the beauty of life revealed itself in unexpected moments. Like now. He had engaged in an uplifting conversation with a charming woman and hadn't thought for a moment about his impending marriage to the Scottish bride. He swung his cane, tossed a coin to a beggar on the corner, and tried to hold on to the feeling that made his steps wide and directed his gaze towards the good things in the world. Perhaps he should speak directly to the Prince Regent. Tell him that marriage was out of the question. After all, they lived in a progressive era, and George was not a despot. Just a well-meaning fool who wanted the best and achieved the worst.

An older woman, with grey curls peeking out from her plain bonnet and carrying a basket of eggs, sidestepped a few street urchins. Her cargo shifted as she tried to take a giant step over a puddle of mud. Nash jumped to her aid, shielding her body from the cheeky boys and simultaneously grabbing her arm, where she carried the basket. "Allow me," he said, guiding her past the obstacle onto the relatively clean footpath. Skilfully, he caught one of the eggs that threatened to break free. What had Frederica Fitzroy said about nature? *In nature, the harmony of form prevails.* For a heartbeat, he looked at the unremarkable thing and saw nothing but a perfect oval. She was right. Beauty wasn't just everywhere; it truly lay in the eye of the beholder. What he had always taken for granted – that hens laid eggs that served him as food and were indistinguishable in shape – seemed like a miracle to him in this moment.

"Would you like to continue worshipping the egg, or may I have it back?" A mocking smile illuminated the woman's face.

"Forgive me," he replied, "but for the briefest of moments, this was much more than an egg." He placed the egg back in the basket among the others. "It was and is a revelation like no other." From the corner of his eye, he saw the boys who had nearly knocked the woman over watching him with grins. One used his fingers to twist his face into a grotesque likeness of a madman.

The grey-haired woman took a step back as she looked into his face. Inevitably, her feet landed in the puddle that Nash had just saved her from. Looking around for help, she retreated further and muttered something about "opium dens" and "sin," if Nash understood her correctly.

"Forgive me," he said, baring his teeth in a laugh that he knew made most people turn pale. The scar, which he had forgotten as easily as the Scottish bride, stretched painfully. "I didn't know that helping someone was a sin." He pulled his lips further back from his teeth, as Mrs. Fitzroy's damned cat did when it issued its feline death threats. The old woman's free hand flew to her bosom. Nash indicated a step forward, causing her to let out a sharp scream. The basket of eggs threatened to fall to the ground again. This time, Nash did nothing to catch it. The old woman managed to regain her balance on her own before she hurried away.

"Shame on you," one of the boys called from a safe distance, "scaring an old lady like that!"

Nash turned around. The sun had disappeared behind the clouds. The lightness he had just enjoyed was gone. Mrs. Fitzroy's house was in sight, as was his coachman, waiting for him at the street corner, unaware of the unpleasant scene. For a moment, Nash pictured himself going back. He saw himself knocking on Mrs. Fitzroy's front door. She would open it herself because her maid was busy elsewhere. The cat would occupy itself with hunting mice. Nash would ask her to accompany him to Almack's this afternoon. They would have tea and continue the conversation from this morning, this time without him having to buy every word from her with his stillness. He would make her smile, perhaps even laugh. He would kiss her hand. The delicate underside of her wrist where he would feel her pulse beneath his lips. Her mouth would open, her moist, rosy lips offered in anxious anticipation like the petals of that Queen of the Night she had raved about. He would... what would he do? Seduce her?

No. No. None of this was right. Frederica Fitzroy was still a married woman, even if he suspected it was in name only. He had no doubt he could lure her into his bed. Nor did he doubt that she would enjoy it. But then... he was promised to another woman. There was no denying that. Until he found an honourable way to persuade Lady Annis Stewart to dissolve the union, he would not drag himself and Mrs. Fitzroy through the mud. Even if she were a free woman, she wasn't the type for a brief affair that one enjoyed and then forgot. Frederica Fitzroy was unique, and if he were to seduce her, it would only be with her consent and in full openness.

To his own regret, Nash doubted that she would ever agree to even extend her hand for him to kiss once she learnt that the Prince Regent desired his marriage to another woman. No, no, and again, no! The game had got out of control today. She might not be in love with him, but on the day they met, she had put his face on paper dozens of times. According to her own words, she painted only what was meaningful to her. It wouldn't take much – at least in Nash's imagination – to make her fall in love with him. Out of harmless flirting, more had developed, and of all the nuances of the game, this was the most dangerous. She made him think things that were simply not possible.

With a soft sigh, he turned away from Mrs. Fitzroy's house and marched to his carriage. As he got in, a fresh breeze picked up and dispersed the last clouds before the radiant sun.

Even the weather mocked him today.

"To the club!" he barked at the coachman and drew the curtain over the window after he had entered. The world wouldn't fall into chaos if he discharged his duties for the rest of the day and let Providence take care of the rest. Today he wanted to drink, gamble, and eat, far away from anything even remotely related to the female sex. Aunt Matilda, Lady Annis, and especially the disconcerting Mrs. Fitzroy could be left behind. On this day, he didn't want to hear the rustling of a skirt anymore.

24

FREDERICA

Frederica had worked on Lord Burnwood's portrait until shortly before sunset, spurred on by his probing questions that forced her to look deep within herself. What was beauty? How could she convey her feelings for the man on the canvas while still creating what he valued most: a lifelike representation of himself? It was a nearly impossible task that pushed her to her limits and beyond. He had thrown her into the dark heart of her fears, and yet she had never felt more alive, more determined. With the realisation that she was her own greatest obstacle in her pursuit of happiness came a bittersweet knowledge: she and no one else was the forger of her destiny. As the light faded and she could no longer discern the nuances of colour well enough to continue, she reluctantly cleaned her brushes and decided to check on her soaps. The drying of the next batch should be far enough along that she could cut the large blocks into smaller pieces and prepare them for sale. And so it was. As she sorted the bars and placed them in crates, Frederica felt a little better. If her plan failed and Lord Burnwood disliked the portrait, at least she had something to bring her milk, bread, and cheese.

. . .

Just as they had the morning before, her first steps led her to the studio, where she took the painting from the canvas and carried it, along with the cloth, to the window to view it in natural light. After a tiny moment of hesitation, she let the fabric drop and emitted a sound that lay somewhere between surprise and delight. No, delight didn't even come close. There were still numerous details missing, and the eyes hadn't yet captured the expression she wanted to convey, but by all the saints of the Church of England, it would be magnificent! Frederica could not only see but also feel how the portrait would look when she had finished it. Under her fingers, Lord Burnwood would come to life, enchanting the viewer.

With trembling hands, she placed the painting on the floor and leant it against the terrace door. Without caring that she was only in her nightgown, she sat down before the painting in a manly fashion, with her legs crossed, and looked at her work.

It was all there: the square chin, the curved nose, the proudly arched eyebrows, the wide mouth that always seemed ready to form a mocking smile. The most difficult part was the eyes, which she had only hinted at so far. And then the scar… Frederica squinted and leant back. The longer she worked on the portrait, the more the injury became a part of his face, just as expressive as his mouth and nose. Frederica decided to paint the scar as she saw it: present but by no means dominant. Yes, that was how she would proceed, and as quickly as possible. She couldn't wait to continue painting.

When Millie arrived, Frederica had placed the painting back on the easel and was mixing various shades of blue for the eyes. How should she create the background to highlight Lord Burnwood's eye colour? Tidbit, curled up on the chair by the window, dreaming with twitching whiskers, woke up with a lazy meow and stretched luxuriously. After a brief greeting, Millie cleared away the tea service that had been left untouched from yesterday. "You must eat the stew today, or it will go bad," Millie warned, unfazed by Frederica's absent-mindedness.

Caught off guard, Frederica turned around. "I'm sorry, I just forgot to eat," she admitted ruefully. "When I paint, I am..."

"... in another world, I know," Millie completed the unfinished sentence. She set the tray down for the second time and rested her hands on her hips. "If you continue like this, I will not be able to get married. Who will take care of you and the cat when I'm no longer here?" Her voice grew softer and eventually fell silent.

To Frederica's surprise, she noticed tears in Millie's eyes. "I'll manage," she said, putting her tools aside. She went to Millie and hesitated, but then wrapped her arms around her maid's neck and pressed her forehead against Millie's. "Don't cry, my dear. I'm so happy for you and Mr. Solomon." A lump formed in her throat as Millie silently shook her head, not pulling away from Frederica's embrace as she normally would. "And I swear on all seven of Tidbit's lives that I will not forget to eat regularly." Now she was crying too. What saved them both from flooding the entire studio with their tears was the Tiger of Lambeth. Frederica heard his growl and saw out of the corner of her eye a red-striped flash head towards the hallway.

"If that isn't His Lordship," Millie snorted and wiped her tears away with her apron in embarrassment. The gesture was so typical of Millie, with her always energetic demeanour, that Frederica's sorrow doubled. "I'll let him in and keep the cat from giving him a second scar."

The thought of the two combatants fighting each other made Frederica chuckle briefly. How would the battle between man and cat end? She'd bet on Tidbit, but Lord Burnwood would certainly have a few tricks up his sleeve as well.

She decided she would show him the painting today so he could comment on any changes he wanted. Perhaps her client had an idea for the background because the more Frederica thought about it, the more undecided she became. If only she had more time to turn an already excellent portrait into a perfect one! Could she ask Lord Burnwood for a few more days?

She heard his steps before she saw him and made an effort to impose a neutral expression on her face. After he had left yesterday, she had made great progress on his portrait. But now doubt pierced Frederica.

"This man looks *friendly*." He spat out the word as if it were spoilt meat. "He smiles. Furthermore, he lacks the distinctive character that sets me apart." He twisted his lips. "Look at me, Mrs. Fitzroy. Look closely." His voice grew quiet. "What do you see?"

Frederica felt like a rabbit who had been cornered by a fox. Or like a woman feeling a man's hard mouth on hers for the first time. Her throat was parched, and even if she had thought of an answer, she wouldn't have been able to speak.

"Where is the man I saw in your first sketches? That's the person I want to see in your painting, not this... weakling you've painted here in a highly mediocre way." He gestured to the easel. "Your first pictures were *brilliant*." He spat out the last word as an insult, not a compliment.

He was talking about the pictures she had drawn on the first night, as if in a feverish delirium. The ones where she had captured his wildness, as well as her reaction to him, that mix of attraction and repulsion.

Frederica swallowed her tears. She would paint him, this Lord with two faces, and if he didn't like the result, he could go back to where he came from: Hell.

25

NASH

The feeling of having overlooked something important wouldn't go away. He had set the painter on the right track. That was good. Excellent, even. He would get the painting he needed. She had promised that only two, perhaps three more sessions would be needed.

What had she been thinking, painting him so... attractively?

Nash pondered half the night. Eventually, Mrs. Fitzroy sneaked into his dreams, and they were by no means pleasant. In his nightmare, she joined forces with Aunt Matilda, who gave her detailed instructions on how to complete the painting. And Mrs. Fitzroy – from his dream, of course – had nothing better to do than to dress him in a dark violet suit and paint his hair in waves over the side of his face where he had suffered the injury. The more dream-Nash raged, the more lovely the painting became under her skilled fingers, while Aunt Matilda cheered her on enthusiastically. To complete the procession of charming femininity, the Scottish bride also appeared and expressed her desires, which Mrs. Fitzroy promptly fulfilled. Just as she ordered the painter to place a damn lapdog with a fluffy white and diamond-studded collar next to Nash on the canvas, he woke up drenched in sweat. Even on waking up, he still heard the three-part female chorus with their tinkling laughter in his ears.

But that wasn't the worst part.

The second dream that Nash vividly remembered was even more disturbing. In this dream, he and Frederica had shared a bed. There was nothing inherently wrong or disturbing about that. No, what terrified Nash was the intensity of his experience, which still had a tight hold on him, even after waking up. His masculinity was rock hard and ached as Nash believed he could smell her and feel her silky skin under his fingers. In the dream, she lay on her back, legs willingly spread for him to bury his head between her thighs and bring her to a pleasurable climax with his tongue. Nash thought he could taste her and, most importantly, hear the lustful, muffled sounds from her mouth. Part of him half-wished the dream would continue so he could at least penetrate her in his fantasy and find relief from the agonising ache in his loins, but nothing of the sort happened. He was awake and remained so, no matter how hard he tried to recapture the dream-Frederica.

THE REST of the morning also left a lot to be desired. Aunt Matilda beamed with satisfaction as she informed him that she had completed the guest list for the soiree. He waved it away as she began to read the names to him. His thoughts were everywhere but on an evening social gathering. Arden House would soon be buzzing like a damned beehive! Aunt Matilda's laughter from the dream echoed in his head. Absentmindedly, Nash grunted his approval and wondered silently what he had done to deserve this regiment of women.

He rose from the breakfast table. It was too early to head to Lambeth, but before he said something he would regret later, he retreated to his study. He felt Aunt Matilda's thoughtful gaze on him long after the servant had closed the door behind him. As if he were fleeing, he stormed up to his desk and sat down. This was the perfect time to answer Lady Annis Stewart's letter. He used his current mood to compose a polite but cold reply.

As soon as he signed his name, he tore the paper and threw it into the fireplace. The girl who was looking forward to marrying him was not to blame for his foul mood. Lady Annis was as much a victim of circumstances as he was, and it was not fitting to punish her for his misery.

Mrs. Fitzroy did not deserve it either. Nash groaned and buried his head in his hands. He cursed the day the bullet had torn half his face open, and also the one when the Prince Regent had embraced the absurd idea of a marriage between the Beauty and the Beast. He cursed himself even more for not simply leaving the country and forcing the royal matchmaker to find another, more willing victim.

"My lord, the carriage is ready." His valet reminded him that it was time to leave.

Nash's streak of bad luck continued mercilessly. There had been a collision between a beer cart driver and Lord Thunderville's carriage on Westminster Bridge. It was impossible to get through. Nash's carriage was stuck. His valet couldn't even turn around and take the route over Waterloo Bridge. Progress was at a snail's pace at best. Nash could either stay inside the carriage and wait or walk to Lambeth. It seemed that the two wedged vehicles hadn't blocked the entire width of Westminster Bridge but had left a passage for pedestrians.

Nash opened the door and jumped out. "Come after me as soon as possible," he instructed his coachman. "I'll expect you on Charlotte Street." He made his way through the crowd of onlookers. At least, Nash thought as he reached the scene of the accident, no one had been hurt, neither man nor beast. Everything remained intact except for the unfortunate beer cart driver's cargo. Nash waded through the puddles of beer that were slowly but steadily pouring into the Thames.

He threw a coin to a one-handed beggar on the street who asked for alms with a monotonous voice. The surprising dexterity the man displayed in catching it caught his attention. "Thank you, my lord!" the man exclaimed and hid the coin under his shirt. He eyed Nash's scar. Nash, in turn, looked at the stump wrapped in dirty bandages where a healthy hand had once been. Once again, Nash thought he had been lucky with his injury. Others had lost much more than their good looks.

"France?" he asked and stopped, even though he was in a hurry to reach his beautiful painter.

"Yessir," the man replied. "Waterloo."

Oh yes. The famous battle in which the English and the Prussians had finally routed Napoleon. Nash hadn't forgotten a single second of that three-day confrontation. The beggar's gaze seemed as laden with memories as his own. He scrutinised the man, made his decision in seconds, and spoke before he could regret his soft-heartedness. He gave the man his address. "Report to the kitchen and tell them Lord Burnwood sent you and that they should serve you a decent meal." The beggar gasped for air. He didn't utter a word of thanks, but that wasn't necessary. "For a man who risked his life for the Empire, there's always a place in my house. Provided, of course, that this man is capable and willing to earn his roof over his head and his meals through honest work. Consider it, and if you want more than a free meal, let my butler know." He nodded to the bewildered war veteran and continued on his way. Public displays of gratitude had always been distasteful to Nash.

Half an hour later, he stood in front of Mrs. Fitzroy's house. The condition of his boots and the hem of his breeches was lamentable, but he couldn't change that now; besides, the painting only showed his face and upper body.

As usual, the neat maid opened the door and invited him in with a curtsy and a muttered "Lord Burnwood." Her nostrils flared. That probably meant he carried the scent of the tavern, which the crossing of beer puddles had bestowed upon him. Barely had he removed his hat and coat when the cat made its appearance. Nash braced himself for the usual exchange of hostilities, but nothing of the sort happened. When the red-striped tiger came closer, instead of hissing at Nash and raising a threatening paw, it lovingly rubbed against his beer-soaked legs. What the hell had gotten into the beast? Cat hairs were as unwelcome on Nash's tailored clothing as sticky beer. The creature mewed shrilly but also longingly, if one could claim that from an animal sound, and stuck to Nash's legs as he followed the girl into the studio.

"Lord Burnwood for you."

Mrs. Fitzroy turned around. "Thank you, Millie." She blocked his view of the progress she had made since yesterday, but the painting became secondary the moment Nash saw her face. Under the brown eyes that had looked at him appraisingly yesterday lay dark shadows. Her already fair skin was a shade paler than usual, and her movements were marked by a weariness that hit him like a punch in the gut.

"Bring tea for your mistress and me... Millie," he ordered. "And something to eat for Mrs. Fitzroy." The girl acknowledged his instruction with a satisfied nod. Still besotted, the cat circled his legs. "And take the Lambeth Tiger with you before he changes his mind and tears me apart while I'm still alive," he added.

Mrs. Fitzroy seemed too tired this morning to lift the brush. She furrowed her brow and stared at him darkly. "I'm not hungry. Thank you, my lord, for your concern." If she knew how appealing she looked despite her exhaustion, she would consume something invigorating, even if it was only to tease him. Nevertheless, her ironic tone lacked emphasis, so Nash allowed himself to ignore it.

"Wouldn't you like to inspect my work?" Mrs. Fitzroy's brown eyes had a feverish gleam. With a step to the side, she gave him a clear view of the portrait.

What in the name... He stepped closer, dumbfounded.

Staring back at him from the canvas was a face that was unmistakably his own. Everything that defined an Arden was there, and she had painted the scar without the slightest hesitation. But while yesterday he had looked at a lovable version of himself, he was now confronted with a monster. The lips were pulled back, revealing his white teeth in a predatory grin. Were those horns on the top of the forehead? Or perhaps his dark hair, whose whorls happened to take the position and shape of horns by chance? The man's eyes on the canvas seemed to track his every movement. The gaze mercilessly pierced his skin and bones, looking deep into his soul. *I know you,* the man on the canvas beckoned, *and I know your secret desires, your hidden lusts. Come, and I will fulfil all your wishes, even those you dare not admit.*

Out of the corner of his eye, Nash noticed Frederica – Mrs. Fitzroy, he corrected himself absentmindedly – retreating further, as if she wanted to get away from his burning anger. "Burning" was a fitting keyword. The background of the painting was shrouded in shadows, but somehow she had managed to create the impression of flickering flames.

This was no monster she had conjured onto the canvas.

She had painted the Devil of St. James.

26

FREDERICA

His Hot-headedness stared wordlessly at the painting. Frederica could only guess what was going on inside him, but his tense posture told her everything she needed to know.

Since his departure, she had been painting non-stop. In a frenzy, she had applied layers of paint and completed the background, which filled her with some pride because it had been damn difficult to create the impression of fire without actually painting the flames. In a moment of madness, she had even given him devil's horns, which could just as easily be interpreted as swirls in his hair. Her masterpiece had become the face, just as it should be in a portrait. She had put all his seductive power into it, the ruthlessness with which he had treated her yesterday, and as a masterful contrast to the inferno, the icy coldness of his character. She would much prefer if Lord Burnwood despised her portrait, rather than calling her "mediocre" again.

She had held a mirror up to him.

Frederica awaited the storm of outrage that would soon descend upon her. Lord Burnwood seemed to have overcome the initial shock because the muscles in his broad shoulders relaxed, and he stepped closer to the easel, almost nose to nose with his likeness.

He would surely demand a refund of the advance.

Well, at least she had Mr. Kingston's down payment for the house. She could return Lord Burnwood's money and, in return, keep the painting. Destroying it was out of the question, but she would banish Lord Burnwood to the farthest corner of the attic, where he would remain hidden under a blanket. No, she corrected herself in her thoughts, not him, but his likeness. Then again, the portrait had become too good for that. She would keep it and show it to the next potential client looking for a painter.

Lord Burnwood straightened up. Frederica braced herself for the inevitable outburst. Her heart raced, and the fear in her stomach clenched like a fist. It had been all well and good to create a devilish seducer in a revengeful trance and tell herself that he deserved it. But standing before him in anxious anticipation of his justified anger was far less satisfying than Frederica had hoped.

Her own anger at the arrogant Lord had dissipated. She had created a magnificent painting, which only needed a few more brushstrokes to be finished, but it wasn't what the Marquess of Arden had paid her for. Frederica didn't dare to look at him but lowered her gaze to her shoes and focused on a bright red paint splatter on the leather. Her footwear was ruined, but who cared? The buzzing of her father's bees echoed in her ears. It had a mocking undertone, as if the creatures were rejoicing in her defeat.

Now he stood before her. The leather of his shoes was stained and showed signs of the puddles he had waded through. The bitter smell of beer filled her nose. She felt like a defendant awaiting the judge's verdict.

"Don't you want to look at me?" Lord Burnwood asked in a subdued voice.

With great effort, Frederica raised her eyes to his chest. The buttons of his Spencer no doubt cost more than a horse because they were not only embroidered but also studded with jewels. At least, Frederica believed they were real gemstones, as she couldn't imagine a man like Lord Burnwood displaying fakes. Strictly speaking, they couldn't be called fakes because they were just buttons, not a necklace or earrings, and besides...

"You surprised me," he continued in an unexpectedly soft tone.

Her throat felt dry. The greatest danger was not always concealed in a loud voice. Predators were also silent and deadly. When would Millie bring the tea?

"I cannot say that I like your view of me, but the painting serves its purpose."

What was he talking about? Frederica finally dared to look at him. She wanted to ask what he meant, while a thousand thoughts raced through her mind, each crazier than the other. She liked his eyes when they looked so gentle as they did now. Despite all it had cost her, she loved the painting and would rather keep it. She would miss the sessions with him, which had torn her out of her daily routine. Lord Burnwood was not the easiest man, but it was never boring to be in his presence. He was the first one to give her a chance, even though she was a woman. He was demanding but generous. Now tears were welling up!

She heard Millie enter and set the tray on the table. "I'll take care of this," Lord Burnwood said, causing Millie to withdraw without comment. Although Frederica couldn't see her, she knew how Millie would look right now: satisfied because Lord Burnwood was taking care of Frederica, and suspicious because his behaviour was so ungentlemanly.

This man was a walking contradiction.

"Come," he murmured and led her to the chaise longue. "You need to eat something."

Frederica shook her head. "Later," she pleaded. "I cannot eat a bite right now."

The blue of his eyes darkened. A storm was brewing. "When was the last time you had something to eat? Here, at least drink a cup of tea. For heaven's sake, has the girl forgotten the sugar?" Sudden heat rose in Frederica as he accused Millie of a crime – or so it sounded – that she hadn't committed.

"We don't have sugar in the house," she said, sharper than intended, and with increasing hysteria, she watched him pour the tea with his sinewy hands. She also liked his fingers, which were slender but not bony, as they were with many thin people – like her, for example.

"Drink!" he commanded and settled into the chair across from her. "You've done good work, but today we're taking a break." She thought of the time pressure he had mentioned so often over the past few days and shook her head. Only then did she realise that Lord Burnwood had not done anything she had expected, from the first angry brushstroke until this moment.

He hadn't stormed out of the house in anger.

He hadn't rejected the painting.

He hadn't rejected *her*.

The Devil of St. James was still in her house.

27

NASH

It was a sign of her exhaustion that she fell asleep on the chaise longue in his presence. Nash watched as her eyelids drooped lower and waited for quite some time, motionless, before he dared to get up. Mrs. Fitzroy had overexerted herself, and Nash felt responsible for it. Taking a day off was the least he could – indeed, had to – do if he wanted to continue looking at himself in the mirror with a clear conscience.

Speaking of mirrors. In the first moment, the painting had given him a damn shock. Yes, he was aware that he instilled fear in most people, but for him, displaying his scar was nothing more than a game. Mrs. Fitzroy had captured more on the canvas than that one facet of his being. For the beautiful painter, he had truly been the devil during the hours she had worked on the painting.

Mrs. Fitzroy's eyelids twitched as she slipped deeper into sleep. Was she dreaming of him? Surely, she was currently chasing him through the studio with a palette and brush in hand, hoping to make him stand still.

Well, as long as she only dreamt, Nash was satisfied.

He went back to the easel and examined the painting once more. Now the shock of the initial view had faded, Nash recognised more than the monstrous features he had perceived when he entered. There was something in the eyes and in the way his likeness curled its lips that spoke of more than the painter's disgust. He took two steps back and let the portrait work on him again. Yes, Mrs. Fitzroy had undoubtedly put something seductive into the diabolical appearance, there was no doubt about it. It wouldn't be enough to drive Lady Annis into his arms against his intentions, even if she were one of those romantics drawn to dark gentlemen, but it was sufficient to fill his heart with confidence: the beautiful painter also felt some of the attraction between them.

A sound behind him redirected his attention to the sleeping beauty. Involuntarily, his gaze slid to her full breasts outlined under her dress. The plump hemispheres pushed out of the neckline. How he would love to bend down to her and gradually lure her out of the realm of dreams into his arms. First, he would kiss her neck and move gently until his mouth found the curve of her breasts. Her breath would tell him about the slowly growing excitement that spread from fingertips to toes in her worshipful body, gathering in her moist lap. He wondered how her face would look in the moment of the highest physical and emotional ecstasy when he... Enough! As much as Nash enjoyed imagining their union, the growing excitement in his loins was distracting him.

He got up and left the salon. The girl came out of the door, which he assumed led to the kitchen, and closed it quickly before the love-stricken cat could escape. Nash heard its offended meowing, followed by scratching at the wooden door, and smiled to himself. Who would have thought that a little beer on the cuffs of his breeches would be enough to turn bitter enemies into friends? Tomorrow would determine whether it was a lifelong alliance or if the fragile peace would vanish along with the scent of hops and malt.

"Your mistress is asleep," he said to the girl. "Tell her I will come back tomorrow at the usual time to..." He hesitated. He had originally intended to say *to pick up the finished painting*, but he didn't want to put more pressure on Mrs. Fitzroy in her exhausted state. So he finished the sentence with the next best thing that came to mind: "...to see her." He didn't even wait for the girl's response but nodded briefly and stepped out onto the street.

His carriage had just turned the corner, and Nash didn't spend much time looking back. He hopped inside and had himself driven home. It was still early in the day, and he intended to devote an hour or two – probably closer to three – of the unexpected free time to his correspondence. First, he reread the letter he had written to Lady Annis last night to correct any remaining mistakes that had crept in at the late hour.

Respected Lady Annis,

Thank you very much for your letter about the virtues of your homeland. I sincerely hope I will succeed in making you appreciate the virtues of my hometown, London. Hyde Park will surely appeal to you once you become accustomed to the noise and learn to avoid the rowdies (and their horses' leftovers) on Rotten Row.

After a brief hesitation, he struck out the words in parentheses about the horse droppings. That was too crude and unworthy of him.

The air may not be as clear and pure as in Scotland, but you will surely not take offence after some time. On my estate in Yorkshire, it is undoubtedly as lonely as in your homeland, and my esteemed old nanny, Mrs. Dolittle, will accompany you on your walks through the moor if you ever decide to leave the grey walls of my house so it does not swallow you up. Since it rains on nine out of ten days anyway, you need not worry about it.

He briefly considered whether he should paint a more dismal picture of life in the barren landscape of Yorkshire and its unsociable, taciturn inhabitants, but decided against it. In the end, he left the lines as they were, hoping that Lady Annis would think him a boor. And when she saw the portrait, it would turn him into a fearsome boor!

Lady Matilda, my beloved aunt, is eagerly looking forward to welcoming you into the family.

What mattered here was what Nash omitted and hoped Lady Annis would notice: namely that he didn't speak of his own joy.

I remain your devoted servant,
Nash Burnwood, Marquess of Arden

There. That should suffice. Did he overestimate the young lady's ability to read between the lines? Nash didn't think so. Her letter indicated education and a reasonable level of intelligence, and he hoped the letter would prepare the ground for the effect of the painting. Or had he perhaps gone too far? No, he didn't believe so. Satisfied for the moment, he folded and sealed the letter, ready to send it to Scotland tomorrow at last.

Thanks to his reliable steward, Nash kept up to date with the account books of his estates in Yorkshire, although it was almost time for his quarterly visit there. Nash wasn't worried about the state of his properties, but he preferred to make it clear to the people in his domain that he cared for them. If that meant spending a few days every three months in Yorkshire and settling border disputes like a medieval landowner, he could live with it very well. In fact, he loved riding out on the moors, enjoying the rugged beauty of the landscape where he had spent his early years. Sometimes he even missed the taciturn farmers, who refused to respect a man just because he held a title. Nonetheless, living in London was unavoidable for a man of his standing, and he appreciated the conveniences that life in the capital of the British Empire offered.

For a moment, Nash imagined himself evading the Prince Regent's matchmaking plans and leading the life of a hermit in Yorkshire, with a wild beard and long, shaggy hair. He would breed dogs and tame some of the wild ponies that roamed the moors. Surely Lady Annis Stewart would not willingly follow such a barbaric stranger into the wilderness. If his plan with the monstrous portrait failed, he had an alternative in mind. The question was only how long he could withstand not trimming his beard. Perhaps he should ask Mrs. Fitzroy to accompany him to his estate in Yorkshire and commission a second portrait.

Nash smiled mischievously. He sprinted up the stairs, bypassing the study. The idea of snatching Mrs. Fitzroy away from the hustle and bustle for a few days was appealing. The two of them alone in the great outdoors... Their pale cheeks would gain colour. Mrs. Redcliffe, the cook, would pamper them with local specialties until Mrs. Fitzroy gained a few pounds. He would like that. Some women looked good with the ethereal pallor of a wilting rose, but Mrs. Fitzroy was not one of them. Even though she constantly restrained herself, she had the temperament of a Southern woman and the matching dark eyes. Together with the reddish shimmer of her hair, it painted the picture of a passionate, vivacious lady, missing only a few curves for his taste.

He still smiled as he rushed into his bedroom. He was going for a ride. The rest of the correspondence could wait until the afternoon. Right now, Nash needed some movement to get rid of the restlessness that had a firm grip on him. He rang for his valet and started to undress, tossing his clothes onto the bed without waiting for the servant's help. Mason appeared. "I'm going riding," Nash explained, pulling on his riding breeches.

Half an hour later, he mounted the broad back of Thunder. The stallion was restless, and Nash leant forward to pat the muscular neck of the horse. Originally, he had planned to take a few rounds on Rotten Row, but now he decided on a ride to Hampstead Heath. The area around the village in North London was open enough for a gallop, something he desperately needed to clear his head. He wanted to feel the horse's power beneath him and the wind in his face while he considered how to prolong the pleasure of Mrs. Fitzroy's company. Another painting was a good idea, but he couldn't keep her busy painting for him for a lifetime.

He was about to start riding when he heard someone calling his name. For the briefest of moments, he was determined to ignore the call, to pretend he hadn't heard anything. But it was Aunt Matilda, standing in the doorway, waving frantically. With a growl that made Thunder prick up his ears nervously, Nash leapt off the horse and threw the reins to the stablehand. By the time he reached the steps, he had regained his composure.

"Good morning, Aunt," he said. "What's the matter?"

Aunt Matilda flinched at his harsh tone but then smiled. "Your betrothed wrote to me," she said and beamed.

"You correspond with Lady Annis Stewart?" His mood reached a new low. "Since when? And why?"

Aunt Matilda gave him a reproachful look. "She will soon be part of the family," she answered his last question, sounding only a bit defensive. "I did not know I needed to ask your permission to write to her." It sounded half-snippy, half-regretful. "Besides, Prinny personally asked me to write to the young lady. I can hardly refuse his request to take her under my wing until she becomes your wife."

Nash felt his impatience growing. Heaven and hell, all he wanted was a ride to be able to think undisturbed. Couldn't a man be alone with his thoughts for even two hours? He took a sharp breath. A premonition of imminent disaster brushed against him. "And what is it that you want to tell me?" He suppressed the urge to snatch the letter from her hand and read the *good news* with his own eyes. "What will you help her with?" He knew what was in the letter. With every fibre of his black soul, he felt what Lady Hastings was about to reveal to him.

"Your bride and her father are coming to London. They will be here by the end of next week at the latest, probably earlier if Lord Stewart's business permits." She descended the steps until she stood directly in front of him and placed a hand on his arm.

Nash felt as if he were frozen inside and out.

Mrs. Fitzroy would delight in his immobility.

28

FREDERICA

It took a while for Frederica to overcome the embarrassment of falling asleep in Lord Burnwood's company. Even by the late afternoon of the following day, she wasn't completely over it, which was probably because she was preoccupied with nothing but the painting. She had given Millie the weekend off, and the Tiger of Lambeth was probably lurking in some backyard where his amorous pursuits were appreciated. Millie had delivered Lord Burnwood's message to her and told her about Tidbit, who seemed to have overcome his aversion to the Lord.

At ten o'clock, the appointed time, she was barely ready to face him, but Lord Burnwood had sent her a message with a servant, stating that he would be delayed today and could only come for the final session in the afternoon. His politeness had surprised her. Grateful for the time to gather herself, she had indulged in a leisurely breakfast.

Frederica chuckled as she remembered Millie's words about Tidbit and the Lord. It was not surprising that the cat didn't appreciate His Lordship. For a long time, the cat had been the only male presence in the house, and when she thought about it, she had shamefully neglected him in recent days. The work on the portrait had consumed all her attention. If Tidbit treated her with disdain, perhaps she deserved it. Even the mackerels she gave him every day, which were a true feast for him, did not make the Tiger more forgiving.

She turned her attention back to the painting, blocking out the street noise, which seemed particularly intrusive today. Frederica felt like she could hear every hoofbeat on the pavement and every door slam, every shout of the newsboys.

As far as the absence of the model allowed, Frederica had continued to work on the portrait. The background with its hint of hellfire was finished, as was the upper body. Lord Burnwood's hands were not in the painting, which made her work much easier. Hands and fingers were the body parts that gave her the most trouble, and the time it took to paint them was enormous. The nose was perfect, as was the mouth, on whose mocking expression she secretly prided herself. It – the mouth – seemed as if Lord Burnwood were about to open it and speak every second. What would he say? Frederica didn't know, couldn't imagine it. He was so… unpredictable. She was convinced that she had a good understanding of people, but with him, she reached her limits.

She took a step back, then another. "Are you really a devil?"

"Only when the situation calls for it," came the voice of that devil behind her.

Frederica let out a muffled scream and dropped her tool. "What gives you the right to sneak up like that? Don't you know that it's polite to knock and request entry before entering someone else's house?"

"I did knock," he explained, "more than once. It looks like your thoughts were not in the present moment." He glanced significantly at the painting before getting down on one knee, picking up the brush, and handing it to her. Their fingertips touched as she took the tool. "Where is Millie?"

Frederica did what she seemed to do half the time in his presence: she stared at him silently. It was extremely strange to hear Millie's name from his mouth, almost as if he were at home here.

"Millie has the day off. Not that it's any of your business," Frederica replied. "Thank you," she added belatedly, holding up the brush to make clear what she was talking about. She shook her head. What was wrong with her? "Excuse me, I'm nervous. Tired." It occurred to her too late that he had seen her sleeping, as only a husband should. She quickly continued, "I'm sure I'll only need you for today."

His eyebrows twitched upwards.

"To model, I mean." Oh God! She had to pull herself together. Why did her mind play tricks on her whenever he was nearby? And why did she constantly think about what lay beneath his layers of clothing?

"It looks finished to me," Lord Burnwood said casually as he stepped beside her and examined her work with narrowed eyes. Then he reached out and drew her back. "When will it be dry enough to transport?"

"I'd like to touch up the eyes again," Frederica said, thinking. "I don't know how quickly Mr. Ackerman's drying substance reaches the lower layers of paint, but I would say you should be patient until the beginning of next week."

"It doesn't matter when it's finished anymore," he said nonchalantly.

Although Frederica only saw Lord Burnwood's face in profile, she noticed the effort he made to banish any emotion from his expression. She had known him for a whole six days, five of which she had spent studying every detail of his appearance – who did he think he was fooling? Certainly not her. More like himself.

"I know you better than to ask about the reason," she said, feeling how the prospect of painting his eyes awakened a strange mixture of calm and nervousness within her. The calmness stemmed from the certainty that she had painted the best painting of her life with the last brushstrokes. The apprehension, on the other hand, had a different source. One she had tried with all her might to push away.

She would miss Lord Burnwood. His strength. His unexpected kindness. His biting remarks and his ability to push her to her limits and beyond. He stepped away from the painting and turned to her, faster than Frederica could hide her feelings behind a mask of composure.

For the duration of a heartbeat, they looked at each other. Forgotten was Lord Burnwood, the Marquess of Arden, and especially the Devil of

St. James. Forgotten was also Mrs. Fitzroy, the widow of the once-famous painter, who had mostly hidden herself, and who every gust of wind frightened. In that one second, they were... not friends, no, but a man and a woman who had spent a lot of time together in recent days and had caught a glimpse into each other's souls.

"My lady," he said softly, in a voice that sent a shiver down her spine with its roughness. "Let's finish this."

Although his words expressed the opposite, Lord Burnwood reached out his hands towards her, as if he wanted to hold her instead of letting her go. Without thinking, Frederica returned the gesture and allowed him to take her hands. She felt the calluses, those strange hardenings on the palms that were unusual for a gentleman, and wondered dizzily where they came from. His head lowered, and he leant ever so slightly toward her. His scent of shaving soap and starch surrounded her. It contained something wild, untamed, a masculine fragrance that intoxicated her senses and made her tremble with anticipation.

Frederica's heart beat so fast that she thought it would burst at any moment. She raised her head and wanted to say something, anything, to break the spell, but not a word escaped her lips. Her knees still trembled, but strangely, her thoughts were of crystal-clear sharpness. *I don't want him to disappear from my life. He's the first man since... Francis who has sparked interest in me and who motivates me, who cares about me, as strange as that may be.*

Frederica raised her head just a fraction, but it felt like she was bridging a distance measured in miles and years. She saw the change in his eyes even before he stepped back. His chest rose and fell in rapid rhythm.

"Of course," she replied breathlessly. *Before I do things I will regret and that will break my heart a second time.*

29

NASH

Nash wished the day would never end. Even standing still didn't feel difficult for him today. Something had changed after the almost-kiss, not just within him but between him and Frederica. Without asking her, he had intended to assume his usual position in front of the terrace door, but she had asked him to take a seat nearby. "The light is different now, and I want to see your eyes."

Although Nash couldn't refute her claim, he believed there was something more to her request: she sought his closeness. Perhaps she wasn't even aware of it herself, but the fact remained that she had offered him her lips. The trembling of her admirable body had been one of excitement, not fear, as her rapid breathing and the warmth in her cheeks had revealed. If he hadn't realised at the last moment that he still had no absolute certainty about the status of her relationship with her invisible husband... He sighed and pushed his heated, but currently inappropriate, fantasy to the back of his mind.

"You're unusually quiet today," she remarked after a while, her eyes focused on the palette.

Nash shrugged. Unlike during their previous sessions, this motion didn't earn him a furrowed brow, which meant he was allowed to move. He stretched out his legs and relaxed. The beautiful painter followed his movement with her eyes before returning her attention to the canvas. "I'll miss our time together," he said languidly.

A delicate, barely noticeable blush crept onto her cheeks.

"I'll miss painting," she replied. The colour in her cheeks deepened.

"This doesn't have to be the last painting you do for me."

The hint of a smile flitted across her face, but it didn't reach her eyes. "That's very kind of you," she responded formally.

"Kind? Not at all!" Nash disagreed. "You're an outstanding artist, and I don't understand why you shouldn't continue doing what you do best and what you obviously love. I'll pay you handsomely. You could become famous if you wanted to, Mrs. Fitzroy."

The brown of her eyes grew slightly darker. "I don't want to be famous. I've seen how fame can change a person, and it's not something I want to experience again, least of all in myself."

"You're talking about your husband," Nash said softly. This time, her face didn't close up at the mention of her spouse, but her movements became more agitated. With a deep sigh, she forced herself to calm down, though the pain in her face was unmistakable. Here was his chance at last! He had to know if her husband still held a place in her life and if the almost-kiss had been nothing more than a whim. Nash took a deep breath and reminded himself to be gentle.

"Yes."

"Your husband couldn't handle the fame." Nash paused. "My aunt was an avid patron of the arts before the war and often told me how difficult it is for many artists to cope with sudden fame and all the money that comes with it."

Mrs. Fitzroy continued to dab paint onto the canvas, but Nash recognised from her posture that she was listening.

"There's no shame in stumbling," Nash said in a gentle voice, even though he wondered what this Francis Fitzroy had put his wife through that made her withdraw so deeply into herself. "We all make mistakes. Falling down isn't the problem; it's finding the strength to get back up."

He had her attention. She turned her dark eyes to him, studying him intently. "And what if you don't have that strength? What if you just want to lie there and watch life go on without you participating?"

Alarmed by the sorrow in her tone, Nash didn't take his eyes off her. Was she talking about herself or her husband?

"Then you should confide in a friend and accept the helping hand that assists you in getting up." Despite the turmoil of worry and anger towards the unknown husband, Nash forced himself to speak calmly. Her eyes widened. "What happened? Tell me, Mrs. Fitzroy. I can be a good listener if you allow me."

With a distant look in her eyes, she lowered the brush onto the palette. "My husband couldn't handle the fame, as you suspected. He... was a very talented painter, but the more famous he became, the less he was able to pursue his art. Francis... only came alive when he indulged himself." She pressed her lips together as she remembered. "He froze as soon as he stood in front of the canvas."

"So, you painted the paintings," Nash noted. Suddenly, he saw her visit to Arden House, where she had identified her husband as the alleged painter, in a completely different light. Thoughts raced through his mind. He still lacked certainty about what had happened to Fitzroy, even though he had a strong suspicion.

In a mixture of defiance and shame, she raised her head. "The truth is that in the three years before his death, Francis didn't complete a single painting by himself."

Two heartbreaking truths found a place in a single sentence. Her husband was no longer alive, and she was the artist who had established the fame. This meant he was free to win her over! Was he a monster for both sympathising with Mrs. Fitzroy and feeling unaffected by the death of a stranger? Nash chose his next words carefully.

"Thank you for your trust," he said in a subdued tone. He didn't want to voice aloud that he wouldn't disappoint her, hoping she understood it. "It must have been very difficult not to receive the recognition you deserved."

Mrs. Fitzroy shook her head and set aside her brush and palette for the moment. "Yes and no," she admitted. "It wasn't quite easy when he was alive, but I don't miss the fame." She furrowed her brow. "I didn't want it back then, and I don't want it today, at Francis's expense. All I desire is a fresh start."

"That's why you never revealed your husband's death," Nash observed. "You hoped to keep the secret about the authorship of the paintings forever and make a name for yourself with your works. One that belongs solely to you." Oh, she was a wonderful woman who didn't deserve that scoundrel of a deceased husband. Nash vowed to give his all to prove himself worthy of her.

Mrs. Fitzroy smiled sadly. "I don't want to tarnish his memory, even if it means I'll never step into the public eye as a painter."

The signature! "FF" could stand for both "Francis Fitzroy" and "Frederica Fitzroy." All the clues had been right there in front of him, Nash had just not looked closely enough! He suspected that the difference in the signatures would be noticeable in a direct comparison, but she hadn't yet marked her painting. Her nervousness when she had made the first brushstrokes provided a retrospective reason, as did her decision to apply for the commission with him. In the months following her husband's passing, Mrs. Fitzroy had not painted, and it had been sheer financial necessity that had driven her to break her resolution.

His beautiful painter possessed everything a man could wish for in a woman: she was smart, charming, loyal… and more beautiful than ever, now that she was confiding in him. His heart swelled with pride and desire, each emotion competing for the top spot. "Tell me more about how you got into painting," he said. He would do anything to dispel the sorrow that had her in its grip. "It was your mother who taught you to paint, you said?"

She hesitated briefly, taking up the brush again. "I inherited my talent from my mother," she said and walked over to the table to add new colours to her palette. Her slender back was tense, her shoulders hunched. When she turned back to him, she straightened her shoulders and continued speaking. "Her father – my grandfather – was a free spirit and allowed her to receive painting lessons," she recounted. "When she was my age, she was known for her miniatures. People came from far and wide, from Rome and Venice, to have their portraits painted by her." She fell silent.

So her maternal family originated from Italy, as he had suspected. That explained her dark eyes and, above all, the temper simmering beneath her cool exterior, which Nash felt and wished to draw out. "And then?" He didn't dare to say more, not wanting to interrupt her flow of words.

She smiled bitterly. "And then my father came," she replied, as if that explained everything, which it did in a way. "They fell in love with each other, and he brought her to England against her parents' wishes. They were happy for a while, at least I think so. Then my father got a parish position and forbade her from taking commissions. She could still paint, but only things befitting a lady. Boring things," Mrs. Fitzroy added. "Flowers, children, kittens. Safe still lifes. Nothing improper."

"I suppose that was long before the birth of the Lambeth Tiger," Nash remarked. "Judging from our brief acquaintance, I'd say he was never boring, not even as a newborn kitten."

Her smile touched his heart. He reached for the handkerchief in his breast pocket, which he had intended to give her as a parting gift, but it suddenly felt so inadequate. The moment he had first seen her pressed into his thoughts. *Not young anymore*, he had thought, and imagined himself holding her in his arms. He had wanted to seduce her. Now, he wanted to be the only man in her thoughts, the one she thought of first thing in the morning, and who accompanied her through the night in her dreams.

He wanted to *conquer* her.

He wanted to love her, every day and every night.

He wanted to show her what passionate love felt like.

He would do things with her that she had never experienced, and awaken feelings in her that she had not dared dream of.

He...

"Whatever you were just thinking," her voice interrupted his plans, "don't stop. That's the expression in your eyes I need." With flushed cheeks, she guided the brush to the canvas.

A triumphant feeling surged in his chest. Now he just needed to steer the conversation in the direction he had in mind. "I was thinking about your tiger," he said casually. He approached his goal like a hunter closing in on its prey.

"I doubt that," she muttered to herself, examining her work critically. "If you present this expression when you think of my cat, he'd better stay away from you."

"What would you say if you had the opportunity to paint a real tiger?"

It took a few seconds before she replied. First, she set aside her tools, then she cleaned her hands with a rag that displayed all the colours of the rainbow. "I can only dream of that. I'll never travel to India, and even if I had the money for the journey, I'd never get close enough to a tiger to paint it. It would probably be my first and last painting of a predator. Or, if I did manage it, no viewer would recognise the tiger. My hand would tremble so much it would be nothing but a mess of tangled lines."

Nash's sense of triumph reached alarming proportions. He had made her crack a joke! He stood up, reaching for her hands for the second time that day, and pulled her closer to him. She hesitated almost imperceptibly, looking into his face with curiosity. Only her dark eyes with dilated pupils revealed her excitement. Feeling the warm, delicate skin of her fingers in his almost drove him mad. Nash had to focus to not lose sight of his actual purpose.

"There's a way," he whispered and tilted his head. At the same time, he drew her fingers to his chest, and he saw her eyes widen. Her pupils grew larger until only the narrow rims of her luminous brown irises were visible. "Less than a day's journey from London is Loring Hall, the country estate of Lord and Lady Castlereagh." He spoke quickly, not wanting her to reject his proposal before he could voice it aloud. "Lady Castlereagh has established a zoo there, and it includes a tiger. Paint the tiger for me, my lady."

Her eyes lit up.

For a heartbeat, everything Nash desired seemed possible. He lowered his head. Simultaneously, she lifted her beautiful face. There was barely a hand's breadth between them. Nash could almost feel her breath on his lips. Bare longing filled her face. Was it meant for the tiger or him? It didn't matter because he was the one who would make her happy and erase the expression of vulnerability from her face forever.

But not now. Nash had to muster all the strength he possessed not to kiss her, but he was not yet free. Once the Scottish bride was no longer his, he would do anything for his beauty with reddish-blond hair. He wanted to roar, scream, rage, but just once – only once – he couldn't unleash the devil.

He had to exercise patience, even though passion for the beautiful painter threatened to consume him. For her sake. She deserved to be treated with respect.

It was the most challenging thing he had ever done.

30

FREDERICA

It was close, he almost kissed her. His restraint had saved her, not her common sense. Although he had put an arm's length between them, he still held her hands. And thank heavens, he didn't know what was going on in her mind at that moment. How close she was to touching his lips with hers, perhaps even surrendering to him! Even if Lord Burnwood hadn't rejected her, anything that followed the act of physical love would have been highly embarrassing. He was her employer! How could she ever regain her self-respect if she had obeyed her longing impulse?

"I've heard about the menagerie," she said. With a clearing of her throat, she dispelled the hoarseness and pushed any thoughts of physicality away. "It would be my pleasure to go there with you and paint the tiger." In her mind, images of black and orange stripes accompanied by lush, dark green tendrils with fleshy leaves emerged. Frederica heard the tapping of paws and the terrifying royal roar of the beast. "Thank you, my lord." She knew he wouldn't take her to one of the noblewoman's famous official parties, but would ask the Castlereaghs for a private visit. She was a poor, insignificant widow, he was a lord. Yet the thought of never seeing him again tore her chest with cutting pain. "I..." she began, unable to put her conflicting feelings into words.

Lord Burnwood released her left hand and placed a finger on her parted lips. Given her agitated state, the feeling she experienced was almost too much. "Don't speak!"

She closed her eyes, but that only made it worse. Her proximity to him turned into a delicious, throbbing pain that tasted bittersweet on her lips. "There's something unique between us. Something precious," he assured her. "I feel it too." Could it be? Was this not just a game for him? Frederica lifted her eyelids, and for a second, it seemed as if she saw the devil flicker behind his blue eyes. But the moment passed. The devil disappeared behind the man with the scar and the loving gaze.

"That's not possible..." she stammered, longing to believe what he was hinting at. Her heart raced in her throat. Lord Burnwood, the Marquess of Arden, intended to court her. Of all women, he wanted her, the not-so-young widow, the commoner with calluses on her hands from candle-making and soap-boiling.

"I'll never hurt you, my lady. I swear it on everything sacred to me." His expression was highly concentrated and appeared so serious that it took her breath away.

She didn't know why, but she believed him. Frederica wanted to say something, but couldn't find the words. Instead, she nodded and was rewarded with a spark in his eyes. Lord Burnwood raised his hand and gently stroked her cheek, tenderly and almost reverently. Frederica nestled her cheek in his hand and watched as his eyes darkened. For the duration of a heartbeat, she felt closer to him than she had ever thought possible.

Heaven help me, I want to touch this man. Kiss him. Place my hand on his chest and feel the movement of his muscles. She wanted to feel the stubble of his cheeks under her fingertips and watch him wake up from sleep. The question was not whether he would adhere to the unspoken rules of society, but rather whether she could control her feelings for him until... Yes, until when exactly? Until he proposed to her? Frederica held her breath. Could she dare to dream of a future by the side of a man who was so far above her in society? His eyes told her that everything she dreamt of was within reach. Could she dare to ask him about his intentions, or would speaking the words aloud destroy everything between them?

In the midst of the silence, Frederica said with a husky voice, "Your portrait will be finished tomorrow."

"That's excellent," he replied, just as quietly as she.

"Good!" She took another step away from him.

Lord Burnwood nodded. The flickering candlelight gave his hair a metallic shine. It also shimmered bluish black on his cheeks and chin. The desire to place her hand on his cheek, feel the stubble under her fingertips – the unmistakable mark of a masculine body – or trace the path of the scar with her fingertips became unbearable.

"Here is the rest of your payment," he said, placing a bag on the table. The coins inside jingled. Her first instinct was to refuse the money. The advance payment alone had been more than enough, not to mention his generous gift. "Just in case I cannot pick up the painting myself."

A wild mixture of disappointment and hope choked Frederica's throat. Disappointment because he was considering having someone else pick up the painting, and sweet contradictory hope that she might see him again tomorrow. She looked uncertainly at the bulging bag and struggled with the feeling of not deserving the payment. For Frederica, it had always felt like a miracle to be paid for something that didn't feel like work, and in the case of Lord Burnwood's portrait, this feeling was doubly true.

"You've more than earnt the money."

Again, it seemed like he had read her thoughts. She swallowed the meagre remnants of her pride and nodded. "So, you like your portrait?"

Lord Burnwood looked at the painting and laughed. The thoroughly masculine sound seemed out of place in her cramped house, yet she enjoyed hearing him chuckle. "Well, it's not exactly flattering," he said. "You've given the monster civilised clothing, at least. I like the knot of the tie, though..." He paused, and Frederica's pulse quickened again, "Although I must say, the respectable clothing accentuates the devilish features even more. I, for one, wouldn't want to encounter this gentleman in a lonely alley at night."

Warmth spread in her chest as she heard him joke. Frederica suppressed a smile. "Nor would I, unless he were my ally. I feel like nothing could happen to me if I were with a man like him." Moreover, with Lord Burnwood by her side, she could take on the whole world.

His eyes sparkled. "Then every second of standing still was worth it, my lady." In a lighter tone, he continued, "If I had to choose between a conventional but boring portrait and this demon from Hell, I would prefer the devil anytime."

"Where will you hang it?" Frederica asked. It seemed like him to place it in the entrance hall and terrify visitors to Arden House before they even met him.

His expression darkened like thunderclouds. "That's not decided yet." He extended his hand to her. This time, he settled for a gentle squeeze. "We'll see each other again, my lady. Soon."

She watched him leave her studio. Only when she heard the front door close did she allow her tears to flow freely. She didn't even know why she was crying. Was it because she was afraid? Oh yes, definitely! She felt something for Lord Burnwood that she had thought she had put behind her long before Francis's death. Was it love? She was not only a widow but at eight-and-twenty years old, arguably too old to fall in love again. Yet this feeling existed, spreading from head to toe, pushing aside the rational fear born of reason. She stretched her arms out and spun in a circle. For a few hours, Frederica wanted to be as unreasonable as a young debutante with her whole life ahead of her. She wanted to forget that her marriage to Francis had not been terrible but not exactly happy either. She wanted to forget that she had sold the house and that the being closest to her was a cat. *Apart from Millie, of course*, she thought with a twinge of guilt. The thought of Tidbit reminded her of Lord Burnwood's gift. She would see a tiger! A huge feline with striped fur, golden-green eyes, and paws that could kill with a single swipe. Where was the fear? By Lord Burnwood's side, nothing bad would happen to her.

He had promised it.

31

NASH

He had to break off the engagement, no matter the cost.

Nash had a goal in mind. It was no longer about avoiding a marriage with the Scottish bride, but about winning Frederica Fitzroy for himself. It might turn out to be a stroke of luck that Lord Stewart was coming to London with his daughter. Of course, the portrait had become unnecessary to properly frighten the young woman, but that also suited Nash – he could keep it and look at it whenever he pleased. They would look at it together, he and Frederica, once they were married.

The thought felt entirely natural, as if it had to be this way and no other. Nash was glad he was alone in his study at this moment because no one could comment on his probably quite foolish, idiotically blissful expression. He reached for the handkerchief in his breast pocket and placed it on the table. His fingers caressed the precious smooth silk. He would give it to her at a later time, after the visit to Lady Castlereagh's menagerie, once she had agreed to become his wife.

He would marry her. He wanted to spend the rest of his life with her and no one else. The thought that she might refuse came and went. Why wouldn't she want to marry him? Of course, she was of lower social standing, and so on and so forth, but Nash couldn't care less about where

Frederica came from. He wasn't interested in her past. It was who she was that mattered. Who she would be.

He threw his head back and laughed loudly.

Since the moment Aunt Matilda had informed him of the upcoming visit of the Stewarts, a lot had happened. His world had changed.

"My lord." Ferguson had entered the room. To a stranger, nothing would have seemed amiss, but Nash had known the butler his whole life and sensed there was a problem.

"Yes, Ferguson? What has happened?"

The butler cleared his throat. "One of the maids has gotten into trouble, sir. I wouldn't usually trouble you with this, but Annie has always been a good girl, and I don't want to send her away without a character reference."

For that, Ferguson, of course, needed Nash's permission. Female servants who committed a misstep – possibly with visible consequences, as seemed to be the case here – were dismissed. They were lucky if their misconduct wasn't recorded in the service book, making it visible to potential future employers.

"Annie is the one who came to us from Yorkshire two years ago, correct?" Involuntarily, Nash thought of his beautiful painter. Her situation was not comparable to Annie's, but as an artist and a penniless widow, her social status was only marginally higher than that of a servant. Her manoeuvre of not immediately revealing the truth about her deceased husband had been nothing more than a puzzle for Nash to solve at the beginning of their acquaintance. A pastime, just like his planned seduction. But with every hour he spent in her presence, he had become increasingly aware of how difficult it was for her as a woman in the present day. And now, with a girl in his care having made a single mistake, he couldn't bring himself to put her on the street and leave her to fate.

"Exactly, my lord."

If Nash's memory didn't fail him, the girl's parents lived on his land, not far from the estate. Two weathered faces appeared in his mind's eye. Yes, exactly. Joseph Deering worked a small farm, and his wife Esther earnt a little extra as a kitchen assistant when Nash was in Yorkshire and, which rarely happened, receiving guests. The Deerings barely made ends meet, and sending their daughter back to them, with child by an unknown man and without a ring on her finger, was out of the question.

Ferguson, who was waiting patiently, looked at Nash expectantly.

"Send Annie to me." Ferguson nodded curtly and turned to leave, but Nash remembered something else. "Do you know who the father is?"

The unthinkable happened: for a fraction of a second, the butler's face showed an expression of anger. It disappeared so quickly that it would have escaped a less experienced observer. But to Nash, the butler's expression revealed that the culprit was also to be found in his household. "Who is it?" he asked, dangerously quiet.

Ferguson cleared his throat again. "Joe Blessup, sir."

Joe was one of the stable lads, a good-looking young man who was fantastic with horses. Apparently, not only with horses. "Have you spoken to him already, Ferguson?"

"Yes, my lord. He claims not to be responsible for Annie's condition."

"Bring me both of them. Immediately!"

Three minutes later, a tearful Annie and a pale Joe stood before him. Joe had taken off his cap and was now tormenting it with both hands. Nash searched the man's face for an expression of guilt but found nothing but a kind of panicked stubbornness. The two didn't look at each other and stood as far apart as politeness allowed.

"I will only ask each of you once for the truth," Nash said deliberately slowly, looking from Annie to Joe. "You have nothing to fear as long as you do not lie to me." He paused for a moment to let the weight of his words sink in. "Joe Blessup, did you take advantage of Annie?"

"No, Lord Burnwood." He shrugged. Nash saw that his hands were clenched into fists. "I kissed her once. Well, twice. I admit to that. Nothing more happened." He glanced over at Annie. Besides anger at the accusation, Nash also saw something else: concern for Annie. Joe liked the girl. Nash wouldn't go as far as to call it love, but there was definitely affection there. He turned to Annie.

"Annie Deering, who is the father of your child?"

Annie blushed and pressed her lips together.

Tears streamed down her cheeks, but she didn't say a word. Although Nash had just said that he would ask only once and never again, the sight of the young woman softened his heart. "I assume you accused Joe because you do not want to name the true father, correct?"

A barely noticeable nod was the response.

"My lord, I—" Joe burst out, but Nash silenced him with a look. Annie's hands clenched her apron. She sniffled quietly but didn't dare to blow her nose in Nash's presence.

"He is a married man?" He tried to speak gently.

Again, there was a nod, this time not as hesitant. Joe breathed a sigh of relief. Nash didn't believe the real culprit was among his staff, but he would deal with the man later. For now, the priority was to minimise the damage for Annie.

"You know that your accusation could have put Joe in great trouble?" A sob escaped Annie's chest. Joe moved closer to her, as if he wanted to reach out for her hand, but apparently, he changed his mind.

"Annie, look at me!" Obediently, the girl lifted her head, but she could only meet Nash's gaze for a brief moment. Her eyelids were red and swollen. "We can find a solution, but it mainly depends on what Joe says."

"I, my lord? Why... I mean..." The stable lad stopped in confusion.

"Joe, would you be willing to marry Annie and accept the child as your own if I provide a generous dowry for Annie? Assuming it's what Annie wants."

Joe swallowed hard.

"Annie, if you do not want to marry Joe," which Nash didn't believe because she had named the stable lad as the father, indicating a desire to do so, "there is another option. I would arrange for you to have your child far from London and your parents, and then put it up for adoption. After that, you could resume your position at Arden House." Annie finally looked at him. "The condition is that there are no more mistakes of this kind. I will not be able to help you next time." Nash had no concerns that his care for his staff would be interpreted as weakness, but he had to draw a line somewhere. "Think it over. Talk to each other and let Ferguson know your decision. Neither of you is obligated to accept my proposal. Joe," he turned to the stable lad, whom he had somewhat overwhelmed, as he had to admit. "If you choose not to marry Annie, you will not face any negative consequences at Arden House." When he noticed Joe's bewildered expression, he added, "No punishment, I mean."

As soon as the two had disappeared after a brief farewell – Joe with a furrowed brow, Annie still mostly speechless except for a stammered "Thank you, m'lord" – there was a knock at the door.

It could only be Aunt Matilda, as servants didn't knock. Right on cue, her ice-grey head peeked through the door, and she looked at him curiously. "Is everything all right? The lad looks like he has been struck by lightning, and the girl…" She sighed and cautiously entered his study.

"Annie is in trouble, and I hope Joe will help her." With a gesture, he indicated that the topic was closed for him. Once the two had made their decision, he could inform Aunt Matilda. She opened her mouth to inquire further, but after a searching look at his face, she decided against it.

"What is happening in this house? Since you commissioned the portrait for Lady Annis, you have hardly been home." She shook her head and moved closer. "When you are here, you behave strangely. Yesterday, for example. First, you stormed off on that diabolical horse as if the devil were chasing you. Then you returned visibly agitated."

The ride hadn't alleviated the feeling of helplessness that had held him firmly in its grip yesterday. He hated not being able to make his own decisions and felt like a marionette, manipulated by Prinny, Aunt Matilda, and Lord Stewart, with the man probably being the least responsible. "And today I hear that you have summoned a silk merchant with a selection of his wares before disappearing again for several hours."

"The word 'privacy' doesn't seem to exist in Arden House," he grumbled, unsurprised.

"Do not change the subject," Aunt Matilda said. "I know you. Remember, I am the one who raised you."

Yes, and for that, Nash was grateful. So grateful that he didn't kick her out as befitted a nosy gossip, but instead resolved to count silently to one hundred while recalling her good qualities: caring, loyalty, unconditional love. She was humorous, albeit in a quirky way. Generosity. Magnanimity. Nash got to twenty, not because Aunt Matilda's good qualities were running out, but because she broke the silence.

"I know I can be a bit overprotective sometimes," she admitted, bringing out her handkerchief. Who did she intend to fool with it?

Nash teetered between laughter and the urge to jump up and howl at the moon like a wolf, just to put an end to the notion.

In the end, he chose neither. "I know you only mean well," he said calmly, rang for the butler, and ordered tea for Aunt Matilda and, despite her loud protests, whisky for himself.

When the requested items were before them, Nash smiled at his aunt and took a sip. "But I am a grown man, no longer a child. My happiness is not your responsibility but mine."

Her gaze sharpened. "You have not fallen in love, have you?" she asked, taking a sip of her tea and leaning closer to him.

Nash held her gaze, although it wasn't easy. "My feelings are not up for discussion," he replied. Denying his love for Frederica was out of the question. He had to be careful not to let Aunt Matilda discover the identity of the woman who had captivated him.

She ignored his response. "Who is it? Do I know her?"

"No," Nash said, rising from his seat. "You should go to bed. It's already late."

"Do not treat me like a simpleton or a child," exclaimed Aunt Matilda. Nash tilted his head and allowed the ironic smile to spread across his face. Aunt Matilda blushed.

"Oh, my dear... Nash. I only want what is best for you. What will Prinny say if you do not marry Lady Stewart? And the scandal! The lovely little lady does not deserve that," she lamented, attempting to appeal to his chivalry. With moderate success, Nash noted.

"Don't worry about Lady Annis Stewart," he replied. "I will handle it.

Her reputation will not suffer, I promise you. And as for the Prince Regent... he can find someone else to wed, as far as I'm concerned."

"But..."

"That's enough," Nash gently but firmly interrupted his aunt. "I have made my decision."

"Against Lady Annis."

"*For* another woman," he chuckled to himself. "You'll like her." Probably. Once she had overcome the shock of him planning to marry the Italian daughter of a clergyman. "She's intelligent, beautiful, and educated." *And she can paint. She even managed to wrestle a painting from the devil.*

"So she is a commoner," Aunt Matilda astutely observed, glancing at his whisky glass. Without commenting on her previously vehement abstinence, he poured her a finger's width and pushed the glass towards her.

Now Aunt Matilda smiled. No, she grinned and downed the whisky in two hearty sips. All that was missing was for her to lick her lips contentedly and let out a satisfied "Aaaah."

"But this will remain our secret," she requested, placing the glass on the table with a sigh and leaning back. Her gaze then fell on the handkerchief. She sighed again.

Nash, feeling back on solid ground, took a seat. "I will not breathe a word to anyone," he promised.

"Allow me one final remark," she said, giving him a worried smile. Nash nodded, surprised that Aunt Matilda even bothered to ask for permission. She was more the type to offer unsolicited advice. Well-intentioned advice, no doubt, but "well-intentioned" didn't necessarily equate to "suitable" or "desired."

"Marrying a commoner should be carefully considered." Her voice sounded calm, but her eyes revealed her concern. "You are not only publicly snubbing the Prince Regent if you break off the engagement with Lady Annis in favour of a low-born woman. You will lose many of your friends, and when you appear in public with your chosen one, the majority of our peers will shun you and your wife."

"I'm aware of that," Nash said, meeting her gaze. Aunt Matilda got up and circled the desk. Then she leant over him and planted a kiss on his forehead.

"Goodnight, my dear."

"Goodnight, Aunt."

The door closed with a soft click behind her.

He expected to feel relief now he was finally alone, but all he felt was guilt and worry. Aunt Matilda was right: his marriage to Frederica would cost him much of his social standing. He could live with it, but what about Aunt Matilda and, most importantly, Frederica? The upper ten thousand would look down on her, and her dream of a career as a painter would be shattered. She had said she cared nothing for fame, and Nash believed her. But would she be able to cope with the contempt she would inevitably face as a presumed adventuress and social climber? With a muttered curse, he pushed the whisky decanter aside and rang for the valet. For a change, he would go to bed early tonight. He had a few challenging days ahead, and he would do well to approach the battle for the beautiful painter as rested as possible. He had a feeling he would need all his wit and strength.

32

FREDERICA

For six days, Frederica had lived solely for Lord Burnwood's portrait. When she rose on the seventh day, the morning inspection of the painting had already become a routine, and she only realised what she was doing when she found herself in the studio. Once there, she might as well check if the painting was dry enough for transportation, as Ackerman's quick-drying promises suggested.

She ran her finger over various parts of the portrait. The background and the body, completed the day before yesterday, were in good shape so far, although she couldn't directly check the lower layers of paint. The recently finished eyes also seemed dry. Frederica had a feeling that caution was necessary, but the painting was transportable. "Perhaps I'll keep you with me for another day or two," she said to the painting, blushing, even though no one else was in the house to hear her. Millie had the day off, and Tidbit was either entertaining the neighbourhood cats in Lambeth or engaging in a skirmish with his rivals. She was alone, and an endlessly long day lay ahead of her.

With all the determination she could muster, she tore herself away from Lord Burnwood's likeness and shuffled into the kitchen. She curled her toes when her feet touched the cold tiles and took a detour back to the bedroom for her slippers. Finally, she put the kettle on, added leaves to the teapot, and waited, while her thoughts kept returning to yesterday evening's almost-kiss.

Was there a future for her and Lord Burnwood?

Her heart said yes, but her mind had a myriad of objections. There was the difference in their social status. They lived in modern times, but nobles who married commoners were still in the minority. By societal standards, she was no longer young, even though in the past few days, she had started to feel as lively as she did ten years ago. Moreover, she didn't possess the radiant beauty of those women who had managed to marry above their station, like that famous actress who was now Lady Albright and, according to the newspapers, had a blissful marriage.

She poured herself some tea, cradling the cup with both hands and blowing on the steaming liquid. Yes, she was getting ahead of herself, Frederica knew, but she couldn't help it. Not a single word had been spoken between them that sealed any kind of agreement, and yet it felt that way.

Suppose she became his lover. As his mistress, nothing would prevent her from continuing to paint. However, as Lady Burnwood, she'd be expected to limit her painting to a pastime. Hadn't she learnt her lesson? Her father had forbidden her mother from painting. She had even had to beg him for needle money, let alone money for paints. How many times in her childhood had she heard that "dabbling," as her father called it, was the last item on the expense list?

She took a sip and tasted the bitterness of the tea. Frederica had used too many tea leaves and let it steep for too long. Now it was undrinkable. Did she have any milk left in the house to dilute it? She couldn't muster the energy to check.

And Francis... He hadn't believed in her potential as a professional painter either, even though she had proven him wrong day after day. Even if she mentioned the famous artist Angelika Kauffmann, who had become one of only two women appointed as founding members of the Royal Academy by the King, Francis had stuck to his opinion: women lacked the physical and mental constitution to create works of art. According to Francis, if God had intended women to perform herculean tasks like painting a masterpiece, He would have endowed them with the necessary strength. Eventually, Frederica had given up arguing with him and withdrawn further into herself.

For once, her parents had agreed in their dislike of Francis, albeit for different reasons. The Reverend had feared she would end up in the gutter and sell her body to feed Francis. Mama had considered Francis a profligate and warned her that he would exploit her talent. In the end, her mother's prediction had come true. Frederica had been allowed to paint as long as it benefited Francis.

Perhaps she should stop dwelling and let the future unfold. Thanks to Lord Burnwood's generosity, Frederica's most pressing financial worries were in the past. Perhaps she could even convince Mr. Kingston to undo the sale of the house.

But did she want that?

Frederica felt like a leaf being blown here and there by the wind. She pushed the now-cold tea away and thought of her mother. When had she last written to Mama? The worse Frederica felt, the more she had distanced herself from all the people who meant something to her. Perhaps it was time to gradually change her life. A letter to Mama and Papa would be a good start.

The Reverend hadn't spoken a word to her or answered her letters since she had run away with Francis, but perhaps time had made him more inclined to forgive her. Ink and paper were ready on the table in the studio. What was she waiting for?

Frederica jumped up and then hesitated. She had forgotten to get dressed amid all her contemplation. It would be embarrassing if Lord Burnwood's servants came to collect the painting, and she opened the door to them in her nightgown. Perhaps he would come himself... *Enough of this!*, she ordered herself. Hadn't she just decided to take small steps? She was behaving like an immature debutante. It was no wonder, as she felt like one.

With what she hoped was a self-ironic smile, she returned to her studio. She winked at the Devil of St. James, who even as a painting dominated the room. *No one can resist his dark charm*, she thought, rushing past the easel to the double-winged terrace door. She swung the doors wide open and turned her face to the sun. The mild early-summer air went to her head like old wine. It wouldn't be long before the balsam flowers bloomed and filled the night with their sweet scent of almonds. With its delicate white blossoms, it was one of Frederica's favourite plants in her night garden, perhaps also because it was one of the first things she had planted here.

Back then, she had believed she would grow old with Francis in this place.

With a sigh, she turned around. She left the doors open, not wanting to shut out the sun and air. As she turned, her gaze fell on the boxes from Mr. Ackerman's store. The box of watercolours remained untouched. Frederica didn't enjoy working with watercolours, but her mother would love the painting kit.

No, this one was a gift from Lord Burnwood, and it wouldn't be right to give it away. But what she could do to bring joy to her mother was something else. First thing tomorrow, she'd buy one of the kits from Ackerman's and send it to Mama, along with the long-overdue letter to her parents. She rubbed her eyes to suppress the rising tears and approached the table. Then she began to write.

33

NASH

He would never admit it in front of another person, but Nash could be honest with himself: he missed Frederica. She was absent from his life, even though less than a day had passed since he had stepped out of her front door. The urge to get into the carriage and, under the pretext of personally picking up the painting, check on her was unbearable. However, since Nash didn't know how much longer Frederica had to work on the painting, he decided to restrain his impatience until the afternoon. Around four o'clock, he couldn't bear it any longer and was about to give the order to harness the horses when Ferguson announced Lord Wingfield's visit. Wingfield was a close associate of Lord Liverpool, the current British Prime Minister, and Nash remembered that the man had requested a confidential meeting with him a fortnight ago. Driven by curiosity, Nash had assured him that Wingfield could visit him at any time; he would be at home. How fortunate it was that he hadn't made a firm promise to personally collect the painting. As he feared, something – or rather, someone – had come between them. Nash resisted the urge to pull his hair out. He liked Wingfield, but the man had a tendency to be long-winded. It was now a few minutes past four, and Nash knew their conversation would last two hours or longer, depending on the reason Lord Wingfield had come to Arden House. An evening visit was out of the question if he didn't want to harm Frederica's reputation. All in all, it was better for Nash to send a servant for the painting and visit her tomorrow. Or even better, to avoid any falsehood or evasive behaviour on his part, he would first bring the matter with the Scottish bride to a satisfying conclusion for all parties involved, and then explain himself to Frederica. Yes, that was the honourable solution. One that required a great deal of self-control, but the right one nonetheless.

He was an idiot. A conscientious idiot whose moral compass prevented him from approaching her before the knot was untied because it felt wrong. His plans to break off the engagement with Lady Annis Stewart were on hold until the Scottish bride arrived in London. He couldn't speak to the Prince Regent to clarify the situation since the heir to the throne had left for Bath yesterday. Officially, to undergo a water cure. Unofficially, to fully enjoy the company of one of his numerous mistresses.

Conscience is a cold bedfellow, Nash thought as he descended the stairs to face the conversation with Lord Wingfield. As it turned out, Wingfield wanted Nash's support against the demands of "dubious blue stockings" who – shockingly – were organising a protest march in front of Parliament. Nash was puzzled by what this had to do with him, as the only blue stockings he knew of were educated women of the middle and upper classes with whom he had no contact whatsoever. He didn't even know exactly what these otherworldly dreamers were protesting for or against. Even when Wingfield confided that the women were demanding an easier divorce procedure and, heaven forbid, the right to vote, he didn't understand why the man had come to him. Presumably, Lady Astor-Blackwell and her circle of militant women were behind it, always demanding more rights for women and even aiming for economic independence from their husbands, but they had been doing that for years.

Half an hour had passed by now, and Nash was gradually losing patience. Just six months ago, perhaps even just a month ago, he would have readily pledged his political support to the visitor. Today, he hesitated and boldly asked Wingfield whether it wouldn't be better to sit down with the women at the round table and listen to their demands first. After all, Nash argued, women made up half the population, and many of them worked just as hard as men in their own way.

Nash's suggestion left the man speechless, and when he had recovered from his initial shock, he gave Nash a taste of what Aunt Matilda had warned him about: the contempt of one man for another who seemingly had lost his mind, along with his class consciousness. Wingfield rose and cast a look at Nash that fluctuated between contempt and pity. "Allow me to offer you some friendly advice, Arden. Lady Hastings is rumoured to be actively involved with the troublemakers, especially in the planned demonstration. If you do not want to see your relative in jail soon, you should sit down with *her* at the round table and make it clear to her that she is damaging the family's reputation."

Nash was too busy extracting the information from Wingfield's convoluted sentence, and when he had succeeded, the man had already left the room. So, Aunt Matilda was collaborating with the activists? Granted, the idea of her shouting slogans and demonstrating in front of Parliament was strange, but wasn't it her right? If he tried to talk sense into her or tried to forbid her participation in Lady Astor-Blackwell's circle, he would be as hypocritical as most of his peers. Perhaps he should accompany her to ensure she didn't come to harm, even though the idea of marching amidst the enraged women didn't sit well with him.

Nash downed his glass of whisky in one go. He chuckled because good old Ferguson had served him and his guest the second-best malt, as if the butler had anticipated that offering the top-notch whisky wasn't worth it.

Even Aunt Matilda was out of the house. Well, now he knew why he had seen her so rarely lately. When she wasn't discussing matters with Lady Astor-Blackwell, she was issuing invitations for her soiree. His chuckle deepened as he imagined his Frederica and Aunt Matilda in one of the upcoming gatherings. It would do his beautiful painter good to be protected by Aunt Matilda, no doubt. Frederica was an outstanding artist, but she was so unsure of herself and her talent. That, he would change, together with his aunt.

A noise from outside drew his attention back to the present. His carriage had arrived at the house. He walked down the steps measuredly to oversee the transport of the painting.

As the devil would have it, at that very moment, the old-fashioned two-horse carriage in which Aunt Matilda had been riding appeared. Barely had Ferguson taken off her coat and hat when she rushed to him. "Have you heard? Rumour has it 'the Priest' is back in town! Oh, I wish I knew who was behind that mask. Such as dashing fellow. If only I were twenty years younger…" Her eyes took on an expression that could only be described as "transfigured."

Nash, who knew exactly who the mysterious man was, nicknamed "the Priest" because of his all-black attire, suppressed a smile. The Priest had become a legend for boxing masked in the Whitechapel taverns and distributing his prize money to the needy. His one-year absence had not changed his status as one of the most sought-after men in London. Even Aunt Matilda hadn't forgotten him, as her infatuation clearly showed.

"Is that your portrait, by any chance?" The boxing unknown was forgotten as two men brought in the crate. With her unerring sense for the wrong question at the right time, depending on the perspective, Aunt Matilda targeted Nash. "I cannot wait to see it." She attached herself to the heels of his two servants, who cast him helpless glances, but Nash held onto his aunt's arm.

"Take the crate to the drawing room. You can lean the painting by the fireplace, but hold off on unpacking it. And you, Aunt, calm down." He turned to Ferguson, who had a watchful eye on the commotion in the entrance hall, ready to intervene and restore order if necessary. "Tea in the drawing room. And tools to open the crate."

A few minutes later, tea was served, the two servants had opened the crate under Nash's watchful eyes, and all traces of it had disappeared as if by magic. Now, as per Nash's instructions, the painting leant by the fireplace, wrapped in a blanket. He pushed aside the odds and ends on the mantel, bent down, and uncovered the painting while Aunt Matilda huffed impatiently behind him. Nash straightened up and placed the painting on the mantel.

The spoon clinked against her teacup as Aunt Matilda's stirring ceased.

Nash stepped aside, revealing the portrait of the Devil of St. James.

"Oh my... What... I..." Aunt Matilda put her cup down and stood. Her eyes were wide, and she struggled to close her half-opened mouth. She approached slowly and cautiously, as if approaching a wild beast. Which, in a way, was true. "This painting is..." She searched for words and delivered her verdict in a voice that was nothing more than a whisper: "Out of the ordinary."

"You could say that," Nash muttered, suppressing a grin. Aunt Matilda's gaze darted between him and the painting as she murmured to herself, "New impulses in art, of course, but oh my, this painting, it is truly... I have only been away for a few years... It has indeed changed a lot." Nash concealed his smile by turning his head to the side.

She exclaimed, "That is unmistakably you." She sounded surprised by her own words. "Although an eccentric interpretation of your essence." She stepped even closer to the painting. "This brushwork... it seems familiar to me." Nash held his breath as her eyes landed on the signature. "FF – Fitzroy painted this?!" She spun around to face him, not giving him a chance to answer. "I must say, he has made tremendous progress during his time away. Even though in a way, it is a bit unsettling. But perhaps I have been absent too long, just like Fitzroy." She frowned, and her words poured out so rapidly that Nash had no opportunity to respond. "Did you know there are rumours that he comes from one of Henry VIII's bastard lines? Oh, my dear boy, it is a sign from Heaven that you have chosen this artist of all people!"

Nash could only agree with that, although in a different way than Aunt Matilda assumed.

"I will host the soiree entirely for Fitzroy," she continued, marching toward the door. "I am the first to know of his return to society, and I will help him achieve new fame." Her skirts rustled as she turned to Nash and beamed at him. "I am so looking forward to deepening my acquaintance with him. It has been years since I met Fitzroy at Lady Wilmington's. Back then, he was just starting his career."

"Let's wait a bit longer," Nash interjected. It was important for him to settle his affairs first, as then he could introduce Frederica not only as the creator of the artwork but also as his future wife. "Perhaps a better opportunity will arise. I have very little time for diversions like your soiree at the moment."

"What opportunity could be better than now? Carpe diem, my dear boy, as the old Romans knew!"

His chest tightened as he read the silent plea in his aunt's eyes. A thousand words were on the tip of his tongue, and none of them made it past his lips. Heaven and hell, he loved her, but could Nash trust her? Precisely because she always wanted the best for him, her unfortunate tendency to meddle could cost him the woman he loved. His aunt's view of what constituted his happiness and his own were miles apart in this case, even though she meant well.

"Don't worry, Aunt." He gave her a kiss on the cheek. "A week from now, Lord Stewart and his daughter will be on their way back home, and I'll have more time to spend with you, I promise. I'll introduce you to my future wife, and you'll love her, I know it." Like all lovers, he was tempted to speak his beloved's name and tell Aunt Matilda about her, but he restrained himself. Nash let go of her hands, kissed her on the cheek once more, and walked into his study. He only hoped he had spoken the truth when he had confidently spoken of Lord Stewart and his daughter's departure. The best-laid plans had a notorious tendency to go disastrously wrong.

34

FREDERICA

It was late afternoon when Frederica finished the letter to her mother and folded it. At first, she had struggled to find the right words, but then the words had flowed almost uncontrollably. She had only allowed herself a pause to feed Tidbit, the victorious hero of the battle against the mouse plague, as he strolled in through the terrace door. He devoured the mackerel offered to him, followed Frederica into the studio, and spent some time grooming himself under the table before curling up. His soft snoring provided a soothing counterpoint to the restrained Sunday-morning sounds drifting in through the open doors. London in general, and Lambeth in particular, were always bustling, but on Sundays, everything was more subdued, except for the church bells, of course, calling the faithful to worship. Later, as the shadows grew longer and the taverns filled up, the usual drunken arguments or brawls would disrupt the Sunday mood, but for now, Frederica relished the rural-like peace in the midst of the city. Even the Thames fishermen observed the day by holding still.

The imperfect silence was the reason Frederica noticed the arrival of the carriage. *It's him*, she thought and jumped up. Tidbit complained about the disturbance and perked up his ears. Frederica rushed to the door, paused, brushed her hair away from her face, and cast a critical eye over her second-favourite dress. Everything was in order. The green fabric accentuated the red shimmer in her hair, and the white trim was white, not speckled with paint splatters. She had even put on the tiny pearl earrings she had received from her parents for her sixteenth birthday and couldn't bring herself to sell. Not that she would have gotten much for them – the delicate jewellery was modest, and the pawnbroker would probably have given her something out of pity rather than seeing it as a great deal. While running, Frederica fixed her hair once more. At the last moment, she slowed her pace, opened the front door, and recoiled. Before her stood a liveried servant, hand raised to knock. Frederica peered past him and saw Lord Burnwood's carriage in front of her door, as she had almost every day of the past week. But why was he sending a servant instead of coming himself? Her heart sank. Even though he had expressly mentioned that he might be busy, Frederica had firmly expected Lord Burnwood to pick up the painting in person.

"Mrs. Fitzroy? Lord Burnwood has sent us to collect the painting."

Frederica nodded and suppressed the rising tears. She stepped aside and gestured into the hallway. "Please come in. The painting is in the studio. I'll lead the way." The liveried servant signalled to another one who was perched on the carriage's coachbox and followed her. Less than two minutes later, the two men carried the painting, packaged in a crate, outside. Frederica watched them gently place it on the carriage seat, and she quickly closed the door before bursting into tears. Selling a painting had never been easy for her, but today it seemed many times harder than usual. In *The Devil of St. James*, she had painted as much of her own soul as Lord Burnwood's, and now she didn't even know where it would hang. Would it get enough light for the play of flames in the background to shine properly? Or would it be exposed to too much sunlight and fade over time?

To calm herself, Frederica marched into the kitchen and put on a kettle for tea. The familiar actions had an almost magical effect, combined with the robust scent of the tea leaves, and when she poured her first cup, she felt better. The hot tea revived and warmed her. Her life had taken a turn for the better, and she was determined not to give in to the deep-rooted pessimism within her. If she wanted, she could start sketching for her next painting today. Frederica had an abundance of everything she needed, thanks to Lord Burnwood: paper, pencils, paints. She could just as easily take a break and go for a walk or sit in the garden to read or dream.

That was an excellent idea, but surprisingly, it turned out to be challenging to implement. Sitting still was a challenge after two years of rarely finding peace. Frederica caught herself reading the second page of Byron's *Childe Harold's Pilgrimage* for the fourth time and set the book aside. The intricate verses didn't have their usual effect on her today. Tidbit, who had followed her into the garden and curled up on her lap, didn't appreciate it when she brushed his ears while turning the pages, and he gave her a reproachful look before moving away. Without Tidbit, Frederica felt even more like a layabout, and without the purring cat on her lap, she lacked a reason to sit still. "I'll tidy up the studio," she decided and got up. Lord Byron wouldn't run away, and doing something felt more meaningful than forcing herself to rest.

An hour later, Frederica examined her work. She had washed the brushes again and sorted the paints. She liked the order and cleanliness in her workspace. All the tools seemed to be waiting for her to start a new painting.

The loud knocking on the front door startled her. Frederica wasn't expecting anyone, and the thought of Lord Burnwood, who might have found time for a quick visit after all, crossed her mind. While she reminded herself to stay calm and brace for another disappointment, her heart raced nonetheless.

For the second time that day, Frederica faced a servant in the dark blue livery of the Burnwoods. Was something wrong with the painting? Had it been damaged during transport, or had His Lordship changed his mind and no longer wanted it? In that case, Frederica reassured herself, he wouldn't have returned it but would have simply disposed of it or consigned it to oblivion in a dark chamber.

"Lady Hastings inquires if..." The man didn't get to finish his sentence, as a female voice from inside the carriage called him back.

"That is all right, Thomas. I see someone is at home." With the expressionless demeanour of a well-trained servant, the young man turned around and hurried to the waiting carriage.

Who was Lady Hastings, and what was she doing in Lord Burnwood's carriage? Had he possibly revealed their shared secret? She wasn't ready to go public and face the competition! Panic flooded her mind. In her mind's eye, a future unfolded where she would be ridiculed by male painters and forced to leave the city in shame. She heard a voice suspiciously resembling Francis's bright tenor, asking her how she, as a woman, could ever have believed she was better than a man.

The sound of the carriage door slamming brought her back to reality. Where was Lord Burnwood? She looked past the imposing female figure into the carriage but saw only an empty space. Meanwhile, the lady hurried toward Frederica, leaving the servant behind. Grey curls peeked out from under the precious bonnet, which exactly matched the shade of her coat. A lace-trimmed shawl added a splash of scarlet to the iron-grey ensemble. The luxurious clothing spoke of more than just wealth, but it also unmistakably revealed that the wearer paid no heed to fashionable conventions – no one in the lady's advanced age wore red. "Eccentric" was the word that described her most accurately, but who cared about that? Frederica certainly didn't. She would wear brightly coloured clothing too when she reached the lady's age – and her confidence.

"Good day," the woman said with a melodious voice that resonated with generations of wealth. "I am looking for the artist Mr. Fitzroy, who painted the portrait of my nephew."

Frederica knew she should say something, but her throat felt tight. "My husband is not at home" would have sufficed, or perhaps "The artist is not at home." The latter came close to the truth because Frederica was standing on the sidewalk, not inside the house. But besides the fact that no words came out of her mouth, it was sophistry. Furthermore, it was too late for evasion. The lady gave her a not unkindly once-over from head to toe.

Following the lady's gaze down to her black shoes, Frederica immediately understood the reason for the lady's lingering eyes on her plain footwear: red and blue paint splatters marred the leather. When she lifted her head and looked into the lady's face, she read a sequence of various impressions in her open countenance: it began with barely concealed curiosity, followed by surprise, and ended in comprehension.

"It is *you*," the lady said.

The world seemed to stand still as Frederica tried to decipher the meaning of the statement. Her thoughts were still revolving around Lord Burnwood and the connection he had with her visitor when Mrs. Wheedon, Frederica's neighbour, approached with her children in tow and greeted them warmly. Mary Ann, the eldest of the bunch, cast a shy glance at the lady's expensive coat, while Georgie, the only boy, made moves to approach the horses.

"Please come inside, my lady," Frederica said to her visitor, to buy some time. She smiled at Mrs. Wheedon, who had just unlocked the front door, and curiosity was written all over her face. From the corner of her eye, Frederica noticed that the servant, whom Lady Hastings had called "Thomas" earlier, was giving Georgie a friendly smile and gesturing for him to come closer.

After Frederica had closed her door and taken the lady's coat, she hesitated. Politeness dictated inviting her into the sitting room and offering her a cup of tea, but her peculiar remark – *It is you!* – made Frederica pause. It could only mean one thing: her visitor knew that Frederica was the creator of the portrait. Should she outright deny it? Could she even do that? No, with the tell-tale paint splatters on her shoes, it was not only impolite but also futile to fabricate a lie. The attentive expression and sharpness reflected in the older woman's eyes would make any lie a futile endeavour.

Finally, Frederica's good manners won out, and she asked Lady Hastings to follow her. "Please, have a seat," she said, indicating the most comfortable chair. Lord Burnwood had sat there during his first visit. "May I offer you a cup of tea?"

"No, thank you," the lady declined after looking around searchingly. She was probably wondering where Frederica's maid was. "I would not mind a glass of lemonade."

Frederica took a seat opposite her. "I'm sorry," she said, wondering in a surge of defiance what she was apologising for, "I don't have lemonade in the house." *Of course I don't,* she added in her mind. Lemons from Italy and sugar were expensive. Did Lady Hastings really expect royal hospitality in a small Lambeth house? Her gaze must have revealed more than Frederica intended because a strange expression of embarrassed horror flickered across the older woman's face. Her eyes were similar in shape and colour to Lord Burnwood's, although not in expression. Frederica couldn't imagine him ever being horrified by something he had said or done.

They could sit here and stare each other down forever, or Frederica could try to figure out why Lady Hastings had come to her. "You are related to Lord Burnwood?" Frederica attempted to steer the faltering, almost non-existent conversation into sensible territory. At that moment, Tidbit chose to stroll into the sitting room. Knowing how hostile the Tiger of Lambeth could be towards intruders in his territory, Frederica jumped to her feet to pick him up and carry him out, but the cat eluded her with a graceful movement and trotted straight up to Lady Hastings. Frederica's warning "Tidbit, no!" caught in her throat as Lady Hastings bent down with an exclamation of delight.

"Well, my beauty, who are you?" she cooed and reached down to pet him between the ears. To Frederica's surprise – and relief – the cat extended his head toward her hand and began to rub against it. Was that a purr emanating from his throat?

Some of Frederica's tension dissipated in pleasure. If Tidbit liked the visitor, and she, in turn, loved cats – the sounds coming from Lady Hastings' mouth left no doubt about her delight – then she couldn't be harbouring ill feelings toward Frederica.

"Forgive me," Lady Hastings said after a while, straightening as Tidbit curled up at her feet. She appeared embarrassed. That was another thing that set her apart from her relative. When Lord Burnwood apologised, it sounded as if he were celebrating a victory. Another reason for Frederica's growing sympathy was the fact that Lady Hastings didn't bother picking Tidbit's red cat hairs off her clothing. "Let us start over. I am Lady Hastings. Lord Burnwood is my nephew." She raised her chin challengingly. "And you are the woman who painted that extraordinary portrait."

35

NASH

English brandy, French cognac, or Scottish whisky? Nash thought it was less a matter of patriotism and more a matter of taste. Black's offered only the best of everything, whether it was food, drinks, or company. Some club members were less than pleased that the club had opened its doors to non-noble men after the war, but Nash had no problem with it. He had fought side by side with them in battles and recognised that courage and honour were not privileges of the nobility. It was about the heart, not the lineage.

He opted for the cognac and strolled with the snifter in hand into the club's library. This room, more than any other, demonstrated that Black's was a strictly male domain. The shelves were filled with works on warfare and science, all subjects that were not in the domain of the fairer sex. His thoughts involuntarily drifted to Frederica. Perhaps Nash needed to reconsider his views on not only the fairer but supposedly weaker sex. She excelled in a field where men traditionally dominated. As Nash saw it, her late husband had exploited her talent, passing it off as his own and constantly suppressing his wife, like a plant given only a certain amount of light and water. The plant didn't die, but it also didn't grow to its predetermined height, much like his beautiful painter. So why else would Frederica be so afraid to face the public? As his wife, she would have nothing and no one to fear. Would their marriage be the fresh start she longed for, or was her sole ambition to succeed as a painter?

He recalled Aunt Matilda's suggestion of the soiree. Perhaps Frederica would prefer to say "I do" only after achieving her goal.

The thought of Frederica's pursuit of independence made him smile. It was an endearing trait, one he had often observed in other women, though not to this extent. Nash admired his beautiful painter for her ability to blend determination and femininity. Most women striving for independence did so with a masculine obsession and went overboard.

Or was it just his perception that those ladies were overdoing it? If he was honest with himself, before meeting Frederica, it had never crossed his mind that a woman should pursue work for reasons other than financial ones, especially not a lady. Well, Frederica was a commoner, but she had received the education of a lady and possessed the corresponding manners. The passion with which she spoke about painting showed Nash that some women wanted much more than a wealthy husband and a house full of children.

The warmth of the cognac spread in his stomach. It was a moment of heavenly tranquillity, and Nash savoured it. Unfortunately, this didn't last long, as another club member had decided to seek the library's silence. It was Lord Aldekirk, Nash recognised. He cleared his throat to announce his presence.

"Is that you, Arden?" Aldekirk approached. "In this half-light, one can hardly see a hand in front of one's face." He avoided a stool. "I hope I'm not disturbing you?"

Nash laughed. "Not in the least. Join me. You look like you could use a cognac as well." Nash made a move to ring for the servant, but Aldekirk waved it off.

"Thank you, my old friend, but I've had enough wine with dinner, and I need to keep a clear head tonight. My brother-in-law and his wife are returning from Scotland."

In the dim candlelight, Aldekirk probably couldn't see Nash raise an eyebrow. "Cavanaugh hasn't turned into a teetotaller, has he? I cannot imagine that." Even a well-meaning friend wouldn't call the Marquess of Cavanaugh Brother Temperance, but he had never been averse to indulgence. Nash suspected he was a secret admirer, especially when it came to the fairer sex.

"No, no, it's not that. Cavanaugh and I just don't get along. He still hasn't forgiven me for marrying his sister late, and he lets me know it. He's practically looking for a wrong word to come out of my mouth and enjoys dishing it out. If you're wondering why I put up with it—"

Nash raised his hand defensively. "It's none of my business, old chap."

Aldekirk leant forward and grinned. "Wait until you're married," he said in a mock-doleful tone, "then you'll understand why taking it is one of the qualities you naturally develop as a husband, especially when you love your wife to bits, and there's a little child in the house just starting to walk and pulling down anything that isn't nailed to the wall."

Nash couldn't help it; he threw his head back and laughed. Then he rang for the servant and asked him to bring a bottle of cognac and another glass. "As I see it, Aldekirk, you could certainly use a cognac. If you want, I'll accompany you home and shield you from your wife."

Aldekirk joined in Nash's laughter. "You've always been a big mouth, Arden. But Helen fears nothing and no one, not even the devil incarnate."

So, he had heard of Nash's nickname. Nash raised the snifter. "To the women! If we don't frighten them, we'll have to seduce them."

"To the women!" Aldekirk agreed. They emptied their glasses. Nash refilled, personally, as he didn't want to call the servant back. "I hear you're also about to tie the knot. Is that true, or is it just a rumour?"

Nash leant back, staring at the ceiling with wide-open eyes. "Where did you hear that?"

"I read it, in the *Sunday Times*, if I recall correctly. Along with a very telling caricature of you, I might add." Nash saw the flash of white teeth as Aldekirk grinned. Gloating, unmistakably. "Rumour has it you're set to marry Lord Stewart's wild child."

"The Prince Regent proposed this match," Nash said calmly. He didn't deny it but didn't confirm it either. "What do you mean by 'wild child'?"

Aldekirk leant back, took another sip of cognac, and did everything to stoke Nash's curiosity – or unease. Finally, he deigned to give an answer. "I've met her a few times up in Scotland. Lady Annis is a good friend of my sister-in-law Felicity and often visits her."

"And?" Impatiently, Nash drummed his fingers on the armrest. As long as the connection between him and the Scottish bride wasn't severed, he couldn't reveal to Aldekirk what he was truly seeking: an answer to whether the girl's heart belonged to someone else. That would greatly facilitate Nash's plans.

"She's a remarkable young lady in every way," Aldekirk finally said. "Beautiful, if you ask me, and clever for her age. She has a soprano voice that could grace the stage, and she plays the harp like an angel."

Nash snorted. She was pretty, that was true. The painter of her portrait hadn't exaggerated. "So, Lady Annis is the embodiment of perfection."

"I agree."

"But?" Nash felt an urgent need to put his hands around Aldekirk's neck and shake the truth about the wild child out of him. Strangling would be counterproductive, after all, how could the man speak if Nash cut off his air supply? A few encouraging kisses from his dagger would serve the purpose better.

"But only as long as her father is in sight. As soon as he's gone, she shows her true colours. Oh, don't get me wrong, she's still smart and beautiful and highly musical. But all that garnished with a dash of stubbornness that packs a punch."

Wonderful. The prospects were improving by the minute.

"Felicity says it's because her mother died too early, and her father never remarried. He oscillates between excessive spoiling and extreme strictness."

"Does she have serious admirers?" Let Aldekirk believe it was jealousy driving Nash to ask the question.

"That's why I didn't believe the rumours about you and Lady Annis getting married. She always talks about Lord Alfred Douglas during her visits, and in a way that seems rather obvious. I assumed there was an understanding between her and Alfie, as she prefers to call him, and they were just waiting for the young Lord to come into his inheritance."

"Perhaps her father has something against the Douglas clan. Up there, they're all at odds with each other unless they're sliding on their knees in church."

"Believe me, if Lady Annis didn't want to marry you, her father could move Heaven and Hell, and in the end, she'd still choose the man she wants."

"She sounds like an interesting young woman," Nash said.

"More like a spoilt princess," Aldekirk retorted bluntly, only now realising what Nash had said. "Does that mean you don't even know her?"

"I've never met her, nor her father."

His friend shook his head in disbelief. "That's more than strange."

"Lady Annis may be a stubborn young lady, but in the end, she's just a girl who must bow to her father's will."

"You poor fool," muttered Aldekirk. Now he was the one pouring them a generous portion of cognac. "I wish you good luck. You're going to need it."

36

FREDERICA

The woman who painted that extraordinary portrait. Frederica felt a wave of heat followed by coldness wash over her as she heard the words. Countless conflicting thoughts swirled in her mind. "Yes, that's me," she confirmed. "I am Frederica Fitzroy." What had Lord Burnwood told his aunt? He must have spoken about her, or the woman wouldn't be here. What did she expect from her? "What can I do for you, Lady Hastings?"

The woman looked at her in surprise, as if the question had caught her off guard. Frederica couldn't fathom what had led Lady Hastings to her. Outrage over the unconventional portrait? Well, she had called it "extraordinary" and not "abominable" or "horrible." That was at least one point of agreement between them.

"My original intention was to personally invite the creator of the work to one of my upcoming soirees."

What was going on here? What kind of invitation? Nobility and commoners rarely attended the same social events. Their circles didn't intersect. Society was structured so simply, and yet it was so complicated. "That was before I realised you were not a man." If not for the smile accompanying the sentence, Lady Hastings' words would have sounded like an insult.

So Lord Burnwood hadn't told his aunt that a female artist had painted him, and probably not that there was a closer connection between them than that of a patron and a painter. Frederica returned the smile and found something in the older woman's face – a certain understanding among women – that encouraged her to give an unconventional response. "I formally apologise for being a woman."

Lady Hastings' smile spread across her entire face. The many wrinkles at the corners of her eyes crinkled, and she let out a cackling, almost unrestrained laugh. "No need for that, my dear. Now that I know you are a woman, I will not settle for one of the next appointments. Please come not just sometime but next Friday to my soiree."

"I thank you for the kind invitation, but I'm afraid I am unable to attend." Frederica had never heard of Lady Hastings' salon. Then again, she hadn't been out since Francis's death and had cut off all contact with her late husband's colleagues. In the past, Frederica had accompanied her husband to many such social occasions. Among artists, securing a place as a protégé of an influential lord or lady was highly coveted, but she wasn't quite there yet. To soften her abrupt refusal, Frederica added, "I regret it deeply and appreciate your generosity, but I have nothing to show, and I consider the timing too early."

She had no intention of showing Lady Hastings the sketches by Lord Burnwood she had retrieved from the fireplace and ironed out.

Against her will, Frederica felt sympathy for the lady. She was sure it was not easy to be Lord Burnwood's aunt. "I can show you some paintings of my cat," she suggested.

"Do you have nothing to show except paintings of a cat?" Lady Hastings shook her head incredulously. "My nephew entrusted you with the creation of his portrait after throwing every other renowned artist out? I can hardly believe it!"

"Nor can I."

"You are not one to mince words. I can understand why Lord Burnwood values you. He has no love for sycophants."

"He must have inherited that from you." Frederica allowed herself a small smile.

"Do you not even possess a few unfinished paintings? Sketches? You surely still have the preliminary sketch of Lord Burnwood's portrait." It didn't seem like Lady Hastings would settle for a no. Frederica didn't know what had come over her – the Devil of St. James, probably – but she felt... confrontational.

The blue-grey eyes of her interlocutor sparkled mischievously. "So," Lady Hastings said, and it sounded like the loving but stern admonition of a teacher trying to save her student from making a mistake, "let me tell you something. Before the rise of that dreadful French dwarf, and probably a while before your time, I had a salon where the most famous painters and poets came and went. You are not the first artist to have your knees tremble at the thought of presenting yourself and your work."

Frederica could feel her cheeks getting hot. Lady Hastings had seen through her.

"Besides," her visitor continued, pretending not to notice Frederica's embarrassment, "I would by no means describe my nephew's portrait as 'nothing.'"

"I don't know if Lord Burnwood even wants to present the painting to the public," Frederica replied. "You... have seen it, haven't you?"

Lady Hastings seemed to understand what Frederica was getting at. She winked at Frederica. "Oh, I have seen it! It is breathtakingly daring and the most exciting work I have come across in years. Do me a favour and come on Friday. I cannot imagine that my nephew would object to presenting his portrait to the public." A hint of doubt crossed Lady Hastings' features. "By the way, are you by any chance related to Francis Fitzroy? I only met him briefly once before he gained prominence, but I am familiar with some of his works. His landscapes are solid, but his portraits are excellent. I love his portrait of Lady Hearst with her poodle. Actually, the brushwork on yours is quite similar."

Frederica had the impression that Lady Hastings was peering directly into her soul.

"Francis Fitzroy was my husband," she said softly, wishing she had insisted on tea. Her throat felt parched.

"My condolences for your loss," Lady Hastings replied. A furrow appeared between her silver-grey brows. "I didn't know he passed away. He was still so young! I regret that he didn't have the opportunity to perfect his style." An expression of sorrow crossed her features. "My words may seem hollow and empty to you, but I promise you, with time, it gets easier." Her fingers twitched as if she wanted to take Frederica's hand and offer comfort. "A person you do not forget lives on in us, my dear Mrs. Fitzroy, and your husband will also be remembered through his works."

Frederica bit her lower lip to hold back tears. If only Lady Hastings knew that the portraits she had praised, supposedly painted by Francis, were actually her own works. "Thank you, my lady," she finally managed to say. "For your sympathy and understanding. Francis…" She trailed off.

"Yes?"

"Francis would have greatly appreciated your praise," Frederica completed the sentence. She blinked to suppress her tears. In truth, Francis wouldn't have been the least bit pleased with Lady Hastings' praise, considering that the landscapes he had painted hadn't fared well. "He would have been delighted to meet you, though." That, at least, was true.

"May I ask… if it is not too delicate: how did your husband pass away?"

Oh, heaven! Could she confide in this stranger whom she had met less than an hour ago and for whom she felt a deep sympathy that transcended age and social status? Frederica looked at her and found in her face an unspoken understanding that only women could feel towards each other.

"It was late when Francis returned home from a gathering with his fellow artists."

He had come back staggering from the tavern. She had used his absence to paint in peace and had lost track of time. Normally, she would have gone to bed by the time he returned to avoid a confrontation. She had heard from his footsteps that he was no longer sober. At that moment,

Frederica had only wished for him to lie down on the sofa and fall asleep so she could slip out of the studio unnoticed.

"I was just finishing a portrait when he arrived." She swallowed. It had been a self-portrait, the one she had lost to the Thames. "Francis hadn't completed a painting for a long time, and he detested it when I painted. When he saw me at the easel, he became angry. He... called me an amateur and said I was a woman who merely imagined she could paint. He said I lacked the expressiveness that only male painters possessed, and I would never be successful."

Lady Hastings indicated an understanding nod but remained silent.

"He had been having severe mood swings for the past few months, and I knew that when he was in this state, I should not engage in an argument. I was tired and angry because he squandered all our money on these... pleasures. But he was my husband, and I had vowed to be there for him in good times and bad. So I turned around and intended to go to bed."

For the first time since Frederica had started speaking, there was a reaction from Lady Hastings. She retrieved a handkerchief from her reticule and dabbed a tear from the corner of her eye. "I understand," she whispered, even though she and Frederica were the only people in the salon. "My husband – may he rest in peace – was a drunkard and a womaniser in the eyes of the lord. I know what it means to love a man who tears your heart out of your chest."

"That's exactly how it was," Frederica whispered. "To look at him and know that I couldn't help him, that my love wasn't enough to save him, tore my heart apart. Normally, I would have avoided a quarrel and let him sleep off his drunkenness, but that evening he wouldn't let up." Frederica licked her dry lips. "He became malicious and made fun of me. When I tried to leave, he grabbed my wrist and tried to hold me back, but I managed to break free. Francis took a step back."

As if on cue, Tidbit perked up at Lady Hastings' feet, his ears twitching. Was he dreaming of the night Francis died?

"Tidbit was with me as always when I painted. When he heard us arguing, he woke up and came to us. He stood right behind my husband as Francis stumbled backward and tripped over the cat."

Lady Hastings put her hand to her mouth, her eyes widened.

Francis had bled from a head wound. When Frederica knelt beside him and searched for a pulse, she already knew his heart had stopped beating. No one with a spark of life in them stared so lifelessly at the ceiling.

"He fell and hit his head on the mantelpiece. He must have died instantly," Frederica whispered with a choked voice. She placed her hand on her chest, as if by touching it, she could force her heart to beat more slowly.

Frederica's cries had brought the neighbours out of their beds. From that moment on, she had felt as though she had died herself: cold and numb.

The day after the funeral, she had gone up to the attic and burned all the sketches, all the paintings by Francis that she still possessed. Even those he had started and she had finished. Frederica had kept the daring self-portrait, half as a remembrance of their early, loving years together, and half as a reminder never to forget the events of that night.

For a while, the two women were silent. Frederica wondered if she had made a mistake by confiding in this stranger, who was also Lord Burnwood's relative. Would her unspoken confession of having felt relief at Francis's death strain the relationship between Lady Hastings and Frederica? But then Lady Hastings took her hand and gave it a gentle squeeze. In that moment, Frederica knew she had done the right thing by telling the truth about the circumstances of Francis's death to her newfound confidante.

"What an unfortunate way to depart from life," Lady Hastings spoke up. "I understand why you did not make his death public."

It had been an undignified, embarrassing death that Francis had brought upon himself but didn't deserve. "I wanted to prevent him from being remembered as the man who stumbled drunkenly over a cat," Frederica agreed. "By maintaining silence, I hoped people would remember him as a painter."

"And because you felt guilty, as is in our female nature, you stopped painting yourself," Lady Hastings observed. Her compassionate words had the effect Frederica had desperately tried to avoid: tears welled up in her eyes. She lowered her head, but of course, her visitor noticed her grief nonetheless. "My dear Mrs. Fitzroy," she continued, patting Frederica's hand, "in the absence of a clean handkerchief, I offer you something else that will provide solace."

Frederica raised her head and smiled through her tears. "That's not necessary," she began, but Lady Hastings regarded her with a stern look that was only partly playful.

"Come to my soiree on Friday." She stood up. "Friday, from four o'clock in the afternoon. I want you to create a portrait for me, and I already have an idea of whom you will paint for me. Let me make it clear: I will not accept a refusal."

As if she could have resisted the determined lady! Frederica felt dizzy with joy. The offer had come so suddenly she could hardly put her feelings into words. "Who then?" Frederica followed Lady Hastings into the hallway and helped her into her coat.

"Lady Annis Stewart. Has Lord Burnwood not told you about her?"

"No, that name has never been mentioned. It sounds lovely. I think I would remember it."

"I would like to give Lady Annis Stewart the painting as a wedding gift."

Frederica held the door open for her guest. "That's a very nice idea for a wedding present," Frederica agreed. The lady must mean a lot to Lady Hastings if she wanted to give her such a personal gift. "When is the big day?" Frederica stepped aside so she wouldn't obstruct Lady Hastings in the narrow hallway. Her heart was pounding loudly and quickly, but this time from happiness. Thanks to the kindness and friendliness of her visitor, Frederica had a second commission!

"My nephew has not set a date yet, but I know he cannot wait to bring his young bride home." She approached the footman who held open the carriage door.

A freezing coldness settled over Frederica's heart as she finally understood: Lord Burnwood was about to marry another woman! The casual manner in which Lady Hastings had mentioned it struck her to the core.

Before getting into the carriage, the older lady turned around one last time and smiled at her, but her thoughts were clearly already elsewhere. "Come to my soiree on Friday, then you can meet the young lady, and we will discuss everything further."

Frederica managed to nod. She just barely locked the door to the world before she allowed her tears to flow freely.

37

NASH

It was Wednesday, and the time had come. Lord Stewart and his daughter had arrived in London the day before, Nash learnt from the message Lord Stewart had sent him. To his pleasant surprise, they were staying at Layton's townhouse during their visit to the capital. Nash and Layton had belonged to the same merry group in their younger days, along with Trevelyan, Roxleigh, St. John, and a few others. Aldekirk had joined them later. The war had turned carefree boys into responsible men, most of whom were now married. Once a year, at the start of the hunting season, they gathered at one of the estates and enjoyed themselves without their wives. Nash chuckled as he remembered the first of those gatherings. "What does your wife think of you leaving her alone?" he had asked St. John, one of his oldest friends.

St. John's response had been a lazy grin. "I suppose she keeps the servants busy and has them clean the house from the roof to the front steps." Nash didn't know what to say to that. Marriage was foreign to him, and a woman consoling herself with housework in her husband's absence either seemed dull or was an illusion St. John indulged in. It was only when St. John and the other married men in the group burst into roaring laughter that Nash understood St. John had been joking. "What do you think the mice do when the cat's away? Our wives will amuse themselves to the fullest, just like us. They'll go to the theatre, meet their friends, and empty all the shops on Bond Street."

Apparently, he was the one who had been under an illusion. Nash still remembered what he had thought at the time: if a marriage could be so relaxed and free of suspicion or jealousy, then perhaps marriage wasn't a catastrophe after all.

Nash was in the stables when Ferguson sent a servant to announce the arrival of the guests. He took the shortcut through the servants' staircase and hurried to his room, where he made himself presentable with the help of his valet.

As he stepped into the corridor and heard voices coming from the entrance hall, Nash knew he had timed it perfectly. Lady Annis and her father were in the house and were just removing their coats. Nash stepped onto the landing and prepared to go downstairs to greet his guests. He paused for a moment to compose himself because the encounter would not be easy.

"Is that one of Lord Burnwood's ancestors?" The deep voice with the rolled 'r' must belong to Lord Stewart. "For an Englishman, he carries his wound with dignity, I must say." He was probably referring to Frederica's portrait, which Nash had left in the entrance hall now that he no longer needed to scare her away with it. Nash hesitated when he heard the horror in Lord Stewart's voice. He was curious to know what Lady Annis would say about the Devil of St. James, and although it was ungentlemanly to eavesdrop, he did just that.

But before the young lady could say anything, Nash's aunt spoke up. She was not pleased, and the tone of her voice revealed it. "This is the current Lord Burnwood."

Nash thought he heard someone gasp, and he sincerely hoped it was the horrified and shocked Lady Annis. "Of course, he carries his wound with dignity," Aunt Matilda continued. "Lord Burnwood does not like to talk about it, but he earnt it when he saved thirteen soldiers entrusted to him from the hands of the French. His scar is a symbol of his bravery in the face of the enemy, with which my nephew defended all the British values we hold dear: honour, patriotism, and loyalty. So there is no reason for squeamishness."

It was time to intervene before his aunt disclosed more secrets that Nash preferred to keep to himself, or challenged the Scottish Lord to a duel.

With a calm step, he entered the entrance hall and greeted his guests. When Lady Annis tore her gaze away from the portrait and looked him in the face for the first time, she didn't startle, but her eyes widened, and her smile became so rigid that it couldn't be anything but fake.

Lord Stewart seemed as contrite as a scolded schoolboy, and Nash heard him trying to appease Aunt Matilda. He escorted the Stewarts and his aunt to the drawing room, where Ferguson served them tea, and the atmosphere relaxed.

An hour later, Nash knew what his friend Aldekirk had meant by his remark about Lady Annis. He was equally sure that Lady Annis Stewart was not the woman with whom he would find happiness, as his friends had with their wives. When she stood before him, on her father's arm and a seeming image of humility with her lowered gaze, he couldn't deny that she was truly pretty. Her dark red hair and milky-white skin, without a single freckle, did not conform to the prevailing beauty standards, just like Frederica's unique face. This, in a way, endeared Lady Annis to him. The promise of future beauty was hidden in her face, which belied humility with her impudent glances. But that was the problem: she was still half a child. Her figure didn't suit his taste either. Lady Annis didn't even reach his shoulder and was too slender to please him – like a foal that was still unproportioned and had yet to grow into itself.

He was certainly not the man who would help her grow up.

While they drank tea and ate pastries, Nash's unfavourable impression of Lord Stewart, which he had gained from the man's talkative letters, vanished. He was by no means the ambitious man Nash had suspected behind his pompous, insistent lines. It was clear he wanted a good match for his child, but wouldn't Nash want the same for his daughter if he had one? Overall, the afternoon was more relaxed than Nash had expected, probably because, despite Aunt Matilda's efforts, the topic of the wedding did not come up. Nash felt less like a prospective son-in-law being scrutinised by a stern father than like a man conversing with new acquaintances, and couldn't help feeling that these strangers could become friends.

The only regrettable thing was that there was no opportunity for him to speak with Lady Annis Stewart privately. Aunt Matilda had her in tow and was talking to her about the Crown Princess, the Prince Regent, and her soiree, which she would host the day after tomorrow. The day after tomorrow? What had he missed? In the presence of their guests, it was too late for objections.

Aunt Matilda described her high-ranking guests in such glowing terms that Nash wondered if she had been sipping sherry. He noticed Lady Annis's growing impatience, although she made a great effort to conceal it. He wasn't faring any better; he was now only half-listening to his aunt. Lady Annis's feet shuffled restlessly on the Persian carpet, and she kept glancing at her father, as if she could hardly wait for him to give the signal to leave. Lord Stewart made no move to get up from the sofa early, except to join Nash in the garden for a cigar. Nash took the opportunity to ask Lord Stewart for permission to take Lady Annis for a drive in Hyde Park, of course, accompanied by a maid or a trustworthy servant.

"You have my permission," Lord Stewart agreed, rather quickly in Nash's opinion. "Annis's old nanny has travelled with us. If you would be so kind as to send a servant to Layton's to inform Fiona, you can both set off right away." The Laytons lived less than five minutes from Arden House. Nash and Lady Annis could leave in a few minutes and return before nightfall.

"One more thing," Lord Stewart said, holding Nash back when he was about to return to the house. The look of cheerfulness in his grey-blue eyes gave way to a certain coolness. "Can I speak openly?" The Scotsman was of small stature, but his demeanour left no room for misunderstanding: this was a man who would not hesitate to stand up to Nash.

"By all means," Nash replied. "The more openly we speak to each other, the better." He suspected the freedom of speech Lord Stewart expected did not extend to Nash outright rejecting his daughter's hand, but it was a promising start.

"I know the Prince Regent did not arrange the marriage between my Annis and one of his relatives out of pure kindness," Lord Stewart said, rubbing his red-streaked beard. The laugh lines at the corners of his eyes disappeared, and his impeccable pronunciation faded into the background. "Even though in his letter, he claimed to be merely seeking a wife for a wounded war hero who is dear to him."

"The Prince Regent wants to strengthen his influence in your homeland," Nash agreed. "I am aware of that." He paused for a moment. "Why did you agree to the marriage if you see through his intentions? With all due respect, you don't strike me as a man who lets others use him as a political pawn."

"I can return the compliment exactly," Lord Stewart replied.

Nash waited. When nothing more came, he continued, "You're worried about your daughter, aren't you? That's why you agreed to a marriage with an Englishman in the first place."

Lord Stewart's sigh seemed to come from the depths of his heart. "Do not get me wrong, my Annis is a good child. The best daughter a father could wish for. But she grew up without a mother, and her nannies and governesses could not stand up to her stubbornness. It will do her good to be married to an older man."

Nash nearly choked on his own breath when he heard Lord Stewart talk about him as if he were an old man. But then it occurred to him that he thought almost the same about Annis – namely, that she was far too young for him.

"What does Lady Annis think about it?"

The Scottish Lord smiled grimly. "Stubbornness or not, this time she will do as I say."

If he wasn't mistaken.

38

FREDERICA

She had the pain under control. Absolutely. At least when she occupied herself with something that didn't remind her of Lord Burnwood.

In the first two days after Lady Hastings' visit, Frederica had no trouble working herself tired from morning to evening. Her first task on Monday morning was to go to Ackerman's Art Supplies to buy the watercolour set for her mother and send it along with her letters to Sussex. By chance, Frederica also found a gift at a bookstore by the beach that would please her father. The treatise on beekeeping had just been released, as the bookseller assured her. Before packing it into the box with the paints, Frederica looked at the illustrations of the copper engravings that adorned the pages. Even the plain images in strict black and white would earn her father's approval. Technically, the letter to her mother was no longer current, but Frederica couldn't bring herself to compose a new one. Let her mother believe that she was doing well. That way, Frederica would be less tempted to turn her back on London and crawl home defeated.

She had reconsidered selling the house. She had now definitively abandoned her initial impulse to reverse it and continue living there. Instead, she had notified Mr. Kingston that she would expedite her move. The house on Charlotte Street offered no opportunity for the fresh start Frederica envisioned. She had started sorting her belongings and given away everything she no longer needed to the neighbours. Together with Millie, Frederica cleaned the house from the attic to the front door. In the fortnight Mr. Kingston had given her for the handover, she intended to get rid of everything that bound her to the past, and to her foolish, foolish hopes of a future with a man she loved.

That rascal had never mentioned he was engaged. He had almost kissed her. She had nearly reciprocated the kiss! Was it her fault? Had she misinterpreted his signals and fallen in love with a man already bound to another woman? Yes, he had invited her to accompany him to Lady Castlereagh's residence to paint the tiger. He had said there was something unique and precious between them. What woman wouldn't have interpreted those words as a sign of his love? Well, probably any woman who wasn't as naïve as she was. For a few precious moments, she had dared to dream, and now all her wishes and hopes had collapsed like a house of cards.

Absentmindedly, she scratched Tidbit, who had curled up on her lap, behind the ears. The purring of the cat did not fail to have its soothing effect. It never did. Frederica leant down and gave him a quick kiss on the forehead. At the moment, he was the only male presence she could tolerate. Since the moment Lady Hastings had left the house, she hadn't entered the studio – not even to clean with Millie. Her old friend, despondency, had knocked on her door and settled in her heart to take command.

She couldn't avoid the studio forever, especially if she wanted to figure out her future. There were so many things Frederica had to decide in a short time. Where would she live? And could she bring herself to accept Lady Hastings' invitation, despite her pain over Lord Burnwood's lie? If she settled all the debts accumulated during her years of marriage, she would have a meagre remainder from the sale of the house, plus what Lord Burnwood had paid her for the painting. If she was thrifty, she could live for a year on that. Additionally, if she accepted the commission for Lady Annis' portrait, she would have a small income from candle- and soap-making.

Frederica didn't need to worry about starving or being forced to make a living in one of the less appetising ways.

Frederica pushed away the ale she had been sipping and looked out the window. She would make it! With Lord Burnwood's portrait, she had proven to herself that she could paint and make a living from it. All she needed was a little courage. She decided that a walk would do her good, and picked up Tidbit from her lap. She could swear the stately cat had doubled its weight recently. He let all four fluffy legs dangle and even sagged a bit when she put him down on the floor. "You should go on the stage," Frederica murmured. She met his gaze and smiled as the tiger turned his back to her and, suddenly regaining control of his limbs, strolled elegantly toward the hearth. Once again, a wave of sorrow washed over her as she noticed the movement of the muscles under the striped fur.

"I'll be back in no more than three hours," she promised Tidbit and put on her bonnet. One day she *would* see a tiger, even if she had to write a plea to Lady Castlereagh and kneel before the lady. She could also book passage on one of the impressive ships of the East India Company and seek her fortune there. Or at least seek an old, toothless tiger she could paint. She paused in the act of buttoning her coat, surprised at herself. It seemed she didn't need to make a conscious decision after all because her heart had already made it for her. Her daydreams, inspired by defiance and pain, revolved around painting, not a man. What was she waiting for? If she ever wanted a portfolio of paintings to get more commissions, now was the time to start. She would go to the park and sketch everything that caught her eye.

Swiftly, Frederica entered the studio. She ignored the empty easel and reached for the smaller of the two sketchbooks and a handful of pencils. All together, they just fit into her reticule. The bag was too big to pass as a fashionable accessory, but it was practical. She didn't need a servant to carry everything for her.

With her head held high, she marched towards Westminster Bridge. It would take her more than half an hour on foot to reach Hyde Park, and she intended to savour every minute of it.

. . .

How many times had she walked over these well-trodden cobblestones in the past few years? Here, in burgeoning Lambeth, she had lived with Francis since she had married him against her father's explicit command. At first, it hadn't been easy. They had rented a room in a side street, right next to a laundry. During the day, the laughter and cursing of the women reached them from below, and at night, they heard the owners arguing. And just around the corner was the Golden Whistle, where they had often eaten at the beginning of their marriage, which coincided with the start of Francis's success as a painter. Since his death, she hadn't set foot inside the tavern, even though the landlady, Mary, had invited her for a glass of wine more than enough times.

She turned onto Bridge Road and passed Lambeth Palace. The residence of the Archbishop of Canterbury was located on the south bank of the Thames. Francis, who had not been a religious person, had always made a wicked jest about the bishop and laughed at Frederica's discomfort. "You're still far too much the obedient vicar's daughter," were his words. At first, he had smiled and kissed the tip of her nose as he made this observation. Later, his amusement had turned to condescension, and in the end, he had sounded contemptuous.

Frederica continued quickly.

The absolute regularity with which the arches of Westminster Bridge spanned the Thames amazed her every time. On the other side, the stream of wagons, riders, and pedestrians dissolved, all heading in different directions. Hyde Park was not far now, and the district clearly displayed that here, wealth and power were taken for granted. Every child was accompanied by a nanny or governess. The footpaths were clean, the houses magnificent. You wouldn't find tired horses here. Even the occasional beggar would have passed for wealthy in Whitechapel, thought Frederica, and she was relieved when the park came into view.

She let herself be carried along by the passers-by and kept her eyes open. She eagerly absorbed various impressions, but nothing she saw seemed worth drawing. It was only when an obviously overworked servant in a green livery passed by that she felt the urge to put her pencil to use. He was walking four tiny dogs that behaved as if they were the masters of the world. Apparently, they considered themselves larger than they actually were, as they fearlessly barked at pedestrians and even horses. The unfortunate servant had his hands full trying to keep the unruly bunch in check.

Frederica sat down on one of the benches and captured the scene with a few quick strokes. She had chosen a good vantage point, far from Rotten Row, where the dandies engaged in reckless races in their single-horse carriages and on horseback. She was in the process of drawing a young woman, whose face was hardly visible under a daring hat, when her heart nearly stopped.

An open carriage passed by at a leisurely pace.

It wasn't the sight of the man, whose scarred face was clearly visible in the bright sunlight, that broke her heart for the second time in a few days. It was the smile with which Lord Burnwood looked at the very young beauty sitting opposite him.

39

NASH

Either Aldekirk had ruthlessly exaggerated when he referred to Lady Annis as a "wild child," or something had seriously dampened the girl's spirits. When her father had granted her permission for an outing, she had thanked him politely and included Nash with a weak smile of gratitude. She seemed lifeless, making Nash wonder if she had even understood what Lord Stewart had said to her.

That changed abruptly when she was out of sight of the house. First, she untied the ribbons of her bonnet and tore off her headgear. "I hate being confined like this," she explained, starting to unbutton her coat. Nash wavered for a moment between laughter and horror before he put his hands on hers to prevent her from catching pneumonia. The governess who sat up front on the coach offered no support, and Lady Annis deliberately ignored her. Either the governess was too old to notice the behaviour of her former charge, or this was a routine part of Lady Annis's behaviour that she paid no attention to.

"I understand that you want to enjoy your freedom, but if you don't stop behaving like a child right away, I'll return you to your father. Do we understand each other?" He had no time for such nonsense and hoped he had been clear enough.

"Don't be such a killjoy. If you want to marry me, you'll have to learn not only to tolerate my whims but to love them. Otherwise, I will not marry you; I'll flee to Gretna Green with the coachman and get married there." Her supposed threat ended in a trilling, artificial laugh.

Nash leant forward and tapped Lady Annis's new suitor on the shoulder. "Perkins, turn around and take me back to Arden House. After that, you're welcome to elope with Lady Stewart if you wish. You have my blessing."

"Stop!" The muffled cry was music to Nash's ears. Lady Annis closed her mouth and audibly exhaled as Perkins, who knew his master well enough to know what to do – or rather, not to do – continued to drive calmly.

Nash leant back in relaxation. "Lord Aldekirk told me you were not only beautiful but also clever. I trust my friend's judgment, and I assume you have a good reason for the performance you're putting on here, Lady Stewart."

He watched as all traces of playfulness disappeared from Lady Annis's face. Even her voice sounded different now when she spoke. "I apologise, my lord," she said calmly. She pushed a few strands of her red hair back, put her bonnet back on, and tied it under her chin with brisk movements. "I apologise sincerely for my behaviour."

"Accepted," said Nash, smiling at her. "Why don't you tell me what prompted this impressive performance, Lady Stewart?"

"Impressive? Yes, perhaps, but apparently not convincing." She pursed her lips, and her blue-grey eyes studied him seriously.

"You can trust me," he said simply.

Lady Annis tilted her head. She didn't take her eyes off him for a second. "You are the last man I should trust," she said slowly. "According to my father and the Prince Regent's wishes, I am supposed to marry you."

"It's about young Lord Douglas, isn't it?"

Nash's concise words elicited an immediate reaction. Lady Annis's fair skin turned scarlet. Her cheeks flushed. Out of anger or embarrassment? Anger, Nash decided, as he saw the fire in her eyes.

"I love Alfie, and I will marry him," she declared. Her hands, which she had folded modestly in her lap until now, clenched.

His heart skipped a beat. He was saved! Lady Annis's words seemed like the best thing he had heard in ages. The Scottish bride loved someone else, and that meant the way was clear for him and Frederica! His mood lifted, but Nash refrained from showing it to his companion. Let her simmer a bit, this cheeky child-woman.

"Why... are you so kind to me?"

Now it was Nash's turn to smile. "You mean, even though you intended to use me as a bargaining chip to get Lord Douglas to act?" His smile deepened. "A man holds onto the love of his life when he encounters her. That's all you need to know, Lady Annis."

"But what would you have done if I had wanted to marry you?" She sounded a little hurt.

"We'll probably never find out." Nash imagined that she wasn't used to being rejected. Unlike Frederica, Lady Annis had never had to stand on her own two feet, and had been thoroughly spoilt by her father. It was a wonder she had still grown into an intelligent and, with a little tutoring, insightful young woman. He liked her and even felt a certain protective instinct, similar to what he would have felt for a younger sister.

He hadn't even noticed they had arrived in Hyde Park. How many laps had Perkins already taken? The beautiful weather had lured numerous pedestrians and riders to the paths. Not much longer, and he would be strolling here with Frederica, proudly presenting her to the whole world as his beloved wife.

But first, he had to help Lady Annis find her happiness. He already had a plan on how to get the hesitant Lord Douglas moving.

Life could be so wonderful!

40

FREDERICA

I can do it. I can do it. I can do it. Frederica repeated the words so many times on her way back to Charlotte Street that she almost believed them when she unlocked the front door and bent down to greet Tidbit. Later, as she fell asleep, she repeated the words to herself, and when she woke up the next morning, they were the first thing that came to mind.

When Millie stood in the doorway, Frederica was ready to face the world. Lady Hastings had invited her to her salon and hinted at a commission. The worst thing Frederica could do was sulk like a child and wait for her fate to miraculously turn for the better. She held the reins of her life in her hands, and it was up to her alone!

Frederica didn't assume that every word Lord Burnwood had said to her was a lie. He may have even meant what he said – something precious, unique – but there was something she couldn't forget, even if she wanted to: he was about to marry another woman. She had to forget him and try to banish that moment of soaring fantasy from her heart. Could she do it?

Yes. It was about her future as a painter, and another dream that had nothing to do with a man's love and everything to do with self-love.

Frederica pulled her clothes out of the trunk. One thing became clear to her when she saw the pile of fabric on the floor: it was high time for a new dress. Faded colours and frayed hems, worn sleeves and brittle trimmings... The comparison with the radiant white dress and the precious bonnet of the exquisite beauty in Lord Burnwood's carriage intruded into Frederica's thoughts. But even the headdress of an Egyptian queen wouldn't change the fact that Frederica had never had a chance.

Even Millie, who was more frugal than anyone Frederica knew, looked at the dresses with a disdainful expression. "These are fit for the ragpicker," she declared. Frederica stood up and looked down at the pile of clothes.

"You're right," she agreed. "But until that time comes, I'll have to make do with the old ones."

"Not necessarily," Millie replied with a sly smile. "I happen to know a very fine tailor who has a few beautiful sample dresses in your size he can offer you at a good price."

Sample dresses? Mr. Solomon's business must be doing well if he not only did commissioned work but also had samples he showed to his customers. What else had Frederica missed?

"It's very kind of you to offer me a discount on behalf of your future husband, but thanks to Lord Burnwood, I can afford to pay the full price."

"Madam," Millie said in a somewhat ominous tone, "may I speak candidly?"

"Of course."

"I've been working for you for more than ten years, and I've seen how you withdrew more and more into your house in the months after your husband's death, like a snail into its shell. Forgive me, but you haven't taken care of yourself at all."

Frederica could only nod.

"And then this Lord comes into the house," Millie continued. "I see you smile. I hear you humming a tune when you think no one can hear you. You're not just talking to the cat anymore, but also to me. You're painting again, and when you come out of the studio, your face is radiant. And suddenly, it's over again. The Lord is gone, and the studio is locked again."

Tears welled up in Frederica's eyes. Millie had held a mirror in front of her, and what Frederica saw in it was not pretty.

"I don't know what happened between you and His Lordship, and it's none of my business, but—"

"Nothing happened between us," Frederica interjected.

Millie nodded as if she had expected that. Frederica's cheeks grew warm.

"But if you end up where you were after your husband's death, then everything will start all over again. The sadness. Your refusal to eat. Don't let His Lordship be responsible for your happiness. Please, madam. Do something that brings you joy."

Millie's wise words were true, no doubt. But that didn't make it any easier to follow them.

"Madam," Millie said softly, touching her arm. Frederica saw Millie's face working. "Frederica." Millie swallowed. "We've known each other for so long now. You have to take the next step. Not just think about it or talk about it, but do something. You've sold the house but haven't found a new home yet. You say you're sorting through all your things and you've given away more than half of what you owned. You scare me."

"Millie, I..." *will not do anything foolish*, Frederica wanted to say, thinking of the humming of bees and the brown waters of the Thames. No more lies, not even those she told herself. "You're right. I'm deeply sorry; I must have been unbearable."

Millie nodded.

"Will you come with me to Mr. Solomon's? Right now?" She had to leave immediately, or she would just continue to ponder this opportunity in her mind. Besides... Another decision formed in Frederica's mind. Today was Friday. Lady Hastings had invited her to her soiree. Whether further commissions resulted from it or not, she had explicitly asked Frederica to be at her place today from four o'clock onwards.

Oh, she would go! And not only that, she would accept Lady Hastings' commission and paint Lord Burnwood's future wife, proving to the world that she was more than just a weak woman without discipline and perseverance. No more secrecy, no more hiding within her four walls, and no more hiding behind her husband's name. It was time to prove her talent.

She would do it, with God's help. The secret of Francis's death and the authorship of his portraits would remain hidden, but Frederica would finally get what she had yearned for for years: freedom.

41

NASH

Three or four days were all Nash needed to get the matter of the Scottish bride taken care of. He had only shared the rough outline of his plan with Lady Annis because it was important that she didn't pretend. Her brief display of acting during the outing had convinced him she had a tendency to exaggerate, and that was something he couldn't use.

He spent the morning making the initial preparations and was relieved that Aunt Matilda was busy with the arrangements for her soiree today. The busy comings and goings of the servants reached him faintly, and Aunt Matilda allowed him to work undisturbed, for which he was extremely grateful. When she got to know Frederica and saw how happy he was with his beautiful painter, she would relent, he was sure of it. Not relent, he corrected himself in his thoughts. His aunt wanted the best for him and would understand that he needed Frederica.

His mood lifted as he thought that only a few days separated him from explaining things to Frederica. He sealed the letter to Lady Castlereagh and placed it on the stack of other letters he had written during the morning. He had set everything in motion for today. Now he had to be patient and wait for responses.

If he wasn't mistaken, the first guests were arriving. He glanced at the small clock on the mantelpiece. Aunt Matilda would be pleased if he joined her, and it would cost him nothing but an hour to politely engage in conversation with her friends and make them happy. Nash hurried upstairs to change. He usually preferred clothing in which he could move freely, but for Aunt Matilda's sake, he was willing to make an exception. The tightly fitted Spencer and the knotted cravat were a small price to pay for the satisfaction of the woman who had raised him. His valet straightened the tie pin with the blue gem, and then Nash made his way to the lion's den.

As he entered the drawing room, the murmured conversation fell silent, except for the laughter of a woman whose voice he would recognise among thousands. Frederica. She was here!

Over the heads of the guests, he searched for and found her in the middle of the room. What the hell had she done with her hair? The intricate, upswept style didn't suit her, especially not the artificial flowers that someone had adorned her silky strands with. Since she had her back to him, she didn't notice him. However, it allowed him to see her all the more clearly.

She wore a bright red dress made of soft flowing material that clung to her curves as if it were made for her. The colour reminded Nash of poppies, and the fabric enveloped her in a way that concealed yet hinted at everything he had ever desired: the slender waist, round hips, and arms that were slim and well-shaped at the same time, filling Nash with a burning desire to feel them wrapped around his neck. Her red-blonde hair appeared brighter than usual, and in his eyes, she was temptation incarnate. Nash suppressed a possessive growl as he noticed one of the gentlemen present letting his gaze glide from the graceful curve of her neck to her bare shoulders. Without giving the people blocking his path even a glance, he made his way to her, pushed sharp elbows aside, ignored the snippets of conversation rising again, and sidestepped pompous bellies that kept him away from her. He pushed the man who had stared at her so boldly aside and was only a few steps away from her. She stood upright and spoke to... Lady Annis. It shocked him to see her talking to the woman who, in the eyes of the world, was engaged to him. A touch of desperation rose in his chest, but he pushed it aside forcefully, even though he wondered how he would explain everything to Frederica here, in this crowded drawing room, amidst all the guests. Lady Annis's face was focused. She was half a head shorter than Frederica and looked past her. Nash was so close that he saw Lady Annis's mouth move. She said something to Frederica, whose response he didn't hear, but he watched as she straightened her back and squared her shoulders.

Then he was with them. A look into her brown eyes, and he knew someone had told her everything. Pain flickered across her face like a single cloud on a summer day before it disappeared and made way for a deceptively blue sky. A storm was brewing on the horizon, and he felt it with every fibre of his heart.

"Mrs. Fitzroy," Nash said through gritted teeth.

"Lord Burnwood," she replied, just as tersely.

"Lord Burnwood." Lady Annis repeated Frederica's words and stepped back. She probably would have backed further away if the confined space hadn't prevented it. "You already know Mrs. Fitzroy. Your aunt told me that Mrs. Fitzroy painted your portrait. Lady Hastings kindly invited her so we could get to know each other in an informal atmosphere."

Aunt Matilda had invited Frederica.

Nash forced himself not to immediately look for her and shake her until she revealed what she had been thinking. He could guess.

Lady Annis seemed to sense the tension between him and Frederica because she simply continued talking. "Your aunt is very eager for Mrs. Fitzroy to paint a portrait of me so we have two matching paintings."

"How very kind of Lady Hastings," Nash growled.

"She only has your best interests at heart." Frederica's voice sounded cool and composed. "I look forward to painting your future wife, my lord. I already have a fairly clear idea of how I will depict her." She attempted a smile. It failed.

"Perhaps you should not be too hasty, Mrs. Fitzroy, and delay the painting a bit. Many unforeseen things can still happen." For example, Lady Annis marrying someone else, but he couldn't say that out loud.

"That doesn't surprise me," Frederica replied. "Anyone who stays close to you should expect surprises."

From the corner of his eye, Nash saw Lady Annis's gaze flickering between him and Frederica. "Which doesn't necessarily mean anything bad, unless unauthorised individuals get involved and spread *falsehoods*," Nash made an effort to speak quietly so those around them wouldn't eavesdrop on their conversation.

Frederica's gaze grew even colder. It wouldn't have surprised Nash if the salon's windows had frosted over and the tea in the cups had frozen. "It's good that one can always verify for oneself who is telling the truth." Her eyes brushed over Lady Annis's face and softened for a heartbeat. Or had he been mistaken? When Frederica looked at him, there was no sign of kindness, let alone warmth. "Have you shown your future wife the portrait? Perhaps she will not like my style and may wish to choose another artist."

"Of course I have," he replied, puzzled. How on earth could she believe that he didn't love this painting, from the damn horns to the blazing flames of Hell she had painted?

The irony of it all hadn't escaped him. He had commissioned the painting to dissuade Lady Annis from marrying him, and now the portrait had become a symbol of his love for Frederica, which he couldn't reveal until Lady Annis walked down the aisle with that damn Douglas. "I will gladly show it to the whole world!" he growled. He would never, ever betray the trust she had placed in him by tarnishing the memory of her deceased husband.

Aunt Matilda and her cursed curiosity. Why hadn't she listened to him and waited with her presentation of the creator of his portrait? His triple-damned indulgence of her! He absolutely had to speak to Frederica privately.

That didn't happen. Aunt Matilda tapped her glass with a spoon, and silence spread through the salon.

"Ladies and gentlemen," she began. Nash saw her hand trembling slightly, but during her next words, any outward sign of unease disappeared. "I am delighted that you have accepted my invitation. Most of you had the opportunity to admire my nephew's portrait in the entrance hall upon your arrival."

Nash suppressed a wolfish grin. He had observed Lord Harborough holding smelling salts under his wife's nose to prevent her from fainting at the sight of the Devil of St. James. He hadn't missed the muttered labels like "frivolous" or "outrageous" and "sinful."

"Today, I would like to introduce you to the extraordinary, indeed visionary creator of this painting. Ladies and gentlemen, please focus your attention on Mrs. Frederica Fitzroy. I am proud and happy to be her next client after my nephew. Mrs. Fitzroy will paint Lady Annis Stewart, my nephew's wife-to-be."

Nash went cold.

Aunt Matilda gestured towards Frederica, who did her best to stand upright and bear the bundled attention of the upper ten thousand with her head held high. Only Nash noticed the trembling that ran through her body and moved closer to her. Aunt Matilda's eyes followed his movement.

Her gaze shifted from Frederica to him and back to Frederica. Nash saw Aunt Matilda turn pale and cursed silently. Damn! His aunt had understood what Frederica meant to him; he could see it in her controlled, rigid features.

"I promise you, she will accomplish great things." The last sentence came comparatively quietly from her mouth. He saw her down the champagne and approach him and Frederica.

"Young man!" she hissed in his ear, presenting a smiling face to the world while linking her arm with his. Meanwhile, Frederica was being showered with kindness by the same ladies and gentlemen who had appeared shocked at the sight of the painting just moments ago.

"Why did you not tell me that she is the woman who has captured your heart?"

"What difference would it have made?" Nash, vigilant as Lady Castlereagh's tiger, waited for a gap in the crowd that surrounded his beautiful painter.

"It would have changed *everything*," Aunt Matilda whispered shrilly but still audible only to him. "Oh, my boy, I have commissioned her to paint your *future wife*!"

"I heard that," Nash grumbled. "I was *there*!" He spoke the last word so loudly that some heads turned to look at him. To hell with the gawkers! "We'll talk later," he said to Aunt Matilda and pushed through the bystanders until he reached Frederica.

"Come with me to the garden, Mrs. Fitzroy," he said, offering her his arm.

"I deeply regret," she replied flatly, "that I must leave now. I have preparations to make for tomorrow. It will be an honour to paint such a beautiful young woman as you, my lady." Nash could hardly believe his ears. Frederica sounded like she meant every word as she said it! He should have known. Nothing was further from her than malice or jealousy. He realised that he was still holding out his arm invitingly.

"Five minutes," he said, gritting his teeth when he realised that his words sounded like a request. "My coachman will take you home."

"My carriage is already waiting," she rebuffed him for the second time but made no move to say goodbye to him. She took a deep breath as if she needed to gather strength.

Nash came as close to her as possible in the presence of other people. "Just a moment. You will not regret it."

"Oh, yes I will," she whispered almost inaudibly. She lowered her head, only to raise it again and look him in the face.

Come with me to the garden, my love. I will explain everything to you, Nash conveyed the silent message.

She shook her head.

"I will visit you tomorrow, Lady Annis. Goodbye!"

Before Lady Annis could respond or Frederica could escape, Nash took her hand and raised it to his lips. He felt a tremor run through her reluctant body as he, ignoring all conventions, pressed his lips to the back of her bare hand. Only when he realised that they were attracting the attention of the surrounding guests did he let go of her.

Nash watched her walk across the room to bid farewell to the hostess.

"My lord?" Lady Annis brought him back from his reverie, in which he was giving his aunt a proper scolding. That would have to wait, as would the conversation with Frederica. "I do not wish to appear curious, but this painting that Mrs. Fitzroy has painted – does it have a special significance?"

He could barely tear his gaze away from Frederica's back. For a brief moment, he closed his eyes. Immediately, her face appeared before him again, as cool and impassive as he had seen it just a few moments ago. "Forgive me," he said, turning to Lady Annis. "What did you say?"

"Nothing of importance," she replied softly and linked her arm with his. "Mrs. Fitzroy is an interesting and unusually likeable woman."

He nodded.

"I look forward to the sessions with her."

Nash suppressed a curse. He would never understand women.

42

FREDERICA

No one was more surprised than herself, but Frederica liked Lady Annis. She reminded her of herself at that age. Just like Frederica had back then, Lady Annis looked confidently into the future with a curiosity that was unmatched. Frederica had firmly resolved not to like Lady Annis, but she was powerless against her innocent charm. During their first session, Frederica realised within an hour that the young woman did not love Lord Burnwood, even though she spoke highly of him.

It was painful to hear Lord Burnwood's name from Lady Annis's mouth as Frederica worked on the preliminary sketch. She forced herself to tune out the stream of words while trying to capture the high cheekbones and the arch of the reddish eyebrows. With her delicate but remarkably clear features, Lady Annis's face resembled a statue of the goddess Artemis that she had seen as a child. She and Mama had travelled to Florence to visit Frederica's grandparents, and Mama had always taken her on her walks through the famous gardens and palace grounds.

Should she portray Lady Annis as the Goddess of Hunting? But then she realised that her portrait and Lord Burnwood's would probably hang side by side. A devil and a Greek goddess were not a good combination. She should have portrayed Lady Annis as an angel, but there was nothing angelic, despite her innocence, about the beautiful young woman. The mischievousness in her grey-blue eyes, which sometimes turned into cunning, gave that away.

Since the rooms in her house were filled with boxes and were no longer usable due to the preparations for the move, she visited Lady Annis, rather than the other way around, as she had done with Lord Burnwood. Mr. Kingston had offered her a generous sum if she moved out earlier than initially agreed. His daughter had married, and the house was his wedding gift to the young couple, who desperately needed privacy, as he put it. Finding a place to stay within a week, instead of the originally planned fortnight, that was neither rundown nor too expensive, proved difficult. At least Frederica's belongings were now stored, except for what she needed most urgently. Yesterday, she had given Millie a generous severance, although the young woman insisted on staying with Frederica as long as possible. If they saw each other again after the wedding, it would no longer be as mistress and maid, but perhaps as friends.

The Scottish Lady and her father were staying with friends, the Laytons. Lady Felicity Layton was hardly older than Lady Annis, and received Frederica with such unassuming friendliness that her concerns about working in a foreign environment immediately dissipated. On the second day, the mistress of the house asked if she could watch Frederica work. Even if she had not used the word "work" and thus implied that she understood what Frederica was doing, she would not have declined. Lady Layton had even been so kind as to send a carriage so Frederica could transport all the materials she needed to the Laytons' townhouse.

To Frederica's surprise, Lady Hastings did not appear during the sessions. Was she perhaps angry with Frederica for leaving the soiree hastily? No, Frederica didn't believe that. The day after, a servant had come to her and handed her the agreed-upon sum for Lady Annis's portrait. It was nowhere near as high as what she had received from Lord Burnwood, but at one hundred and fifty guineas, it was still substantial.

As with the portrait of the Lord, she had prepared the canvas so as to finish as quickly as possible. Liking Lady Annis didn't mean it wasn't painful to see her. Whenever Frederica emerged from the painting trance, she realised that this was the woman who would marry Lord Burnwood.

I'm the one who is to blame, Frederica told herself over and over. She should never have allowed herself to hope, no matter how unusual Lord Burnwood was. Ultimately, he was a man like any other, a seducer, incapable of going through life without trampling on the feelings of others.

She noticed she was pressing the brush so firmly into the paint on the palette that its bristles were splaying. With a sigh, she loosened her cramped fingers and urged herself to calm down. Behind her, Lady Layton cleared her throat.

"Can I have tea brought to you, Mrs. Fitzroy?"

Frederica turned around. "No, thank you," she replied. "I have everything I need."

The young woman seemed sceptical, but did not insist. Frederica found it difficult to imagine her as a future duchess, precisely because she was so young. Just like Lady Annis, who would soon be a marchioness.

"Is it too late to express an additional wish?" That was Lady Annis, who couldn't sit still any more than Lord Burnwood.

"You are the client, so you largely determine how I paint you," Frederica replied. It sounded harsher than she had intended, so she added, "I've already started working on the canvas, so it will be difficult to change the pose now. But I can still adjust minor details like the colour of your dress to your wishes, my lady."

"Then I wish for you to include a red heart and three white stars on a blue background. If it is possible."

Lady Annis looked so deliberately innocent that Frederica suspected these ornaments had a secret meaning for the young beauty. She frowned. "I can do that, but perhaps you could tell me the significance of these symbols for you, so I can paint them in the right context." Immediately, a burst of ideas sprang to mind: the Lady Annis in the picture could wear a star-studded dress, and Frederica would hide the heart in a tiara. A dress of starlight and a crown of love would be perfect for Lady Annis.

The rustling of silk revealed that Lady Layton had risen. "Annis, my dear, I do not think that is a good idea," she said. Contrary to her words, which could be understood as a suggestion by an impartial observer like Frederica, her voice sounded firm.

"I think it is the *best* idea," Lady Annis replied, throwing her head back with a defiant gesture and placing her hands on her hips.

Frederica was intrigued. Before her stood an Amazon, a defiant, young but determined warrior. *Wonderful, please stay like this!* Of course, she didn't say that out loud, not wanting to interfere in a conversation that didn't concern her.

"I am not talking about what your father will say, or Lady Hastings, who paid for the painting and will surely consider it an affront to hang stars and hearts from the Douglas coat of arms in Arden House," Lady Layton said, having stopped next to Frederica.

If Frederica remembered correctly, the Douglases were an ancient Scottish noble family. Why on earth did Lady Annis want to show her connection to this clan on her portrait? After all, she was a Stewart!

Lady Layton's pleasant voice continued, "Have you considered what your betrothed will say?"

Frederica's heart skipped a beat when she heard who was being discussed, and unintentionally, she perked up her ears.

"If you are hoping he will not notice, forget about it right away. Arden may be outwardly injured, but he is smarter than you think. Besides," Lady Layton continued quietly but firmly, "I like him. He is a friend of Luke and mine, and one of the most honourable, sincere men I know. I will not allow you to toy with him."

Hearing this apparently deeply felt praise from Lady Layton filled Frederica with a painful pang of doubt. Her knees became so weak she felt she might collapse at any moment. Was Lady Layton talking about the same man who she hadn't opened the door to for two days and had had Millie tell him she wasn't at home? The last time, Millie had looked worried and said she didn't think the Marquess would put up with it for much longer. With a bit of luck, Frederica had replied, she would no longer be living in Charlotte Street in a few days, but somewhere Lord Burnwood would never find her.

A competition of surprise, defiance, and... was that relief? ignited on Lady Annis's face. "But Felicity, I know that!" she exclaimed. Despite her long dress, she jumped towards her friend in coltish leaps, wrapped her arms around her neck, and rested her forehead against Lady Layton's. "And he knows it too. Lord Burnwood, I mean."

What was Lady Annis talking about? What did he know? Frederica held her breath.

"He said he would help me. We will make Alfie explain himself together."

"Alfie Douglas is an idiot!" Lady Layton replied with unwavering conviction.

Frederica covered her mouth to avoid bursting into laughter at the candid comment. She wouldn't want to be in Lord Douglas's shoes when facing Lady Layton.

"He is," Lady Annis agreed, surprisingly. "But he is the idiot I love."

Lady Annis loved someone else. Someone else... not Lord Burnwood. Frederica's head felt like it was wrapped in cotton. She couldn't think clearly and didn't know what to feel. Lord Burnwood had promised to help the young woman? Did that mean he wanted this marriage as little as Lady Annis did?

"I agree with everything you said about Lord Burnwood," Lady Annis's voice continued from a distance. "He is not only honourable but quite clever, if you ask me. Also, I suspect his heart already belongs to another woman. Just to be clear, I do not lay any claim to him, not legally or in any other way."

Frederica didn't look, but she believed she could feel Lady Annis's beautiful eyes turning to her. Frederica's heart pounded so fast she thought it might burst in her chest. Did his promise to help Lady Annis get together with that Lord Douglas mean he did have feelings for her? Had she misjudged him when she had coldly rejected him?

"But... then I do not understand why you got engaged to him," Lady

Layton summed up her confusion, which Frederica shared. She would have hugged the young woman out of gratitude if she could.

Lady Annis sighed. "I thought I could provoke Alfie with it." Suddenly, she sounded like a very young and lovestruck girl. "That fool," she spoke the word affectionately, "really thinks he has to perform some heroic deed to prove himself worthy of me."

"Typical Douglas," Lady Layton replied. "I just wish he was not the man you have lost your heart to."

Frederica's hands trembled. The brush and palette felt a hundred times heavier. If she moved now, the two women would remember her presence and continue their conversation privately. Frederica didn't want to miss what was coming next. Although, she thought, with Lady Annis, she wasn't sure. In a strange way, the Lady seemed to be addressing her words not only to her friend but also to her.

Lady Annis knew what Frederica felt for Lord Burnwood. She had suspected it when she heard him and Frederica talking to each other at the soiree and observed Frederica's injured reaction to the Marquess. And Frederica had been convinced she had her expressions under control!

The three women fell silent.

Frederica dared to look up and glanced over at Lady Annis.

She was grinning – there was no other way to describe it, even if it didn't seem to fit a lady – from ear to ear.

A lump formed in Frederica's throat. Even if she wanted to, she couldn't speak.

43

NASH

After the third attempt to visit Frederica at her house on Charlotte Street, it was clear to Nash that he had to continue his plan if he wanted to win her over. He would have preferred to speak to her alone, to explain the truth about his supposed engagement to Lady Annis, but her maid had made it clear last time that Mrs. Fitzroy would never be available at home, no matter what time he came by. No one had answered the door the last two times, not even Millie. Now, there was no more time to lose. The idea that Frederica doubted his feelings sparked an almost uncontrollable urge in him to act. Reluctantly, because he couldn't possibly force his way in, he withdrew. Persistence was in the blood of the Ardens, as their motto *"audere est facere"* promised. To dare is to do. The only problem was that he was currently juggling so many balls at once that he couldn't do anything but focus on keeping them all in the air. This meant he had to hand over the responsibility for Lady Annis's happiness to that indecisive weakling named Douglas as soon as possible.

Upon returning home, he wrote the letter to the young Douglas and was surprised at how easily the words flowed from his pen.

Dear sir,

Nash wrote and took a sip of the whisky his future-father-in-law – still, but not for long – had brought him from the Highlands,

In a few days, Lady Annis Stewart will do me the honour of becoming my wife.

Nash hesitated briefly. It was important to enrage Lord Douglas, making him react without caring about logic. It was like in war, when you lured the enemy out of hiding with carefully planned skirmishes, and finally delivered the death blow with the full force of thousands of soldiers from the opposing army.

I have heard that you, dear Lord, have behaved shamefully cowardly towards her.

That was not a lie. A man who constantly whined to a woman that he had to earn her was a weakling.

As the man who will share a table and a bed with her in the future, I take it upon myself to defend the honour of my future wife. If you are man enough, meet me this evening at midnight at the Black Heart in Whitechapel and face me in a fistfight.

Nash had thought long and hard about how to boost the young man's self-confidence. First, he had considered a staged attack where Lord Douglas would save his beloved Annis. He liked the idea but realised it involved too many witnesses. Nash would have had to pay and instruct the supposed highwaymen in detail. Besides, Lady Annis would have had to wander alone in a dark alley, not to mention that Lord Douglas would have had to appear at the right time and place. Next, he had thought about a duel between him and Douglas, where Lady Annis would appear at the last moment to throw herself into Douglas's arms. But this option had too many unknowns. He didn't want to risk Lady Annis or himself being harmed by a careless accident like an unintentional gunshot. Moreover, he was sure he was superior to Lord Douglas in the use of firearms and the sword. Since he ultimately wanted it to appear that Douglas had defeated him, he chose a fistfight. Nash hoped the dubious nature of the undertaking would motivate the young man to rescue his beloved Lady Annis from the clutches of a supposed ruffian. The tavern was located in Whitechapel, a London district so impoverished and corrupt that its notorious reputation had hopefully reached a Scottish thickhead. Surely Douglas wouldn't idly stand by as his beloved married a man who frequented London's sin district.

I cannot wait to show my bride how lucky she is to marry a real man.

The phrase was meant to suggest, more or less subtly, that Nash wanted to take Lady Annis with him to the Black Heart when he fought the young man.

When he showed the lines to his friend Layton, he could barely contain his laughter. "You should give up your seat in the House of Lords and consider a career as a writer of penny novels instead," said Luke Thornfield, Lord Layton, wiping the tears of laughter from his eyes. "Midnight? My future wife? Man enough?" he quoted from Nash's letter and burst into laughter again.

"Forget not, the lad is just twenty years old and head over heels in love with Lady Annis, but doesn't dare to ask her father for her hand. I intend to change that."

"Have you considered that he might be one of those poetry-loving dandies who don't care about women?"

Nash felt the colour drain from his face. He hadn't considered that possibility. Could it be that Lady Annis had thoroughly misunderstood the young Douglas? In that case, his plan would be in vain.

"I'll take my chances," he said. "Besides, even if he doesn't desire Lady Annis, I'm confident he likes her. In that case too, he'll feel compelled to protect her from a brutal barbarian like me. Who knows, perhaps he's so noble that he'll marry her anyway."

Layton slapped him on the shoulder. "Calm down, old friend. I inquired about Douglas with an acquaintance after you told me about the wedding. I was just teasing you, that's all. Douglas loves women, so much that he cannot keep his hands off them, not even for the enchanting Lady Annis."

Nash gave him a sideways glance, which Layton returned one to one.

"You cannot fool me. I can see that you're looking forward to this adventure," Nash growled. "Is your disguise washed and ironed? Layton was the man Aunt Matilda, together with half of London, adored as "the

Priest." "What does your wife think about the Priest having a miraculous resurrection tonight?"

"Hmmm," Layton replied with an indefinable sound.

"So she doesn't know," Nash concluded, then patted Layton's shoulder in turn. Not so hard as to make him flinch, but hard enough for his friend to feel it. "See you tonight. I'll pick you up at eleven."

If all went according to plan, Lady Annis would be another man's bride tomorrow morning, and he would be free to finally talk to Frederica.

44

FREDERICA

Frederica didn't know what to think anymore. Without explicitly stating it, Lady Annis seemed firmly convinced that she wouldn't end up marrying Lord Burnwood, but rather this mysterious Lord Douglas. If the radiance on her face was any indication of her affection, she loved him deeply.

The whole situation was peculiar. Frederica couldn't shake the feeling that the young woman had orchestrated the conversation – but for what purpose? To let her, Frederica, know that she had no romantic feelings for Lord Burnwood? But why would Lady Annis be so friendly towards her?

Directly asking Lady Annis was hardly possible. They hadn't known each other long enough, Lady Layton was keeping them company, and besides, Frederica hesitated to reveal her feelings to the woman promised to the man she loved. What if Lady Annis did end up marrying Lord Burnwood? As Frederica understood it, not only Lady Hastings but also Lord Stewart, the bride's father, attached great importance to this union. Frederica would never forgive herself if she was the one to sow doubt in Lady Annis's heart.

Doubts meant the death of love.

Was it too late to confess to Lord Burnwood how much she regretted the coldness with which she had treated him at the soiree? Had she lost him due to her own foolishness, or was there still a chance for them?

With tremendous effort of will, she tuned out the conversation between the two friends and focused on her work. She set aside the brush and quickly sketched the desired stars. If Lady Annis changed her mind, it wouldn't be a problem to paint over them.

"Mrs. Fitzroy?"

Frederica raised her head. Judging by Lady Layton's expression, this wasn't the first time she had addressed Frederica.

"Excuse me," said Frederica, tearing herself away from her thoughts. "I was lost in thought."

"That is quite all right," Lady Layton replied kindly. "Lady Annis and I were wondering if you would like to occupy one of my guest rooms while you work on the painting."

"I... that is very kind, but..." Frederica began hesitantly, as the suggestion had come out of nowhere. She fell silent because she was on the verge of bursting into tears again.

"You would be completely undisturbed and not bound by our daily routines," Lady Layton assured her. "If inspiration wakes you in the middle of the night and you feel the need to paint, you would not disturb anyone." She added more gently, "You do not have to decide right away, Mrs. Fitzroy." Lady Annis acted as if she wasn't listening, but her body language revealed that she was eagerly awaiting Frederica's response.

She wouldn't have to take the carriage back and forth every day, and would thus save money. But she would have to say a final goodbye to the house on Charlotte Street. After that, there would be no turning back.

"Please say yes, Mrs. Fitzroy!" Lady Annis chimed in, hopping up and down like a frog.

"I don't want to intrude," Frederica began hesitantly, but Lady Layton cut her off.

"Nonsense, you would not intrude," she assured Frederica, while Lady Annis emitted an un-ladylike squeak. "So, is it decided?" The delighted expression in Lady Layton's eyes sealed the deal. Frederica nodded and didn't even attempt to hide her own joy. Lady Annis joined them, wrapping her arms around Frederica's neck.

"I know it is not proper, but as a Scot, I have the freedom to let my feelings run more freely than you stiff Englishmen," she said, embracing Frederica. "We will have a lot of fun together."

Now, Frederica had no doubt that Lady Annis was well aware of her feelings for Lord Burnwood. The remark about "stiff Englishmen" was just one of many signs that she was in the know.

Frederica laughed. It was a strangely unpractised sound that she heard coming from her own mouth, but even stranger was the warmth spreading in her chest. The realisation that there were people who liked her just the way she was, with all her quirks, choked her throat.

"One moment," she said, turning to her hostess when Lady Annis released her. "May I bring someone with me?"

The faces of the two women turned towards her in perfect synchronisation.

"I'm talking about my cat," she said quickly, before any misunderstandings could arise. "I cannot leave Tidbit alone. He always acts as if he's independent and needs no one, but I will not leave him behind."

"As long as he doesn't sleep in our bed and earns his keep as a mouse catcher, a cat is welcome in my house," Lady Layton agreed. When she smiled, a dimple appeared on her cheek. "What do you think of a cup of tea?"

She included Frederica so naturally in her proposal that it didn't even occur to her to decline.

45

NASH

"And what do you plan to do if Douglas doesn't show up?" Nash's friend Layton also pondered this question. Nash grinned and gave the answer he had already given himself: "Then I'll insult him in front of his friends until the young lad has no choice but to face me in a brawl."

Layton nodded and looked out of the carriage window. The white collar of his otherwise deep black attire glowed in the darkness. It was no wonder he had become a living legend in London. Luke Thornfield, Lord Layton, was one of the best pugilists Nash knew, duke's heir or not. The always identical black clothing, the disguise, and his never-ending gallantry towards ladies had made the Priest famous not only in Whitechapel. "That should work. I hope the matter goes smoothly for you tonight. If there's one thing I've learnt during my time as the Priest, it's this: the best-laid plans have the unholy tendency to be thwarted by people's unpredictable behaviour."

"I'll just improvise," Nash brushed off the objection. "I'm not claiming my plan is foolproof, but I don't want to leave Mrs. Fitzroy believing that I've played a dishonourable game with her any longer."

"I can understand that, especially after meeting her," Layton said. He still had his face turned away from Nash, but Nash could swear his friend was grinning. He refused to take the bait and let himself be unsettled.

"Then you'll surely understand why I want to make her my wife as soon as possible."

"Indeed," Layton replied unusually pompously and looked at Nash. Expectantly and yes, with a hint of mockery. Nash leant back, closed his eyes, and pretended to be only marginally interested in what his friend was about to reveal. "By the way, Felicity has invited her to stay with us while she works on Annis's portrait."

Nash raised his eyelids sluggishly.

"She accepted and has taken our best guest room. Felicity says she's incredibly talented and insists that your 'beautiful painter', as you call her, immortalises us next."

Nash straightened up. "She's more than just talented," he said fervently. "Frederica Fitzroy is an outstanding artist and the best painter I've ever met."

Layton didn't bother to hide his amusement. "And how many painters do you count among your acquaintances?"

Nash snorted. "Too many, believe me. In the past few weeks, I've met so many artists that it'll last me the rest of my life." Not one of them had been capable, in his estimation, of painting that cursed portrait. Until his Frederica came along.

"What I actually wanted to get at is something else," Layton continued, ignoring Nash's ironic comment. "If Douglas turns out to be a coward tonight, at least you know where to find her. I get a very strange feeling when I see those three ladies together."

Nash sat up, alarmed by the thought of Frederica, Lady Annis, and Felicity conspiring together. "Did you hear what they were talking about?"

"Not directly."

"What do you mean, not directly? Did you hear something or not?"

Women had the unfortunate tendency to meddle in dangerous matters. There were good reasons why he hadn't informed the self-assured Lady Annis about the details of his plan. If Felicity were added to the duo now, he could only hope that Frederica would be sensible enough to curb the enthusiasm of the two ladies.

"They had tea together and, as far as I could tell, only talked about painting. Later, however, my valet told me that my wife saw him preparing my suit. She asked him what I intended to do with it. Thankfully, the man was clever enough to give her an inconspicuous answer, but you know Felicity."

Oh, yes! When she was not yet Lady Layton, but the unmarried middle Evesham sister, Felicity had recklessly put herself in danger a few times. Under the seal of secrecy, Layton had confided that she had even ventured into the night in Whitechapel in the company of her maid to meet a blackmailer.

"But that's not all," Layton continued. "When I gave the order to harness the horses, I found out that the ladies had commandeered our town carriage. They're definitely up to something."

"Do you think your wife suspects that we're resurrecting the Priest tonight?"

"Anything is possible," Layton replied darkly.

"Good Lord, Layton, why didn't you tell me about this earlier?" Nash rapped the carriage roof with his cane and ordered his servant to stop immediately. He opened the door and looked around. They were already in Whitechapel, not far from the Black Heart where he had arranged to meet Lord Douglas. Return or continue? In any case, he couldn't allow the three ladies to enter the tavern in a fit of overconfidence and see things that were not suitable for ladies' eyes. Frederica... she was a widow and probably not as shocked by the spectacle inside a pub that was right next to a brothel. As for Felicity – she wasn't technically his responsibility, but since the plan was on his shoulders, she sort of was. If Lady Annis accompanied the two ladies, as was likely, Nash deserved every blow from Lord Douglas that he received.

"You return and check if the ladies are in your house," he ordered Layton. "I'll go into the Black Heart and look for them there."

"Oh no, my friend!" Layton jumped lightly out of the carriage. At least it was dark enough that the shady characters who roamed the streets of Whitechapel at all hours of the day and night wouldn't recognise him. Still, it was only a matter of time before the first person saw the Priest and word of his return spread like wildfire. "Hogarth," he nodded towards the coachman, "will return and make sure our ladies are safe. I'm coming to the Black Heart with you."

A glance at Layton's stony, guilt-ridden features, and Nash knew he didn't stand a chance. He had to try anyway. "I'll put them in a carriage immediately and send them back," he attempted, but Layton had already started running lightly.

Nash sprinted after him. At the next corner, he caught up with his friend. Without much surprise, he saw Layton pull out the silk cloth that served as his mask and tied it around his neck as he ran. Now the black fabric covered the white collar, and Layton looked like a perfectly ordinary gentleman dressed in black.

"Almost... like old... times," Nash's friend remarked and leapt over a pile of rubbish. A faint wheezing accompanied his words.

"Has marriage made you sluggish?" Nash challenged him, not wasting his strength on too many words. His determination to find Frederica made him forget the uncomfortable stitching in his sides.

"We'll talk... when you're... married yourself," Layton slowed down and gestured for Nash to do the same. "What does he look like anyway? How will we recognise him?"

"I could not glean much sensible information from Lady Annis. According to her, if one were to encounter a Nordic God with light shoulder-length hair, that would be him."

Layton rolled his eyes.

"His accent will give him away," Nash thought aloud, keeping his eyes open. Hidden from the passers-by, they stood in a doorway on the opposite side of the street, keeping an eye on the tavern. "Here's the plan: I'll go in and look for Douglas. You keep an eye on the street in case the ladies show up."

Before Layton could agree or refuse, Nash noticed a young man approaching the Black Heart.

Simultaneously, he and Layton retreated deeper into the shadows. The description the infatuated Lady Annis had given him, which had amused Nash, hit the mark. Nash saw the broad shoulders, the tall figure, and the ease of a predator on the prowl with which the man moved, and he knew exactly what the young Scot had meant. Douglas was dressed in dark attire, had an unremarkable hat on his head, and his hair tied back. His left hand rested inconspicuously on his hip. Nash knew he concealed a dagger there. The gesture revealed that the man was left-handed.

He had expected a pampered young dandy. What he had got was a worthy opponent.

46

FREDERICA

Since her decision to accept Lady Layton's hospitality, Frederica found herself in a whirlwind of activities. Her hostess had provided her with a carriage and sent two servants to transport Frederica's belongings. She had even thought of a wicker basket with a lockable lid for Tidbit. Of course, the Tiger was not thrilled about embarking on the journey, but with the help of a mackerel, Frederica managed to persuade him to sit in the basket.

She only let him out once they had arrived in her room and she had locked the door. The room Lady Layton had chosen for her was at the back of the house, overlooking the garden, and even had a small ivy-covered balcony. Tidbit seized the opportunity and immediately climbed down the thick vines to present himself to the Mayfair cat ladies. It took less than a minute for Frederica to see the self-proclaimed Casanova disappear into the bushes. She had no worries about his return. Anyone who survived the streets and alleys of Lambeth could find their way back in London's upscale neighbourhood.

Most of her luggage consisted of painting supplies, which were already stored in what she called the "painting room." As soon as Frederica had put away her few clothes, a servant appeared in the room, politely inviting her to tea in the salon. Frederica was relieved that Tidbit wasn't in the room to terrify the man. In the hallway, numerous gloomy paintings of men and women hung. She assumed they were Lord Layton's ancestors. The resemblance to her hostess's husband, whom she had briefly met this morning, was evident in their eyes. With a touch of regret, she postponed her inspection of the paintings to later.

She heard Lady Annis and Lady Layton before the salon door opened in front of her. They were engaged in a heated discussion revolving around a priest. "Oh dear," she heard Lady Annis say, and then Lady Layton's response, "Calm down, I know what we need to do." Lady Layton's face was flushed, Lady Annis's pale, but their eyes gleamed as if in a fever.

It was too late to turn back since the servant had already opened the door. "I need to go upstairs again; I think I forgot my stole," Frederica improvised, intending to retreat to avoid causing a disturbance.

"Nonsense!" Lady Layton said, tapping the empty space beside her on the sofa. "Come in, Mrs. Fitzroy. What we have to discuss concerns you too."

Lord Burnwood! raced through her mind. *Something has happened to Lord Burnwood, or Lady Annis has changed her mind, or he's injured and dying, and...* Shock coursed through Frederica's body like a lightning strike. In the past few hours, she had managed to think of him only occasionally. She realised that she stood frozen in the middle of the salon, with trembling knees and probably a snow-white face. Everything left unspoken between her, Lady Annis, and Lady Layton hung heavily between them.

Lady Layton reassured her that nothing terrible had happened and reached out her hand. "Forgive me. I have always been accused of having a tendency towards melodrama. Here." She reached for the teapot on the table in front of her, poured tea for Frederica herself, and added two heaped spoonfuls of sugar after a brief inspection. "Drink up!" When Frederica took her seat next to her, the young woman reached for her hand and squeezed it briefly.

The spoon clattered against the edge of the cup as Frederica stirred. She sipped the sweet drink in small sips.

"We must be open with each other," Lady Annis said. "Given the circumstances, at least we women should keep a cool head and clear all secrets out of the way." She took a deep breath. Lady Layton nodded encouragingly and leant back.

"I couldn't help but notice that you and Lord Burnwood... How should I put it..." Lady Annis paused and ran her hand through her lush red hair. "He loves you, and you love him," she burst out.

Frederica gasped for breath, partly due to the outrageous directness with which Lady Annis had spoken, and largely due to shock: Lady Annis believed that Lord Burnwood loved Frederica. She hadn't said "liked" or "appreciated," but spoke of love. Heat rose in her cheeks, and she had the urgent need to fan herself.

"It was obvious to me and to anyone who paid close attention when you attended Lady Hastings' soiree," Lady Annis continued calmly.

Lady Layton cleared her throat. "You do not have to be embarrassed, my dear. You are among friends. Annis always rushes ahead too quickly. Let me briefly tell you how I met and fell in love with my husband. After that, you will know I am not one of those women who place excessive value on conventions."

"That's quite evident," Frederica replied dryly. Lady Layton laughed, and after a brief hesitation, the other two women joined in.

"So," Frederica's hostess began, "to be honest, I always thought of my husband Luke as quite a... dandy. That was before I got to know him properly. I had foolishly manoeuvred myself into a hopeless situation from which I couldn't extricate myself alone. One day, I received a letter that summoned me to St. Botolph's in Whitechapel in the middle of the night, and..."

With astonished amazement, Frederica listened to a wild story about a suspicious death, blackmail, and a masked gentleman, with Lady Layton, then Miss Felicity, and the mysterious priest at its centre. Frederica had heard of him. No one knew who hid behind the black mask, but his popularity was due to his generosity. The man had distributed his prize money earnt at the boxing matches among the poor and hadn't kept a penny for himself. Miss Felicity had encountered him on that fateful night when she had wanted to pay a blackmailer, and fate had taken its course.

"That's incredible," Frederica said as Lady Layton finished her story and thirstily emptied her cup. "To be honest, it sounds like a story penned by Violet Lilacs." The sensational serialised novels by the woman were the talk of the town in all of London. Everyone, whether rich or poor, educated or not, would snatch copies from the newspaper boys on Fridays to find out how the distressed heroines would fare and if the sinister villains would get their just desserts.

"But what Felicity is getting at is something else," Lady Annis burst out. "She caught her husband's valet this afternoon selecting the clothing Luke wore as the Priest."

Frederica's confusion grew. "I don't understand how this relates to me and Lord Burnwood."

"Lord Burnwood knows I only agreed to marry him because I thought it might prompt Alfie to make a move. By Alfie, I mean Lord Douglas, the Marquess of Queensberry's son. Alfie claims he cannot marry me because he has not achieved anything heroic."

After deciphering the sense from Lady Annis's excited staccato, Frederica began to suspect what this was all about. She felt even warmer. "Lord Burnwood said he would help you," she summarised her understanding. This was necessary to bring some order to her racing thoughts. What kind of assistance was Lord Burnwood planning to offer the hesitant suitor? In essence, Lord Douglas didn't need a real heroic deed; it sufficed to make him believe he had committed one. "He's keeping the engagement with you intact and wants to encourage Lord Douglas, with the help of the Priest, to perform a heroic act so he feels worthy of you?" She paused briefly. "Is that it?" The ladies nodded. "Honestly, I don't know whether to laugh or tear my hair out."

"That is exactly what we thought," both women confirmed in unison.

"The problem is..." Lady Annis began.

"...that we do not know anything specific," Lady Layton completed the sentence. "I know that Luke plans to meet with Arden tonight and resurrect the Priest. He had promised me he would not to get into any more fights." She shuddered. "I will not be tending to his wounds this time, that is for sure."

It was an empty threat, Frederica thought, as the concern in her face said otherwise.

"Is Lord Douglas" – she almost said "Alfie" – "in town? 'Douglas' is the name of a noble Scottish family, and the inhabitants of that wild region don't think much of the English. At least not enough to voluntarily travel to the capital of the Empire."

"Alfie is here," Lady Annis confirmed. "My father told me, and I informed Lord Burnwood."

"What did Lord Burnwood tell you about what he plans to do to help you?" Frederica asked Lady Annis warily.

"Nothing specific," Lady Annis replied. "He said he would set everything in motion, and that I should be patient."

Silence spread.

"So, we suspect that Lord Burnwood intends to use the Priest to persuade Lord Douglas to perform a heroic act," Frederica summarised. Oh, this man! He had the face of a devil and wanted to use that cursed scar to deliver a theatrical performance. No, this wasn't like a story by Violet Lilacs; it was decidedly more absurd.

The faces of the two ladies turned expectantly towards her. "We believe we know when this plan is set to take place tonight."

"But we don't know where they're meeting," Frederica pointed out. "London is vast, and we could search all night without ever finding them."

Lady Layton leant forward and smiled. Frederica wouldn't want her as an enemy. "The Priest has only ever shown himself in one public place so far. I do not think that will change."

"And where is that place?" For the second time in a few minutes, Frederica suspected that she didn't want to hear the answer.

"The Black Heart in Whitechapel."

47

NASH

Without hesitation, Nash crossed the street and grabbed the man he assumed was Douglas by the arm. The man turned around and looked Nash in the face. Douglas flinched briefly when he saw the scar, but it was less of a startle and more of an assessment.

"What do you want?" he asked with the thick accent commonly heard beyond Hadrian's Wall.

"You are Douglas," Nash stated, omitting the title to get straight to the point.

"Arden," the man replied flatly. "What do you want?"

"Nothing," Nash said indifferently. "Now that I've seen you, nothing at all."

Douglas raised an eyebrow. "Are you mad or something?" he growled and stepped aside to let a drunkard out of the Black Heart. "First you insult Lady Annis and me in your letter, and now – nothing?"

"I expected a man. What I see is a coward, not worthy of my attention or that of my bride." Nash bared his teeth.

The reaction was swift. Douglas raised both arms and grabbed Nash by the collar.

Nash pushed both hands into the man's chest to break free from the grip. "Your presence reassures me," he taunted. "I thought the admiration Annis has for you was for good reason." Nash wanted to insult the man and, at the same time, convey that Lady Annis was always on his mind. For this, he had to play the role of a somewhat jealous suitor. Only thoughts of Frederica and their future together gave him the strength to make a fool of himself.

"Don't you dare mention her name!"

Nash tilted his head back and laughed. "What then?" he asked when he had calmed down. "Will you throw your handkerchief at me?"

"You damned—" Whatever Douglas had wanted to say was drowned out by a shrill scream. Nash and Lady Annis's reluctant suitor turned towards the source of this clearly feminine sound.

Good, thought Nash, *very good! Douglas has more honour in him than I suspected.*

In the next moment, every coherent thought was forgotten.

Frederica was here, flanked by two ladies. The pale but determined face of his beloved burned forever into his memory as he saw her shove away a pushy drunkard's hand. There was no room left in his heart for anything other than his overwhelming love for this brave, crazy woman. From a distant place, he heard a two-voice roar and wondered, in a functioning corner of his thought apparatus, why he suddenly had two voices.

Then a thousand things happened simultaneously.

In a single, flowing motion, Nash shot towards Frederica, vaguely aware that he was not the only one roaring like an angry bull and charging forward. Layton crossed the street. At the last moment, he dodged an oncoming carriage and leapt to Nash's side. Later, Nash realised that he and Douglas had acted in astonishing harmony. Now, in this moment, he paid no more attention to the other gentlemen than to a shadow, for his entire thought was focused on his desire to give the audacious tippler the beating of his life. He heard a protest shout, then a cry, "Hey, you dandy bastard, leave my mate alone or—" Whatever the man had wanted to say fell into the category of words that would never be spoken.

Layton's fist came into Nash's field of vision before colliding with the face of the man who had come to his friend's aid. Nash stood close enough to hear the crunch of the breaking nose before it was replaced by deafening screams and quickly turned into a nasal whine. Frederica's face was now so close that he saw her furrowed brows and bared teeth, like a tigress. Just in time, he slowed down, lifted her effortlessly and placed her out of reach of the man with a death wish who had approached her. Next to him came the unmistakable sound of a man whose breath had been knocked out by a punch. That was Douglas, taking on a third man who had joined the fray. In the next moment, Nash was already at his opponent and let Douglas fight his own battle. He saw the clenched fist of the attacker rushing towards his face and ducked under the blow to deliver an unbridled blow to his kidney area. *Ha! Not bad for a devil!* The man rolled his eyes and collapsed to the ground like a marionette with its strings cut. Immediately, Nash turned on his heel and let his still-raised fists drop.

There was no one left for him to beat up. Lady Annis clung to the Scotsman's arm. His left eye was swollen and he was destined to have a proper black eye by morning. With his unharmed eye, he winked at Nash before pulling Lady Annis closer, which Nash chose to ignore. Layton, on the other hand, was surrounded by a circle of people who cheered and celebrated him as if he were the resurrected saviour. "The Priest is back!" echoed towards Nash. Many of the onlookers were women, he realised. For heaven's sake, if Nash had known that all it took to garner female attention was to drape a piece of cloth over one's face and swing fists, he would have used this method long ago. Not that he had ever complained, but it seemed like a fun combination: first, plunge into a fight and then sink into the open arms of a woman. Well, aside from the fact that he would soon be holding the only woman he needed in his arms, perhaps this approach wasn't as fun as Nash assumed. The look Layton threw him over the heads of the rapidly growing crowd seemed almost desperate, but Nash's eyes had already moved on to Frederica, who was staring at him. She was safe. The fight was over. Now, he wanted to explain everything to her. But would she listen?

Nash began to move and looked over at Felicity, ready to put in a good word for his friend who had taken on the disguise of the Priest to assist him, and not out of a desire for reckless adventure. However, Nash quickly realised that Felicity was not at all angry at Layton's excursion into the past. He watched as Layton's eyes sought and found those of his wife before gently but firmly disentangling the arms of a stranger's woman from around his neck and making his way through the crowd to Felicity. His friend pushed the cloth covering his lower face up a bit. The kiss he planted on his wife in full view of the public elicited a disappointed sigh from the circle of surrounding ladies, but then one of the men whistled and applauded. Others joined in the applause, and when Luke finally pulled his mouth away from Felicity's lips after an eternity, still holding her waist, most of the onlookers, including the women, were laughing. "Hold onto him tightly, darling!" shouted an older woman with shining eyes. "A man like him, you only find once in a lifetime!"

"That's my plan!" Felicity called back and pressed herself closer to Layton, who looked down at her with unmistakable pride.

And Frederica...

She just stood there and looked at him. If Nash was honest, her expression scared him more than the prospect of taking on all of Whitechapel. Hesitantly, he approached her, and suddenly there was no holding back. He spread his arms, and in the next moment, she was already with him, pressing her head against his chest, sobbing and laughing, and saying his name and a few unflattering things about his stubbornness, which he promptly forgot as she lifted her head and looked at him.

48

FREDERICA

A sea of love. That was what she saw when she looked into his eyes, and it crashed over her like a wave.

The roars of the drunks swelled in rhythm with her wildly beating heart, just like the neighing of the horses and the sound of the tavern door slamming shut. She blinked to block out the unbearably intense fireworks of colours that exploded in her eyes. For one agonising second, everything seemed to rush at her: colours and shapes, sounds and smells, only to dissolve into nothing the next moment. Her world shrank to a single person.

Finally, she was in his arms, her head against his hard, broad chest, listening to the beat of his heart.

"Frederica," he said with a voice she would never forget for the rest of her life. There was love in it and fading concern. "Are you all right? Are you well?"

She nodded and made a sound somewhere between laughter and tears. "Of course I'm fine. I'm not hurt. What about you? Are you injured?" She reached for the hand he had used to fend off the intrusive drunkard and lifted it to her lips. She didn't care who saw them and might take offence.

Next to her, there was a clearing of the throat. It came from Lord

Layton, who was stepping over one of the groaning men on the floor. The crowd that had just cheered him and Lady Layton began to disperse. "I suggest we take this moment to retreat and head to Grosvenor Square."

Frederica saw Lord Burnwood and Lord Layton exchange a glance. That made it clear that Lady Layton's suspicions about the gentlemen's crazy plan had been correct. She looked over at the two and then quickly looked away again. Lord and Lady Layton were staring at each other as if they had completely forgotten the world around them. The sight of them choked her throat. The love they felt for each other showed in every gesture, in every look. The foundation of their marriage was a tangible respect for each other and the freedom to make their own choices. Lord Layton was an unusual man, just like Lord Burnwood. Marriage to him... Frederica shook her head, torn between years of doubt and the instinctive knowledge that Lord Burnwood felt more for her than had ever been spoken between them.

"Trust your instincts, my dear," Lady Layton said softly. She whispered because Lady Annis, who was huddled in a corner of the carriage with her eyes closed, looked incredibly young in her sleep. Frederica was hardly surprised anymore that Lady Layton seemed to read her thoughts.

In the last two weeks, so many of her unshakable beliefs had been upended, starting with her conviction that she would never love again, to the firm belief that she could never be successful under her own name. Not only her view of herself but also Frederica's perception of other people had undergone a fundamental change. There was Lord Burnwood, who had accepted her as a painter, as well as his aunt Lady Hastings, and Millie, Lady Annis, and Lady Layton – people who had embraced her, even though Frederica had done little to earn that affection.

Perhaps this was the point where she had gone wrong. Affection, especially love, was given without conditions such as good behaviour or fulfilled expectations.

Francis had loved her at the beginning, of that Frederica was sure. It was only later that that love had turned into something else. He had used her – with her consent –for his success. This had thrown their marriage out of balance. Her father had also attached conditions to his affection. The more obedient she had been, the more proof of his affection she had received. Only her mother had loved Frederica unconditionally, always encouraging her to spread her wings and grow.

No, that wasn't true. There was another person in her life who had encouraged her to rise above herself.

49

NASH

The gentlemen followed the ladies' carriage to Grosvenor Square. It was Nash who broke the ice between himself and young Douglas. "That wasn't a bad blow," he remarked casually. "Not bad for a soft-spoken Scot."

"You didn't do too badly yourself," Douglas replied, lowering the hand that had been touching the swelling around his eye. "For an elderly Englishman, at least."

There was silence for two seconds, then Nash snorted and slapped the man on the shoulder. "I don't understand what Lady Annis sees in you." He dared not look over at Layton, who sat across from him, staring out the window with a stern expression. Nash knew his friend well enough to know he was holding back laughter.

It was almost comical how the thoughts played out on Douglas's face: first, the irritation with a slightly pinched look, then amazement with wide-open eyes, and finally, understanding, which turned his fair, freckled skin deep red. "What... How... I don't understand..." he stammered, but Nash could now also see a glimmer of hope in his expression.

"I think you understand perfectly well what I'm trying to tell you," he remarked, making an effort not to overdo it. He didn't want to shatter

Douglas's illusion of heroic achievement, but the young lad wasn't foolish, just blinded by love. Perhaps he had heard too many tales of his ancestors' heroics. Everyone knew a Scot considered himself a fearless fighter if he chased a fly away from his stew. "I've seen the way the Lady looks at you. Do you take me for a fool?"

Lord Douglas opened his mouth to answer Nash's question but thought better of it.

"Listen," Nash said, leaning forward. Hopefully, after the fight, Douglas had been too preoccupied with his lady love to notice how Nash and Frederica had held each other in their arms. He looked the young man squarely in the face. "Let me make one thing clear: I hold Lady Annis in high regard, but I have no intention of marrying her." The Scotsman's hand moved to his hip, ready to exact vengeance on Nash for the perceived insult. "Marrying a woman whose heart already belongs to another is not my custom." In fact, marriage was not a custom of Nash's at all, but the thick-skulled Scot across from him grasped the overall meaning of Nash's statement more than the individual words. Layton had his hands folded in his lap and his eyes closed, although Nash knew he was listening attentively.

"Oh," was all the hothead managed to say before straightening up and puffing out his chest.

"You have shown true heroism by joining me in the fight, even though you were under no obligation as my rival for Lady Annis's favour," Nash continued, giving Douglas a moment to react, but none came. "Considering your honourable and brave conduct, I have only one option left: I withdraw my claim to the hand of the young lady and leave the field to you."

An expression of undisguised pride flickered across Lord Douglas's face. He had taken the bait! "I was a fool to make Annis wait so long," he mumbled.

Layton emitted a snort that got lost in the monotonous clatter of hooves. Nash had better hurry; Layton wouldn't be able to contain his laughter much longer. "Perhaps it's no consolation, but when you're married to Lady Annis, you'll often feel like a fool. That's what some of my friends who have ventured into the adventure of marriage say, at least. But," he smiled, "you'll be a lovestruck and very happy fool. Any man whom Lady Annis loves as she loves you should feel honoured instead of hesitating. So, talk to her father and be happy with her."

"And you?"

Nash considered whether he should tell Douglas about his own feelings and what had prompted him to play along with the charade, but decided against it. Other things were going on in the young man's mind.

It was well past midnight when they reached Grosvenor Square. A muttered "Goodbye" was the last thing Nash heard from Douglas before watching the young lord escort Lady Annis to the front door. Lady Layton kept her distance and moved at a snail's pace to give the lovers a minute or two to talk. She hooked her arm through her husband's, forcing him to slow down as well.

Then Frederica stepped out of the carriage, and Nash only had eyes for her.

A thousand words welled up in his throat, and yet none were enough to describe his feelings. Frederica seemed to sense it because she walked directly toward him and wordlessly extended both hands. "I want to show you something," she said. "But we need to go to Charlotte Street for that." It was half a question and half a request.

He turned to Lady Layton, who had linked arms with Lady Annis. "Tomorrow is another day," he heard her say as she shooed Lord Douglas away with energetic gestures. The young man, who had hesitated for so long to seize his happiness with both hands, seemed on the verge of tears. *What a softy*, Nash inwardly chuckled. He exchanged a brief glance with Lady Layton, and when he was sure Douglas was retreating to wherever he had come from, he refocused his attention on the most important person in his life.

"I'll go with you to the ends of the earth," he promised, raising her hands to his lips. "But we should exercise discretion, at least when it comes to the neighbours and the servants. Come to the back entrance in ten minutes, my dearest. I'll be waiting for you there."

With a heartfelt handshake, he later bid farewell to Layton. "I owe you, old friend," Nash said, but Layton just shook his head as he returned the handshake.

"Not in the slightest. Make sure you make your lady love happy," he said, and with those words, he disappeared into his house.

THE JOURNEY to Charlotte Street felt like an eternity, yet passed in the blink of an eye. The silence between them was not uncomfortable, but that of two people who knew they belonged together. Nash couldn't explain it, but he felt it with every fibre of his heart and soul. Until this moment, he hadn't been sure if his soul existed, but in Frederica's presence, there was no room for doubt.

"Wait here!" he instructed his coachman. Nash had no intention of rushing Frederica, but he also didn't want to linger in her house too long in the middle of the night for her sake. He followed her cautiously into the house, and prepared for the possibility that the cat might ambush him at any moment, but nothing of the sort happened. In the light of a lit candle, Nash recognised that there was nothing left for the Lambeth Tiger to hide behind.

Their footsteps echoed in the empty rooms.

"You've sold the house?"

He sensed the movement of her head as she nodded. "Yes, it was time." She took his hand and led him to the studio. "The daughter of the new owner got married and will move in here with her husband."

"You sound wistful, but not sad," he observed. They stood in front of the terrace door, through which he had glanced a few times during the sessions, without ever paying special attention to the garden.

"So many years I lived here with Francis," she said softly. "Saying goodbye isn't easy, but the thought that a happy young couple will move in makes it much easier." A hint of a smile flickered across her face. "Everything has its time, doesn't it? Tonight," he heard her take a deep breath, "I want to bid farewell to my old life, and I want to do it with you." She opened the terrace doors and extended her hand to him.

Nash took it. "It's an honour," he replied simply and led her outside.

They stood in the middle of the tiny walled courtyard. Frederica lifted the candle to her face and blew it out. The crescent moon provided enough light for Nash to see the contours of her face. As his eyes adjusted to the darkness, white flower petals emerged from the night.

"I created this garden with my own hands," she told him. "I know every plant by name and when they bloom. I've watched them grow, form buds, and flower. I've observed their leaves turn brown in autumn and all life freeze under the snow in winter. And," she took a deep breath, "this is where Francis is buried."

That surprised him. Nash knew it was permissible to bury one's relatives on their own land as long as certain conditions were met: a physician had to confirm that the deceased hadn't died of contagious diseases (the only thing Londoners feared more than the Black Death was a fire like the one that had ravaged the city for three days in 1666). It was also mandatory to bury the body at least six feet deep and to have a permit from the magistrate.

"You're probably wondering why I didn't have Francis buried in a cemetery," Frederica said and led him down a narrow path to the back of the garden. When they arrived, she pointed to a bush, which he recognised as holly with its dark green, thorn-covered leaves.

"No," Nash replied, having pieced together the reason for the hidden grave from his own thoughts. "You didn't want to tarnish his memory, my dearest, and you hoped his death would go unnoticed for as long as possible." He squeezed her hand. Nash suspected that the secrecy also had something to do with the circumstances under which Frederica's husband had met his demise, but he didn't want to press her. She would tell him when she was ready. "I also understand that you didn't want to share your grief with anyone."

"You're so wonderful," she whispered and leant against him while reaching her hand toward the bush. "In the language of plants, holly represents peace," she told him and then withdrew her hand. "I hope Francis has found his peace. In a way," she continued, "he was like this plant that brings colour to the grey world in the deep winter with its red berries. Often, he was prickly like these leaves, but sometimes, when you least expected it, he proved to be warm-hearted and lovable. That's how I want to remember him."

Nash's throat tightened. There was no more loving, generous woman in the world than his beautiful painter. "I understand," he whispered. He loved her all the more for her willingness to forgive the departed, and he would never stand in her way of remembering him, although he himself couldn't think of that man without anger and contempt. Swift forgiveness wasn't in his nature, but it was not for him to show mercy to the dead. No, Nash's task for now and all times was to make Frederica happy. And he would, as God was his witness.

"Come, I want to show you something else." Frederica pulled him back to the front of the garden. "This is my favourite plant, the honeysuckle." She leant forward and closed her eyes, inhaling the scent that emanated from the exotic-looking flowers.

He stood behind her and wrapped his hands around her waist. The scent of the plant was sweet and heavy. It smelled like almonds and roses, underscored by the earthy smell of damp soil.

She leant against him and pointed to another plant. "This is the Queen of the Night," she said with a breathless voice, leaning forward towards the bright flower. "I've waited for years for it to bloom, and today of all days..." Her voice failed her.

Nash knew exactly what she wanted to say. "This night will remain unforgettable to me for the rest of my life. The rarest flower in your garden has opened, and I hold you in my arms." Nash placed a kiss on her neck. Frederica placed her hands on his, which still held her. He felt her lean into him and allowed himself to hold her tightly.

"When we're married, you'll have your own garden at Arden House," he murmured.

A shiver ran through her body. At first, he thought she was crying, but then he heard her laugh. He loved her laughter!

"Haven't you forgotten something?" She turned around without breaking their physical connection. "Don't let go of me," she pleaded, "but you should still ask me."

He bent his knee and released his hands from her waist, only to encircle her right hand with his fingers. Seconds passed as he searched for the right words and dismissed everything as too pompous. "I love you and swear never to let you go unless you want to. Will you marry me?"

"Yes, I will." She leant into him and touched his lips with hers. "On one condition." As Nash stood upright again, Frederica stood on her tiptoes and pressed her soft curves against his body. Under his hands, he felt her supple waist and the absence of a corset. Frederica's breath quickened, and as he felt her sides begin to tremble, he knew she wanted him as much as he desired her. He lowered his head once more. When his mouth met hers, she opened her lips to him. His tongue slid over the small notch in her upper lip and circled every inch of her soft skin. The scent of honeysuckle and the Queen of the Night mingled with hers to create an exquisite composition. But before losing himself in Frederica, Nash had to tell her one more thing.

"I'll never forbid you from painting," he assured her in a hoarse voice. Through the thin fabric of her dress, he felt the seductive curves of her bosom.

"That's good to hear," she replied. Again, he felt her laugh, a little breathless this time. "But that wasn't what I was talking about." She snuggled closer to him. Her breathing had quickened now, and her cheeks had taken on a delicate rosy hue.

He suspected what she was getting at. "I have no objections to moving Aunt Matilda out."

"Your aunt loves you," she said. "I understand that she wanted a good match for you, a respectable noblewoman instead of an impoverished widow. It will take her and me a while to get used to each other, but I don't want you to banish her from your life because of an unfortunate start."

If he hadn't already loved her above all else, he would have fallen for her now.

Finally, it dawned on him.

The cat. She was talking about the beast that hated him more than all the animal catchers combined.

Well, there's a solution for that too, Nash thought and kissed Frederica. He just had to make sure that the beer supply in his house never ran dry.

EPILOGUE: THREE WEDDINGS AND A TIGER

Three weddings within as many months were not few, Lady Hastings thought. Frederica's maid, a certain Millicent, had been the first to tie the knot, and her nephew Nash had naturally been invited as Frederica's future husband. Lady Hastings was not. So, Matilda had asked Frederica quite directly. Amiable as Nash's chosen one was, she had asked her maid to extend the invitation to Lady Hastings as well. Now that the Prince Regent had declared Nash persona non grata, and social gatherings were rare, Matilda had enjoyed every minute of the festivity. By accompanying Nash and Frederica, she had killed two birds with one stone: she demonstrated her full support for her nephew's marriage plans and also got to know her future niece-in-law better.

Nash was still sulking about what he called her "interference." "My dear boy," she had said, "you have only yourself to blame for the mess. If you had not made such a secret of your choice, none of this would have happened." Matilda would never forget the moment she had realised that the painter was the woman who loved Nash from the depths of her soul. The looks they had exchanged at the soiree had given everything away. She didn't regret inviting Frederica to the soiree or the commission she had given her, but Nash could have saved himself some excitement if he had

EPILOGUE: THREE WEDDINGS AND A TIGER

been honest from the start. When he called her "curious," she had called him "stubborn as a mule," and it had taken Frederica's efforts to reconcile them. This stubbornness was typical of the Ardens. "*Audere est facere*" – to dare is to do – was their motto. Matilda thought it should be something like "Rather die than yield." Even her William – may God rest his soul – had remained stubborn to the last breath. Instead of telling her once, just once, how much he loved her, he had instructed her to have the family silver regularly polished. The whole world seemed to believe that Matilda hadn't loved him, but that wasn't true. Despite his escapades and his penchant for dancers and actresses, she had adored him. Mostly.

Well, at least Frederica seemed to get along well with that typical Arden trait. She was exactly the kind of woman a man like Nash needed. Matilda had to admit that at first, she hadn't been particularly enamoured of her nephew's choice, but her reservations about Frederica's station had diminished with every hour she spent in the company of the young widow and soon dissolved into favour. Frederica could not only match Nash's stubbornness and his occasional fiery temper, she was also incredibly talented. What did it matter that she was a commoner? Nothing at all! Besides, they lived in a time when the bourgeoisie was increasingly asserting itself as a serious power, especially in financial terms, from whose cunning the nobility should take a leaf. Matilda admitted to herself that her newfound tolerance had not only to do with Frederica's inclusion in the family but also with the continued social banishment of the Ardens by the Prince Regent. Matilda snorted when she thought of Prinny. It was him of all people, who before reaching his majority, had caused a scandal due to an affair with an actress, but mainly because of his exorbitant financial allowances, and was now playing the role of a moralist. She would have liked to say a few words to him about it, but this spectacle was unfortunately limited to her imagination.

The second wedding took place one month after the first. Lady Annis Stewart and Lord Alfred Douglas exchanged vows. The bride herself had invited Matilda, so she accompanied Nash and Frederica to Scotland. Perhaps even her nephew was aware that a long journey with the woman he intended to marry was better in the presence of a chaperone. Officially, Matilda made sure that morals and decorum were preserved. Unofficially, she turned a blind eye when she saw the lovebirds cooing, which admittedly didn't happen often. Nash and Frederica were very much in love, but they were also mature enough to exercise discretion.

In contrast, the second couple was hardly out of childhood. Nash had been right: marrying Lady Annis was not a good idea. When she unwrapped Matilda's wedding gift, she squealed with joy, and as touched as Matilda was, she thought that such sounds should under no circumstances come from the mouth of a Marchioness of Arden.

Frederica had outdone herself with the portrait. Any painter who knew their craft could capture beauty and loveliness, but what she could conjure from colours was incomparably better than a simple likeness. The Lady Annis in the portrait seemed to breathe, even almost move if you squinted and looked at the painting from a certain distance. A shower of shooting stars rained down on her, and if you looked closely, you could see that some of the falling lights were hearts. Matilda found the symbolism brilliantly done, showing how Lady Annis had captured her Alfie. Also, the artist had opted against a rigid pose. Instead, she had her model running towards a young man, just emerging from the shadows of a forest, with arms outstretched. Although Frederica had only hinted at his features, he was clearly recognisable as Lord Douglas, the groom. When Lady Annis exclaimed upon seeing the painting, "Alfie, look, that is you!" it took Matilda's decades of training not to roll her eyes at the silly endearment.

During the festivities, whisky had flowed freely, and Matilda was glad to finally return home and have a good cup of tea for breakfast. Although her social life had come to a halt, she enjoyed having English soil under her feet. Unfortunately, the plans for her salon were on hold for now. Her plan to open the doors to Frederica Fitzroy would have to wait. Someday, Prinny would relent – or, more likely, forget the issue because he was once again chasing after a woman – but until then, Matilda could only recommend her new favourite artist to her closest friends who hadn't cut ties with her. She would have loved to do much more for Frederica, who assured her time and time again that it was fine to take her career slow, as she had more than enough to do with the wedding preparations. Nash had tried to make her understand that she could leave most of the organisation to the servants, but he was a man and did not know that many decisions were too delicate to entrust even to the best butler. Matilda was touched when Frederica winked at her while Nash was busy staring in disbelief as Tidbit elegantly occupied the empty chair next to her nephew. Nash lifted the cat from his seat, causing the magnificent creature – Tidbit, not her nephew – to strut over to Matilda. She discreetly dropped a piece of smoked herring under the table, and everyone pretended not to hear the quiet munching or the ensuing contented purring. For Matilda, the presence of the proud animal was a great enrichment, and the only thing missing to complete her happiness was the great-nieces and -nephews who would fill Arden House with life in the foreseeable future. Sometimes, when Nash and Frederica went riding or dined at Almack's, Matilda even held conversations with Tidbit, who sometimes seemed more understanding than most people.

While Matilda and Frederica pondered over the seating arrangements, she thought feverishly about what to give the newlyweds for their wedding. Jewellery? No, her nephew was already showering his betrothed with precious gems, and he himself wore no adornments except for the signet ring and obligatory tie pin. The jewel-encrusted buttons on his attire didn't count because she was hardly going to gift him buttons. A complete collection of Shakespeare's works? No, Nash's library was already overflowing with first and second editions, which he rarely had time to pick up. Two noble horses, a stallion and a mare, perhaps, on which they could ride together? That was not a suitable gift either. If Nash wanted a horse, he would buy one. Besides, all of that was far too impersonal.

What would make Frederica and Nash happy? What did they wish for more than anything else? No, that was the wrong question. They surely longed most to finally be married.

Matilda perked up when Frederica mentioned her parents, who would arrive a few days before the wedding. Should she wait for the arrival of Reverend Rawleigh and his wife? It was maddening! By the time Frederica's

EPILOGUE: THREE WEDDINGS AND A TIGER

parents arrived, it would probably be too late to get a unique gift. Matilda needed a brilliant idea, and she needed it right away!

With a sigh, she reached out for Tidbit, who, as so often, was lying beside her, and scratched him between the ears before refocusing on the seating arrangement.

※

A few days later, Matilda sat in the hired carriage that was taking her to Solomon's tailor shop in Peter Street. Lambeth was nowhere near as unsavoury as Whitechapel, but it was also not somewhere Matilda wanted to be alone after dark. The sun was still in the sky, but she didn't know how long she would stay in the shop. She had promised Lady Astor-Blackwell she would take care of a banner that the women could carry in front of them during their march, and her own dressmaker, that fusspot, had outright refused to make it. Matilda's own attempts to sew letters onto a bedsheet had failed. She had painstakingly sewn the words "VOTES FOR WOMEN," only to watch the crucial two letters W and O detach when she unrolled the banner for the first time.

That had been the moment when Matilda knew she needed professional help, and she had decided to ask the wife of the only tailor she knew for assistance.

She still remembered the fresh, rosy face of the girl she had seen once at the Laytons', where her former employer had taken refuge until her wedding to Nash. When the carriage stopped in front of the shop, Matilda felt her heart thud heavily. What would she do if the Solomons outright refused to help her? The coachman jumped down from the box, opened the door, and offered her his hand. Before she could change her mind, Matilda got out and walked towards the door. "Solomon and Wife" was written on the shop sign above the entrance. It showed a man and a woman holding hands. They were surrounded by a dressmaker's dummy and all the tools they needed for their profession: spools of thread, needles, fabrics, and even a pair of scissors.

The vivid faces and the expressiveness of the image revealed who had painted the sign. This was clearly Mrs. Fitzroy's handiwork. It must have been Frederica's wedding gift to the Solomons.

The woman could paint, Matilda had to admit. Imaginative and realistic at the same time, her paintings were of a style she had had to get used to. By now, she was convinced she could recognise Frederica's distinctive style anywhere.

She gathered all her courage and entered the tailor's. A pretty, neatly dressed shop girl rushed up to her and asked how she could assist the lady.

"I am Lady Hastings and I am looking for Mrs. Solomon," Matilda replied.

"I'll inform her. May I bring you something to drink while you wait, my lady?"

Matilda declined. She was nervous and afraid her trembling hands would give her away. It wouldn't do to put herself in a subservient position right at the beginning of the conversation, and—

"Lady Hastings," the woman who had approached her from behind said now. "You?" The woman took a seat in the chair opposite Matilda and studied her with pale blue eyes. She wore a simple-cut dark blue dress that looked elegant and timeless. Laughter drifted in from somewhere into the exquisitely decorated salesroom. "What can I do for you, my lady?"

"I have a request," Matilda said. "Well, actually, two," she added thoughtfully and congratulated herself on her cleverness. If anyone knew what would make Frederica happy for the wedding, it was her former maid!

Mrs. Solomon's eyelids lowered. "Yes?"

Two women, a mother and daughter by the looks of them, entered the salesroom and gave Matilda a reprieve. The girl who had greeted Matilda when she entered followed them, as did the man, who had to be Mr. Solomon. Matilda was surprised at how young he was for a successful businessman. She waited until the customers had left the shop before giving her answer. She noticed Mrs. Solomon responding to her husband's questioning look with a discreet nod.

"I was hoping you might know what I can do to make Mrs. Fitzroy

EPILOGUE: THREE WEDDINGS AND A TIGER

happy for the upcoming celebration. I want to give her something special, but unfortunately, I do not know her well enough, and I hoped you could give me a hint."

Mrs. Solomon leant back and smiled openly at Matilda. "I've been pondering that question for ages myself," she admitted. "Finding a gift for Mrs. Fitzroy is tricky. In essence, her love is exclusively reserved for painting and her cat. You cannot impress her with precious clothes or fashionable trinkets." She shrugged apologetically.

Matilda had suspected as much. "May I ask what you're giving her?"

Mrs. Solomon's face lit up. "She once told me she wishes for a painter's smock tailored to the female figure, with pockets for brushes and holders for the lighter tools."

"That is a wonderful gift and well thought out," Matilda praised. "Which brings me directly to the second reason for my presence," she said, gathering courage. She straightened up and looked her counterpart directly in the eye. "How do you feel about the women's movement, Mrs. Solomon?"

The time until the third and most important wedding for Matilda passed in a flash.

She wasn't the only one planning a surprise. Nash also intended to make the wedding unforgettable for his beloved and had made special arrangements. Thanks to a special license, he was allowed to marry at Lady Castlereagh's estate, Loring Hall. Whether he and Frederica would exchange vows in the presence of Lady Castlereagh's legendary tiger, Matilda didn't know, but she considered it possible. This wild animal seemed to hold a special meaning for the two, but Matilda couldn't quite grasp the exact reason behind her nephew's eccentric behaviour.

She had left for Loring Hall a day before Frederica and Nash to transport her gift away from prying eyes. Frederica's parents, the Reverend and his lovely wife, were waiting with their hostess for Nash and Frederica's arrival. Mrs. Rawleigh had a gentle nature and looked like a dark-haired, older version of Frederica, while the Reverend was more of a reticent type of man, unless the conversation turned to animals in general and bees in particular. Matilda only half-listened to him, but Lady Castlereagh had found an interested conversation partner in the Reverend.

Finally, the moment came. The sound of horses' hooves on gravel reached them through the open windows. Matilda jumped up, and everyone except Frederica's father did the same. Even Lady Castlereagh, who didn't know Frederica, seemed eager to finally meet the painter in person. Matilda could see that Frederica's father had become a little pale around the nose, and her mother was trembling, so she linked arms with both and followed their hostess. Frederica had entrusted Matilda with many details from her past during their hours together, so she could well imagine how difficult this family reunion would be after about a decade with little contact.

Nash reached out to help Frederica out of the carriage. Even from a distance, Matilda noticed Frederica first grew pale, then red, when she saw her parents. At first, it seemed as if she would freeze like a fox in front of the hunter's gun. A choked sob came from Frederica's mother. The Reverend cleared his throat. Lady Castlereagh, who, as a good friend of the Ardens, was also informed about the bride's difficult family situation, held back.

Then the Reverend opened his arms. Mrs. Rawleigh also released herself from Matilda, who promptly took a step back and felt Lady Castlereagh's arm around her shoulders. The support was much needed because Matilda could feel her famous self-control slipping away, even though the young couple hadn't even stood before the clergyman yet! But all of this – the romance filled with obstacles, the reconciliation between Frederica and her parents, and Nash finding the love of his life – was now taking its toll. While Frederica embraced her parents, Nash approached Lady Castlereagh and Matilda. He hugged them both and held them close for a moment. Matilda's tears now flowed freely and didn't stop even when Nash mumbled something like, "Come on, no need to cry." He turned to Lady

EPILOGUE: THREE WEDDINGS AND A TIGER

Castlereagh and attempted to kiss her hand, but the Lady promptly pulled him into her arms.

"I cannot wait to meet the woman who tamed you," she said. She glanced at Matilda and winked conspiratorially.

After a small refreshment, including spirits, the emotional turmoil had settled. Nash, standing off to the side by the window, was subjected to a cross-examination by the Reverend and seemed to be doing quite well, if the satisfied, almost friendly expression on the clergyman's face was any indication of the conversation's positive outcome. The ladies discussed the wedding ceremony, and Matilda made an effort to occasionally contribute a suitable comment, though her thoughts were elsewhere. Finally, Lady Castlereagh suggested that their guests meet the tiger, which, after all, was the reason Nash and Frederica were getting married at Loring Hall tomorrow.

Only Nash's ingrained politeness prevented him from declining the suggestion. Matilda could see he would have preferred to go to the menagerie alone with Frederica, but she would interfere one last time. "May I?" she asked and linked arms with Mrs. Fitzroy.

"Of course," the painter replied and watched Nash longingly as he walked ahead with Lady Castlereagh.

"Are you all right?" Matilda inquired. She wasn't sure where to start.

"I cannot wait to become his wife," Frederica replied and glanced sideways at Matilda. "What about you? You seem almost more excited than I am!"

Matilda nodded, distracted by the scent of fur and animal dung that brushed her nose. She looked ahead and saw the first iron bars separating the animals from the visitors. There was also Matilda's gift, hidden in a wicker basket and at a distance from the tiger's cage.

"Ooooh." Matilda heard Frederica sigh as she cautiously approached Nash's side. "He is beautiful!" She reached out her hand and quickly withdrew it when the sleeping beast opened its eyes. Matilda let the others go ahead. She would have plenty of opportunity to explore her friend's menagerie; besides, this was a moment meant for Nash and Frederica alone.

EPILOGUE: THREE WEDDINGS AND A TIGER

Lady Castlereagh and Frederica's parents seemed to feel the same way, as they also held back, although Frederica's mother kept casting nervous glances toward the cage.

A meow came from the wicker basket.

In response, the tiger let out a deafening roar. For a moment, fear seemed to have struck them all. Then Lady Castlereagh said with a clear voice, "I told you, he is a grumpy witness." Frederica started giggling. Her mother joined in, followed by Lady Castlereagh. Nash's sonorous baritone provided a beautiful counterpoint. Even the Reverend cracked a smile. Finally, Matilda laughed too and handed Frederica the wicker basket. "This is my wedding gift for you," she said. "I am afraid I have to give it to you now because the basket is too cramped to be a permanent home."

As Frederica took the pretty black cat from the basket, she laughed and cried at the same time. "Is this what I think it is? A lady cat for the Lambeth Tiger?"

Nash shot Matilda a shocked look, but Frederica's joy seemed to mollify him. Matilda couldn't wait to see Nash besieged by a host of tiny cats. She sincerely hoped that among the offspring of Tidbit and the as-yet-unnamed lady cat, there would be a black and red-striped one.

Nash sneezed.

The tiger sulked.

End

Dear Readers,

If you liked "The Portrait of the Devil of St. James," you will LOVE "Duke of Night," the next book in the series.

Helen needs a scandal to escape an unwanted engagement, and the infamous "Duke of Night" is the only one who can help. But his aid comes at a price...

MY SERIES CONTINUES

Dear readers,

Reading is one of the greatest pleasures in life – at least until the word "End" appears. For all the romantics out there, I have good news: My series about the romantic summer nights in St. James continues!

Helen must escape an unwanted engagement, and to do so, she needs a scandal of epic proportions. But she can't ruin her reputation on her own. Help comes in the form of the man who spells ruin for any woman seen in his company. Only the notorious Duke of Blackwood is willing to offer his assistance. But every favour comes at a cost, especially when the most dangerous bachelor in the Empire is the one making the offer...

The next book titled "Duke of Night" has everything a reader's heart desires.
    You will find a sample on the next pages.

SNEAK PEEK: DUKE OF NIGHT

Lady Helen sees only one way to escape the dreaded marriage her father has planned for her: she must ruin her good reputation thoroughly enough that no man of rank and name would ever accept her as his wife.

A kiss from an ill-reputed man in broad daylight, and she would be free!

No one else is better suited for this than the one known as the "Duke of Night."

What he touches, spoils.
Those whom he gazes upon, are lost.
Just a minute in his presence is enough to tarnish the reputation of even the most virtuous woman.

She knows he has a cold heart.

And now, the Duke of Night is her last chance.

Reading Sample:

You will marry Rufus Raidenberry.

Her father's voice echoed in Lady Helen de Montbray's head, refusing to be silenced. All her pleading, begging, and crying had not swayed him: in one week, the engagement would be announced at the traditional late-summer ball of the Raidenberry family.

Six days remained for her to escape this trap. Seven, if she counted today. Helen interrupted her umpteenth round of her bedroom and fiddled with the top button of her too-tight collar. Why did this confounded thing resist her? She couldn't breathe deeply, let alone think clearly. She needed air! Finally, the button gave way and squeezed through the tight opening. It was a little better, but far from enough. With icy fingers, she rubbed her burning forehead, but even that brought no relief.

She took a deep breath and walked to the window. Her room, like her father's study, was on the first floor of their townhouse and offered a wonderful view of the garden. And the neighbouring house – unfortunately – where he resided: Rawden Seymour, Duke of Lancaster, also known as the "Duke of Night." The mere thought of encountering him made Helen's pulse race. Determined, she pushed aside thoughts of the man she loathed more than anyone else in the world. For eight years, she had tried to forget him, and she certainly wouldn't start giving him a place in her thoughts now, not even from afar.

There was only one place where she could find peace, and that was the ivy-covered alcove in the garden. *Just five minutes*, Helen told herself. The timespan was so short that no one would notice she was missing. Her gaze fell on her diary. Decisively, she reached for it, grabbed a pencil from the drawer, and hurried down the stairs with her skirts flying. Out through the terrace door and into the far corner of the garden, where no one would disturb her. Here, in this familiar and secluded spot, Helen hoped to calm her racing heart and thoughts.

She ignored the narrow gate, once used as a connection between the two gardens.. Long ago, so many years that Helen could hardly count them, she used to enjoy secretly sneaking over there. However, memories of the connecting gate held little joy for her now: with an angry broken heart, she had thrown the most significant gift she had ever received through it, so it disappeared for eternity in the grass, and if she didn't... Stop! If she started thinking about *him*, she would not be at peace for the rest of the day. However, peace was exactly what she needed now, as she had to find a way to escape her impending marriage to Rufus. She sat down on the wooden bench and assumed her favourite position, with her knees drawn up and her back against the armrest, closing her eyes for a moment. The scent of jasmine, blooming just a few feet away, brushed against Helen's nose. The pounding in her heart subsided, and the rushing in her ears was barely noticeable.

Gradually, the sounds of London drowned out the dull drumbeat in her chest: the clattering of hooves on the pavement, the carefree laughter of a child, likely being scolded by its nanny, as it abruptly stopped, and a faint squeak that Helen couldn't identify and soon forgot.

She opened her eyes, flipped to the page where she had made her last entry, and put the pencil to paper. She preferred writing with ink and a pen, but taking both writing instruments outside would have been too cumbersome. *A systematic approach brings the best results*, she told herself, while simultaneously considering how to escape a marriage in a reasonable manner. Wasn't that a contradiction in terms? Most ladies regarded the day they gave their hand in marriage to a man as the most beautiful day of their lives, and were accordingly happy. The only emotion Helen felt when she thought of marrying Rufus was sheer panic.

One week, she wrote in her diary. *How can I escape an engagement that will be a done deal in seven days? All my hopes of an independent life, of a journey to the Ottoman Empire, will be ruined.*

She raised the hand holding the pencil and tapped it against her lips. She had nothing against Rufus or marriage in general, but she was not suited for a lifelong commitment. Heaven, she was five-and-twenty years old, her first season had been years ago, and her father had always led her to believe that he would never force her, his only daughter, the apple of his eye, into marriage. However, in the last year, his highly progressive attitude had changed. The gentle urging had turned into probing, and from probing into almost desperate insistence on a wedding. All of this had culminated today in the revelation that she and Rufus Raidenberry, Viscount of Marchmont, the son of her father's old friend from Oxford, would marry, come what may.

Helen swallowed and refused to let the tears burning behind her eyelids escape. Self-pity would get her nowhere. She needed a plan, one that would quickly and sustainably take effect.

What if she turned to Rufus and asked him to oppose the marriage as well? But Rufus had no objections to marrying her; he had expressed that often enough. Besides, he was her friend and a nice young man, but one who would never go against his parents' wishes. No, she couldn't expect help from that quarter.

Were there other allies she could count on?

Apparently not. Her only friend was precisely the man she was supposed to marry.

Once, nearly eight years ago, there had been someone who had offered her comfort and help. A man who had sworn to always be there for her and who had broken his oath as casually as a cruel child crushes a fly. That was exactly what he had done to her heart: captured it, dissected it, and burned it to ashes with a smile on his face.

Without realising it, Helen had set her diary aside, stood up, and approached the gate until she stood directly in front of it. Her fingers clutched the rusty iron bars. What was she doing? She would never hear the end of it if Papa got the idea to send a servant to look for her and she was caught lingering around the entrance to that man's property.

They called him the "Duke of Night" for a reason; his heart was as dark as his reputation. Rawden Seymour, the Duke of Lancaster, was the only unmarried nobleman of his rank whom mothers kept their daughters away from, rather than pushing them towards him, hoping he would take notice.

A minute in his presence, and the reputation of any woman was ruined for all time. At least, that was what she had heard.

SNEAK PEEK: DUKE OF NIGHT

Everything that got near *him*, everything he touched, spoiled.

She herself was the best example of the truth in that statement. Helen had been lucky in her misfortune, though it hadn't felt that way back then when she had barely escaped the devil. And today... This time, she couldn't hold back the tears. *Darn it, get yourself together!* She wiped away the salty fluid with her sleeve, and hurried back to the safety of the alcove. She opened her diary again, but the tears stubbornly refused to stop flowing. Now they fell onto the densely written pages of her diary, smudging the letters she had just put on paper. "... *ruined*": Helen read the last word and saw that the paper curled where her tears wetted it.

Her breath caught in her throat.

Ruin. An irreparably damaged reputation. The idea was simple but brilliant.

The pencil flew over the pages, until Helen realised that the five minutes of solitude she had granted herself were long gone. The afternoon sun was low, and it was much later than she had thought. Hastily, she got up and placed the book and pencil beside her on the bench, brushing any tell-tale traces of dirt from her skirts. Helen's legs, a little stiff from sitting with her knees drawn up for so long, gave way, not enough to make her fall to the ground, but enough to stagger.

The next thing she felt were two hands grabbing her waist and lifting her up. Heat emanating from a decidedly masculine body surrounded her. Her eyes were level with jewel-studded buttons as the faint scent of an expensive perfume enveloped her.

Her heart knew before her eyes confirmed it: it was *him*.

Rawden Seymour, the Duke of Lancaster.

Helen raised her head and opened her mouth, perhaps to protest, perhaps not.

...

End of the Reading Sample.

"Duke of Night" is available on Amazon.

SNEAK PEEK: THE COLD EARL'S BRIDE

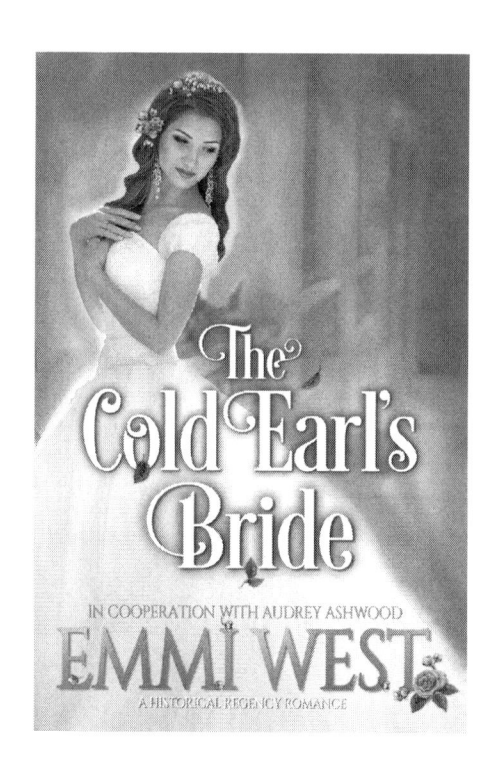

SNEAK PEEK: THE COLD EARL'S BRIDE

They took everything away from him.
His reputation as an honourable gentleman.
His hope for peace.
His faith in love.

Nevertheless, there is one thing that nobody can take from the merciless Marcus St. John, Earl of Grandover – his desire to take revenge on the men who wish for his demise. He is so very close to identifying the mysterious mastermind who is pulling all the strings in the background.

But then he stumbles into a cleverly designed trap, where he is suddenly forced to marry a woman who is clearly an instrument of his enemy.

The longer the ruthless earl has to watch this foe in his own house, the greater his doubts become about the role she is playing. She is smart and beautiful, and somehow, she touches his innermost being in a way that had long since been forgotten. Is it possible that she has completely clouded his mind and confused his heart?

Reading Sample:

In the centre of the garden stood a pavilion, which was perfect for his purposes.

Marcus stood still.

Now that he was almost certain that Greywood had only amorous intentions, he knew that he could just as well turn around and wait for the bastard to come back. So, what was it that made him sneak after the pair? Up until now, it had always served him well to trust his instincts, and he decided to do just that. After a brief moment of internal debate, he stepped from the gravel path onto the grass to dampen the sound of his steps. The moonlight broke through the clouds only sporadically, which worked as much in his favour as it worked against him, but since he did not change old habits easily, he had dressed in dark clothing, which made him virtually invisible.

He started to move forward. In moments like these, his years of experience of working in the shadows was of enormous advantage, allowing him to separate his body and mind. Tiptoeing, searching the surroundings for anything unusual, and making cold-blooded decisions had helped him to survive. Once more he thought he heard a noise that didn't seem to fit the night and the surroundings. Still, his eyes did not see anything that would have made him feel uneasy.

Finally, he could make out the shape of the pavilion in front of him. Only a few steps separated him from his target. Just as he was thinking about how close he could sneak up to the two, and how odd it was that the woman in Greywood's arms didn't make a sound, the hairs on his neck stood up.

But it was already too late.

He bounced against something soft, which he unmistakably recognised as female breasts that were laced up scandalously loosely. Before Marcus could wonder about the reason for his displeasure, he felt a burning pain on his cheek. A tender hand in a white glove pulled back, but not fast enough for him.

His fingers enclosed the tiny wrist, and while he ignored the painfilled but more so indignant scream, he pulled the woman close.

"What have you done to my sister? Where is Felicity?" a voice hissed into his ear, which would have sounded pleasant under normal circumstances. But now, under the vibrating alto, he mostly heard one thing: fury. And fear.

Once more the memory hit him with full force. He heard a similar sounding female voice, which belonged to a different time and a different place.

"Be still," he ordered as he listened to the darkness.

Most likely, her scream had alerted Greywood, but he still wanted to avoid any attention. He knew that the gossip about his transgressions, as well as the rumours about his past, had given him a rather dubious reputation, however, an attentive observer would almost certainly wonder about the reason for Marcus' late-night presence in the gardens.

"I do not think so," the strange woman replied defiantly. "Not until you tell me where Felicity is."

"I do not know, and I do not care," he answered harshly. From the corner of his eye, he thought that he saw the dark dress he had followed all the way out here. "Be still, or I shall see to it that you keep your mouth shut."

He was close to losing his patience with her. For a moment he was hoping that the strange woman in his arms would behave reasonable, but she proved him wrong. She did something no well-behaved young English maiden would ever have considered doing – she opened her mouth and spewed a flood of vociferous insults at him. In all his life, Marcus had heard far worse offences than "monster," which was a ridiculous accusation in the face of the situation, but her lack of reasoning and sheer disobedience angered him.

A short while later, when he was able to think clearly again, he would struggle to find a logical explanation for his behaviour, but in this particular moment, it had seemed like the only way to silence the strange woman. It might have been the warm spring air, the sweet, delicious scent of her soft body in his arms, and, not least, the fact that her sight reminded him of the happiest time in his life, but... he pressed his lips against hers and closed her mouth with a kiss.

She smelled of almonds and something tart, which evoked thoughts of a hot summer's day in the country. Besides her perfume, he smelled the scent of her soap, undeniably some expensive French concoction that more than likely had been smuggled here. However, the most tantalising were her lips, which she opened for him without hesitation. At first, he assumed that she was a versed kisser, but then he realized by her posture that she was simply overwhelmed by the new experience of physical closeness. By now he should have realised that she was a complete stranger to him and not the beloved, familiar, dead woman of his dreams.

But for a fraction of a second, Marcus St. John, Earl of Grandover, a man with a bad reputation and a well-known love of the female grace, forgot to study the situation carefully, and instead lost himself in the innocent but passionate kiss with the young woman.

It was the moment that cost him his freedom.

The moment the moon showed her face from behind dark clouds, and he finally saw who was about to rob him of his sanity, it was already too late to deny that the kiss had ever happened.

Behind the woman with the chestnut brown hair, which threatened to fall into complete disarray, he saw three men approaching with hasty steps.

The first man with his scowling gaze he recognised as the Duke of Evesham, one of the country's most conservative peer and a hater of Catholics.

He looked at the woman he had just kissed. Her eyes darted from his face over to the duke's and back to his. For a short moment, he thought that she would open her mouth and explain what had happened: That she had mistaken him for someone else, that nothing had happened that couldn't be forgotten, as long as all involved swore to absolute silence in this matter – but, she said nothing, not even when the Duke of Evesham let loose a tirade of angry accusations. Her eyes, the colour of which he was unable to distinguish in the flickering light of the torches, widened in fear. He thought that she looked at him pleadingly, but then the presence of the three noblemen demanded his attention and she was pushed to the edge of his mind.

Immediately behind the enraged father loomed the corpulent figure of his friend, the Earl of Warrington. The third man – Marcus froze at the realization – was Greywood. He barely did anything to hide his grin as the two older men stormed towards Marcus. Evesham was held back by his friend, as he waved his fists in Marcus's face. Words such as "honour" and "satisfaction" were thrown around, but they bounced off Marcus like water off a duck's feathers. The only thing he saw was the mockery in Greywood's face, when Marcus realised that he had no other choice, given the Duke's wounded honour.

Either he accepted the duke's gauntlet and met with him for a duel, which he was certain he would win, or he took the only other option open to him – marry the girl and save her honour – while keeping his own actions from being discovered. Marcus St. John closed his eyes and tasted the last breath of freedom before he turned towards his future father-in-law. His gaze brushed over Greywood's face. The desire to catapult the man with his bare hands into the afterlife was almost overwhelming.

Marcus St. John had lost a battle. However, intended to win the war.

Two months later

Annabelle stood before the priest and barely heard what he was saying.

One reason was the monotonous voice of the man. However, what weighed much more on her was the fact that she was about to marry a man whom she hardly knew, and whose coldness filled her with fear, disgust, and anger. Marcus St. John, Earl of Grandover, had agreed to take her as his wife to save her from disgrace.

Those had been his words.

Anger still boiled inside her when she thought of his condescending, arrogant way in which he had treated her since that unfortunate encounter.

"I do not need anyone to save me from a disgrace that does not exist," she had wanted to say to him and "*You* kissed *me*. Not the other way around." But the warning rasp of her father and the disappointing gaze of her mother had finally convinced Annabelle to accept his proposal. With grinding teeth, mark you, and a fake smile that would have earned her a standing ovation in the Globe Theatre.

...

End of the Reading Sample.

"The Cold Earl's Bride" is available on Amazon.

ALSO BY

If you can never get enough of romantic love stories, take a look at my series and standalone titles. Each story can be read on its own, with a guaranteed happy ending.

Summer Nights in St. James:

Dark heroes and strong heroines are the hallmark of my sizzling Regency romance series, all set against the backdrop of the historic St. James's Square. All books can be read as standalones.

The Portrait of the Devil of St. James

Duke of Night

A Duke at Midnight

The Evesham Series:

The Evesham Series features the three Evesham daughters Annabelle, Felicity and Rose on their journey to finding love. While each book is a standalone, starting at the beginning (and going in order) is more fun. *The Evesham Series* is a sweet historical romance series written by Emmi West, and the English edition is co-written by Audrey Ashwood.

Book 1 (Annabelle): **The Cold Earl's Bride**

Book 2 (Felicity): **No Lord Desired**

Book 3 (Rose): **An Unkissed Lady**

ABOUT THE AUTHOR

Emmi West

Emmi West is the pen name of USA Today bestselling author Jenny Foster, under which she writes romantic historical novels.

At times dreamy and gentle, at others passionate and thrilling, the historical romances of Emmi West are, above all, deeply romantic. She has always loved reading, despite her grandmother's warnings that she'd never find a husband with her nose always buried in a book. As she never intended to marry, she simply brushed off the idea and continued reading—especially romances.

Eventually, reading alone wasn't enough, and she began to write. Love is always the heart of her books, even if it isn't immediately obvious. In real life, she's a hopeless romantic, who found her true love and married just three months after they met. She now lives in the Ruhr Valley with two jet-black dogs and a husband who loves to cook for her. Every morning, she takes her furry companions for a walk along the nearby river.

Some of her books are collaborative projects with London-born Audrey Ashwood, who specialises in historical romance for English-speaking readers.

Emmi West on Amazon:
amazon.com/stores/Emmi-West/author/B072193XHH

Audrey Ashwood on Amazon:
amazon.com/author/audreyashwood

Jenny Foster on Amazon:
www.amazon.com/author/jennyfoster

Printed in Great Britain
by Amazon